The Long Room

THE LONG ROOM

Francesca Kay

ff

FABER & FABER

First published in 2016
by Faber & Faber Ltd
Bloomsbury House
74-77 Great Russell Street
London WC1B 3DA

Typeset by Faber & Faber Ltd
Printed and bound by CPI Group (UK) Ltd, Croydon CR0 4YY

For quotation acknowledgements, please see p. 291

A CIP record for this book
is available from the British Library

ISBN 978-0-571-32250-3

FSC
www.fsc.org
MIX
Paper from
responsible sources
FSC® C101712

2 4 6 8 10 9 7 5 3 1

This is for Joseph

We live, as we dream – alone ...

JOSEPH CONRAD, *Heart of Darkness*

Friday

In the long room it is quiet. Winter, late afternoon. Each of the eight desks in the room is islanded in lamplight, its occupant marooned. There are windows along one wall, but as soon as dark begins to fall slatted blinds are drawn across them to bar the view from the building on the other side of the street. In daylight the windows are veiled by nylon curtains. The curtains smell of dust. They are weighted with metal in their hems.

An old man hums in Stephen's ear, and wheezes, sucking deeply on his cigarette; he is chronically short of breath. He has been having trouble with his heating; he cannot get his boiler to stay lit. It has taken several telephone calls and much hanging on the line to secure a visit from a plumber in a fortnight's time. While he waits, the old man hums and sometimes mumbles a few words: '*I'll take the low road and ye'll take the high road – but I'll be . . .*' His voice is raspy with smoking and disuse.

Orders are to fast-forward through material as irrelevant as this. But Stephen is fond of the old man, a superannuated communist; that croaky voice close to his ear is familiar and warm and helps to pass the leaden hours. Time goes so slowly otherwise – those long and boring hours of waiting until he is alone with her again. No one seeing Stephen with his headphones clamped to his ears, his pen poised and a blank report sheet on his desk, would know that what he hears is meaningless, or at least of no significance, to anyone but the speaker.

Quite soon the tape runs out. Last week the old man neither made nor took any other calls. On the empty report sheet Stephen writes the coded case-name in a box at the left-hand corner: VULCAN. Beneath it he notes the date and the time of the scheduled visit by the plumber. Then he writes: 'Nothing further to report.' A fine loop on the 'g'. Other listeners type their reports, and the clitter of their fingers on the keys of their typewriters adds occasional percussion to the sounds of the long room, but Stephen writes his in flowing cursive, with the pen his mother gave him when he was still at school. A Parker pen, in gunmetal grey; it came with a matching ballpoint in a white-lined presentation box. A silky lining, like a coffin's. He has used it ever since. It might be interesting to calculate the miles of ink that pen has travelled, through notes and essays and examination answers, through six whole years of listeners' reports. If all the words that he had written could be laid out end to end, would they reach halfway to the moon and back, or three times round the world? Can I get there by candlelight? No, as a matter of fact, you really can't.

Stephen slides the report sheet into a brown A4 envelope, on which he writes: *Confidential for RWG/Department Two.* He presses the eject button on the tape-recorder and sheaths the disgorged cassette in another, smaller envelope which comes with pre-printed options:

FILE

PEND

WIPE & RE-USE.

He ticks the third. Then he puts both envelopes into the wire-mesh out-tray at the top right-hand corner of his desk.

There are two more cassette-sized envelopes, one thin, the other twice as thick, in the matching in-tray. Stephen breaks the seal of the thinner envelope, which is labelled ODIN, and withdraws another tape. ODIN, unlike VULCAN, does not live alone; he has a wife and a disabled adult daughter and they often use the telephone. This past week they've been trying to get a wheelchair fixed; the obstructiveness that they have met so far has driven Mrs ODIN audibly to tears. Stephen has listened to her plead with various officials in various departments of health and social services, explaining that without her wheelchair her daughter is a prisoner and in consequence her parents too. They do not own a car. He sympathises deeply: he knows how great a toll their loving care takes on the target and his wife.

In spite of all his worries, ODIN has found time to call an extraordinary meeting of his revolutionary group. It will take place next week in order to debate the Labour Party's new inquiry into militant leftists and, as this is a subject which interests the strategists of Department Two, Stephen transcribes ODIN's several conversations in some detail. All the people ODIN convenes are old friends and easily identified, there is nothing new there, and Stephen can predict that the outcome of the meeting will be nothing more than righteous indignation.

Stephen's caseload seldom offers the possibility of drama. His old men – and his targets are all men – are creaking dragons who might once have breathed fire and brimstone across the land but now lie quiescent in their caves. Presumably the strategists believe they still could pose a threat. With one sharp prick from a well-aimed lance, would they erupt again into menacing action? Stephen doubts it. What they mostly do is draw their pensions and send postal orders for small sums to such revolutionary causes that have not yet run out of steam. And they reminisce. But it is not Stephen's place to question the strategists and in any case he quite likes to listen to the chatter of old firebrands, their memories and the small details of their lives.

Time passes. ODIN's travails take Stephen well past five o'clock. Around him his colleagues are beginning to lock their papers and machines away. At the far end of the room Louise, who is the Controller of Group III, is taking something out of a Fenwick's carrier bag to show Charlotte. Yellow-patterned cloth. A shirt? Yes. Louise holds it up against herself and strikes a bashful catwalk pose. Dandelion-yellow bright against her greying hair. Charlotte signals approval. As he takes his head-phones off, the women's laughter reaches Stephen.

There are times when Stephen finds the sounds of the long room restful. Headphones entomb their users in hermetic silence, and Stephen often wears his when no tape is running. But silence must be broken for continuing effect. At intervals he allows the ordinary sounds – the low hiss and click of the machines, his colleagues' voices, the rattle of typewriter keys, a lighter sparking, a telephone ringing – to weave and flow around him and free him from the hyper-acuity that silence brings, when every heartbeat, every breath, the ticking in his veins, can be as loud as hammer blows on metal.

At Stephen's infant school the teacher used to calm a rowdy class by bidding it keep quiet enough to hear a real pin drop.

Stephen remembers that so clearly. Her voice struggling at first to rise above the hullabaloo, the gradual hush as the children composed themselves into attitudes of listening stillness, and then the tension while they waited; the glint of the pin aloft between the teacher's thumb and finger, its swift fall and the relief of hearing the tiny rattle that it made on landing.

Mrs Medlicott, so sweet, and vivid in memory as well. Strawberry-pink, cupcake-icing softness, her dove-like, gentle voice. Reading practice, when his turn came round, sitting very close to her, his cheek against her arm – powdery, scented softness, he'd found it hard to leave her. Impossible, sometimes. He'd cling to Mrs Medlicott, desperate to stay with her in the classroom where he supposed she lived. Mustard and cress growing on damp beds of blotting paper on a window sill, poster-paint pictures on the walls. Smells of biscuit dough, warm milk and glue. Then Stephen's mother, driven inside to find him, after waiting too long in the yard, embarrassed, pulling him away, upset maybe. 'Mrs Medlicott'll think you don't want to go home,' she'd say.

Why had he held on so tightly to his teacher? He hadn't been unhappy as far as he could tell. Was it simply reluctance to face the transit from Mrs Medlicott's small realm of warmth and colour – blue overalls on pegs with names above them in careful lettering – S t e p h e n – to the stark, grey world outside?

Stephen. Re-named a few years later, in the cold corridors of the Juniors: Step hen. Irresistibly comic. Stephen Donaldson. Step hen duck's son. Stephen Waddlecock.

Almost five-thirty. Soon the long room will empty of other people and he will be with her at last. Oh Helen. He has saved this extra time for her; she is too precious now to share, and it is hard to wait. But this evening Louise, Charlotte and Damian are lingering, chattering to each other, Charlotte smoking one more cigarette. Then she skips heavily across the room to Stephen's desk, with a birthday card for him to sign and a plastic box in which she is collecting cash. A button on her blouse has come adrift. 'I hope you've got some change,' she says. 'I'm running short. Rafiq's, on Monday. Don't forget. We're going to the bar for drinks.'

'That's nice,' says Stephen, willing her to leave. But Charlotte wants to talk to him about *Brideshead Revisited*, which she and half the nation watched last night. Stephen watched the programme too but, for some reason he would rather not examine, he pretends otherwise to Charlotte. 'Oh, but', she says, 'you really should. The voyage at sea last night was so romantic. And Sebastian is wonderful and Oxford's so beautiful – well, you know; I mean, in the early episodes, every time they showed the city, I just thought of you. I could see you drinking port in Sebastian's rooms with Charles. And I bet you had a teddy! Actually, I must admit that I still do. But his name is Teddy, which Sebastian would say is frightfully common! He sleeps on my pillow and guards my bed while I'm away.'

Louise wanders up to join them. 'What are you two talking about?' she asks. 'Teddy bears,' says Charlotte. 'I expect you have one too?'

'Of course I do,' Louise replies. 'A whole menagerie, in fact. Not to mention the cats. Do you have a teddy, Stephen?' She pats him on the head. 'Oh bless. Time to go home now, wouldn't you say? Got plans for the weekend?'

'I'm going to the country,' Stephen says.

'Lucky thing,' Louise says without rancour. 'I'm going Christmas shopping.'

'*Moi aussi,*' says Charlotte. 'Oxford Street, not Oxford spires! You coming, Louise?'

'Yes, Lotts,' she says.

Louise and Charlotte return to their respective desks to finish putting their things away. It takes for ever. Damian, quicker and unobtrusive at the best of times, a shadow-man, has already disappeared. Finally, the women leave, calling out goodbyes. 'Don't be long now,' Louise says at the door. 'All work and no play! See you on Monday, Steve.'

Stephen breathes out deeply as the door shuts behind them but at once is jolted by the shrilling of the telephone on his desk. A red light on the handset flashes too; these telephones are modified for headphone wearers. Gingerly, he picks up the receiver.

'Well,' says Rollo Buckingham at the other end. 'Where the hell are you? It's almost six o'clock.'

'The delivery was delayed today,' lies Stephen. 'I'm staying late so that I can deal with it but it wouldn't have been humanly possible to get it to you this afternoon. And anyway . . .'

He leaves unsaid what both men know: that yesterday's tapes are as unlikely to surprise as those of the days and weeks before. There has been nothing untoward so far in the suspect's home life. Rollo's voice is testy. Taking a chance, Stephen offers to bring a transcript up to his room tonight but luckily Rollo has another engagement. 'You'll ring me', he says, 'if anything comes up? Duty Officer has my whereabouts over the weekend.'

'Of course,' says Stephen. 'If not, I'll see you first thing Monday morning.'

7

'Right you are,' says Rollo, briskly, hanging up.

Now there is almost no sound in the long room but for an occasional car passing in the street outside, and footsteps on the pavement. Both are muffled by distance and thick walls. Stephen's is the only lamp left burning; the room is otherwise quite dark.

He prepares his desk. Tearing one blank report sheet from its pad he sweeps the rest, together with everything else he does not need – a bottle of ink, the plastic tray that holds paper-clips and treasury tags, his unwashed coffee mug – into the top drawer on the left. He aligns the cassette player precisely in the middle of the desk and dusts the surrounding area with his handkerchief. If he could, he would light a candle.

The thicker envelope lies before him like an invitation or a gift. It is sealed with a plastic tag that will snap when the packet is opened. He picks it up and holds it for a second to his lips. Then he slits it with a paper knife. It contains two cassettes held together by an elastic band, one unmarked, the other with an orange label stuck across it: Authorised Users Only.

Stephen slots the unlabelled cassette into the machine. He doesn't have great expectations of this tape. Helen is rarely at home during the day in term-time and, in the evenings, the calls that she receives or makes are too often of the practical, brief sort: 'Can she fit in an extra lesson tomorrow? Cover for Mr Burbage? Collect her watch, now ready, from the menders? Meet outside the theatre for a play that starts at half past seven?'

It is only when the arrangements and the diary engagements involve the subject that Stephen must record them. And he does. He writes them down in meticulous detail on each day's

8

report sheet, cross-referencing where necessary, adding information if it might be useful, making carbon copies as required.

8 December 1981:
    Subject of interest and wife expected at Greenwich Theatre on Tuesday 14 December, 9.30. (To see production of *Another Country* – cf. tape dated 6 December, which details provisional plan made by subject's wife and her friend Laura [Cummins, q.v.].) Tickets now booked. Probability of restaurant dinner later, location not yet known. John Cummins also attending theatre. No one else expected to be present.

When he writes these things, he pictures Helen looking forward to her evening, getting ready, getting dressed, and later coming home, in a taxi, half-asleep. He prefers to see her living her life alone.

He knows that Helen is busy. She teaches music to young children at a school in Knightsbridge; she is sociable and often invited out. But even so, she is a kindly friend and a loving daughter. She makes time to telephone, she remembers birthdays, she asks after health and happiness, and she regularly telephones her mother.

Her mother lives in a village by the Suffolk coast, called Orford. When he first heard Helen name the village, Stephen looked it up in the atlas kept in the Institute's library; it is not far from Aldeburgh. She has a gentle voice, just like her daughter, but with the faintest trace of Irish in it, and she evidently lives alone. That's another bond that he and Helen share: elderly mothers on their own.

He presses the play button and the tape begins its smooth

transit from one spool to the other. Recording is activated by incoming and outgoing calls. In a Bravo-level investigation such as this one, where the product is delivered daily, the tapes are often short.

As this one is. One incoming call, at 17.54, unanswered. An outgoing call at 20.17: subject to his father.

'Dad? Hello, it's me. How are you? Just to say we'll definitely arrive in time for supper. That is unless there's a massive hold-up on the motorway; you know how bloody it can be getting out of London on a Friday evening. But I can push off a little bit early, and Helen has a half-day, so with luck we'll beat the lemming rush.'

His father is pleased. He informs the subject that his guns are cleaned and ready in the gun-room. Harry's Saudi millionaire, it now appears, won't be down till Sunday, which comes as a relief. He and the subject's mother are looking forward to seeing their sons. The forecast's good. Should be ideal conditions.

The subject and his father had talked about these plans before. Rollo Buckingham already knows that he will be at his family home in Oxfordshire and that the party will be joined by an Arab businessman (who had been easy to identify, from information already given on the telephone to the subject by the subject's brother Harry). Rollo had not thought there was anything unusual about a weekend's shooting or that extra surveillance measures should be taken. The subject's father was formerly Her Majesty's Ambassador in Buenos Aires, Dublin and Vienna, has a knighthood, and now sits on the boards of several leading companies, including the brewery that Stephen knows to be the source of Rollo's fortune. He is also a personal friend of the Director. There is no way the Director would consent to a covert surveillance operation at that house, even if there had been any point.

The subject was saying goodbye and was about to hang up when his father asked:

'Could you possibly talk Helen into giving it a go? Quite honestly, I sometimes think she sounds like that advertisement: I haven't tried it because I don't like it . . . And it's an awful shame to miss out on such good fun.'

'Really, Pa, I think she made her mind up long ago. But I will try to talk to her again tomorrow, when we're driving down.'

'Ah well, I suppose it could be worse. I mean at least she's not a vegan. Your mother and I were only saying that the other day apropos of Christmas. Mamma's bought her a really rather super leather purse.'

Stephen ejects the cassette and flings it across the room. It strikes one of the metal cabinets that are lined up against the wall opposite the windows, and falls to the floor with an audible crack. He retrieves it and sees that half the outer plastic casing of the cassette has sheared off. In a moment of confusion, as there is no option on the pro-forma envelopes for deliberate damage, he slips the tape into his trouser pocket.

Now for the second tape. The orange label is there to show that no one has tampered with it between collection and delivery to the designated listener. Stephen unpicks an edge and peels the label slowly off.

Orange-label tapes are a uniform length engineered to run continuously for twelve hours. Much research has gone into these tapes and their recording of the sounds relayed to them, usually from a distance and often under circumstances that are technically far from ideal, but this research is none of Stephen's business. He has no idea how the recordings are obtained; he does not need to know. For him the salient fact is that each recording runs from roughly midday to midnight, and from midnight to midday, and that every tape is dated. Someone – and he will never know who that is – removed this particular tape at around 11.59 last night, from a machine that must be located somewhere in the vicinity of the target premises, inserted a fresh one, scrawled 9/12 – 12.00–24.00 on the label of the old one and then, at 11.59 the following morning, repeated the whole process. And that same process happened in dozens of other places from one end of the country to the other. Dozens of anonymous people unobtrusively entering empty flats or lofts or disused offices or hotel rooms or warehouses or vehicles, picking up the plastic spools, dating them, taking them to a central point – and again it is no concern of Stephen's where that is or who controls it – from which they will be delivered to the Institute. He envisages these shadowy people flitting through the midnight streets, their heads down and their collars up, slaves to their machines.

It can happen that an investigation is too urgent to brook even that twelve-hour delay. In these rare cases, specifically instructed listeners are driven by taciturn escorts to addresses that they must not divulge, where they huddle in their headphones over the machines and monitor their targets in real time. Stephen would love to be assigned one of those Alpha-level cases; to be granted that unparalleled intimacy, to hear his target breathe at the same moment that he breathes himself. The possibility that this particular investigation could one day be upgraded from Bravo to Alpha is so deeply thrilling that he hardly dares to give it thought.

In the silence, the sound of the tape docking into place is loud. Stephen presses play and the tape begins its slow passage from full to empty reel, emitting as it slides a sibilant hiss. He replaces the headphones he had for the time being removed, and plugs the jack into its socket.

Yesterday, Thursday, early in the evening. Oh, thou art fairer than the evening air, my Helen. The sound of a key turning in a lock, a door being opened and then closed again and something dropped – a heavy bag perhaps – water running from a tap, a kettle coming to the boil, a teaspoon clinking in a cup. Light footsteps. The swish of curtains being drawn. A few words spoken, only just above a whisper; Helen, talking to herself. She does this often, murmuring some words, far too low to be overheard, with a slight enquiring uplift in her voice. Although he strains to make out her meaning it is only her tone he catches: a woman asking herself questions, who does not stay for answers. Stephen relaxes like a peaceful cat in Helen's presence.

The 5.40 news on television drowns out all other sounds. Stephen and Helen listen to the news together: Andrei Sakharov and his wife Yelena have ended their hunger strike; Michael Foot has won his call for an investigation into Militant Tendency. Stephen has already heard that news – and watched it too – on his own television at nine o'clock last night but he listens to it again with Helen now. When the news is over, she turns the television off. Stephen commends her discrimination as a viewer.

More water sounds. Helen washing up her cup. Then soft rustling sounds that he has heard before: she is leafing through sheet music or the pages of a book. Now it will depend on her frame of mind. Some evenings, when Helen is at home, she practises piano; on others she will sing. Stephen loves her playing – he loves it when he hears the soft knock of wood against the lid prop, her indrawn breath, and then her first experimental scales and the way she takes one phrase and plays it over and over again – bold chords or silvery sad notes – but he is ravished when she sings. He does not know much about music and can seldom put a name to piano piece or song but he is learning; he has bought a turntable and some records. One day he will talk to her about them. In the meantime he shuts his eyes and listens to her songs of love in languages he does not always understand but which speak directly to him. It is by magic, Stephen thinks, that this woman's voice comes straight to him from a room that he has never seen, and catches at his throat, that it stirs in him a yearning that is new, unnameable: a hunger of the heart. It makes her feel so intimately close. It tells him everything about her. And yet, although each time she tells him something new, Stephen knows that he has always known her. From the dawn of time their souls have been entwined and waiting: now hers is calling him. Helen sings for him alone; on occasion she may play the piano for her husband but when he is there she never sings.

This evening she has chosen the piano and she stops as soon as she hears her husband at the door. Greenwood is late. It is 19.33, a time that Stephen writes on the report sheet. Greenwood drops his crackling outdoor clothes beside the door. He has had to finish off a piece of work that couldn't wait, there were problems with his wretched bike chain, he has oil all over his hands, he'd like to have a shower before he rings his father.

Will he have time for that or is he spoiling supper? Supper is the word that Jamie Greenwood uses.

The noise of a cork being pulled from a bottle is curiously disgusting. Cooking sounds: a knife hitting a hard surface, and a match struck, the hiss of a gas jet, hot fat splutter, china against china, metal against glass.

Greenwood makes the telephone call that Stephen has already noted, although on this orange-label tape only his end of the conversation can be heard. Stephen closes his eyes as he listens once again to the confident male voice, the sound of shared assumptions. Let that Saudi millionaire be a hopeless shot, he thinks. Let him swing his gun round wildly and hit Jamie Greenwood, let Greenwood fall to the hard ground dying, bleeding from the mouth. Does blood spurt out in a scarlet halo, in a shower of red raindrops when a bird is shot?

'Smells good,' Greenwood says.

Name it, Stephen urges. He wants to know what Helen will be eating. The scent of onions softening in butter, of herbs and garlic, reaches him through the thin grey ribbon and reminds him he is very hungry. What is the wine they are drinking? He thinks Valpolicella, for the beauty of the word.

When Helen and Jamie have finished their supper it is nine o'clock and they, like Charlotte, like Louise, like Stephen unconfessed, turn on the television for *Brideshead Revisited*. If they speak to each other at all during the hour of the programme, their words are lost in swooning music and the actors' voices. Charles and Julia are falling deeply and adulterously in love on board a ship in mid-Atlantic. Stephen leaves them to it and winds the tape forward to the point where Helen and Jamie make preparations for the night and shut their bedroom door.

For a while longer Stephen shares the noises of the night. Sirens and traffic, voices in the street, a dog barking in the upstairs flat, a sudden swirl of wind in the branches of a tree. He thinks of Helen listening to them with him, as she lies sleepless by the snoring body of her husband. And then he checks his watch and sees with a shock that it is well past nine o'clock. He has kept Helen company for three hours and more; he will have to sign the late list; there is not enough time to finish writing a report.

Every piece of equipment, any scraps of paper that bear even a single word, anything that could identify a member of the Institute, must be locked away at night. Stephen removes the orange-labelled tape and puts it into his in-tray. He carries the tray and his tape player to his allocated cabinet, stows them, clicks shut the sturdy combination lock and checks it, twice.

His coat is hanging on a rack next to the door. He puts it on and walks slowly back to the end of the long room, lightly touching each of the eight deserted desks as he goes past. All the surfaces are bare except for lamps, and on Charlotte's desk a weeping fig, on Louise's a small grove of African violets. Green leaves and pale pink flowers, incongruous in this place of battleship-grey metal: metal desks and metal safes on a sea of carpet tiles that are also grey and dirty. The angled desk-lamps hunch above the empty planes like herons staring into stagnant pools.

Friday night. After the darkness of the long room, the neon glare in the corridor outside stabs Stephen's eyes. He blinks behind his glasses. There is no one in the corridor; the whole building seems unmanned although Stephen knows that there are many other corridors and many other rooms in which feverish activity will continue through the night. And, beyond the reinforced walls of the Institute, other young men will be gazing into the eyes of girls, across restaurant tables, dance floors, rumpled beds. Girls are slipping out of dresses into silky nightgowns; they are standing under showers with water flowing down their breasts. Out there, in the cold December night, new lovers are kissing for the first time and the dying are taking their last breaths. Stephen is aware that these are banal thoughts.

He takes the stairs rather than summoning a lift. He hopes his descending footsteps sound assertive on the bare concrete. At the bottom of the staircase a security guard is waiting.

'Working late,' he says. It's a statement not a question.

'Been a busy week,' Stephen tells him, looking heroically exhausted.

'Even so, you didn't ought to spend your nights in here, son. All work and no play . . .'

'I know, I know,' Stephen interrupts him, 'but it's okay. My girlfriend's waiting for me; she knew that I'd be late.'

'That's more like it,' says the guard, with a leering wink. 'Reg's got the late list.'

Reg is on duty in the guard-post, by the main entrance of the Institute, sheltered by bullet-proof glass. Behind him, flickering screens show what is happening in the corridors and stairwells of the building, and in the street outside. To speak to Stephen, Reg slides open a hatch.

'Working late,' Reg says. 'Put your moniker on this.'

Stephen does as he is told, adding his department and initials to the list. L/III/ SSD. Reg presses a button and the main door opens to release Stephen into White Horse Street and the night.

White Horse Street is dark and empty; Piccadilly, a minute's walk away, is bustling. It is two weeks before Christmas. People have been at office parties in the upstairs rooms of pubs or at the Ritz. In their twos and threes they flow along the pavements, laughing and talking loudly. Girls in high-heeled shoes. They're still chattering beneath the harsh lighting of the escalators at Green Park and on the platforms of the station. Those few who are, like Stephen, on their own seem fugitive and embarrassed.

Dust-metal breath and roar of an approaching train: too bright, too loud, too fast. The doors slide open. To propel himself inside them, to give himself up to those devouring jaws, requires an effort of the will. Within the carriage, when the train plunges back into its tunnel, Stephen's face reflected in the window looks pale and moon-like, imbecilic. He remains standing and he stares at his reflected self. *Mon semblable, mon frère. I never knew death had undone so many.*

At East Acton station he alights. The shop on the corner of the high street will be open; Stephen is in need of food. As he walks past the lit doorway of a pub along the road he considers going in but he has not found it to be a friendly place before and the prospect of the sour eyes of watching strangers puts him off. Safer to drink at home alone.

Home: the lower half of a small and narrow house, the main entrance shared with the flat upstairs, although both also have their own front doors. Stephen's door is painted brown. He unlocks it, pushes it open cautiously, leans in to switch the hall light on while still standing on the threshold. When he comes home to his empty flat he finds at times the waiting silence has an edge to it, as if someone had been there who has only just left, or something was still waiting, with its teeth bared, in the dark.

The flat is very cold. The convector heater in the sitting room will take time to warm it up. Stephen has bought sausage rolls, baked beans, cheese, bread, chocolate, and a bottle of whisky. He holds the bottle up to the light and savours the amber glow of it, its consoling weight, its seal uncracked. Right now, at this very moment, in the dining room of Helen's parents-in-law in Oxfordshire, dinner will be almost over. There'll be guttering candles and silver knives, and dark red wine in crystal goblets; there'll be firelight and golden labradors and Helen will get up from the table without a word, go to the window, catch sight of her own face in the glass and wonder why she feels so lonely.

At that time, on that Friday night, Coralie Donaldson was also contemplating food. Food is a topic that often occupies her mind. It is not that she cares about what she puts into her own mouth – it's her son's diet that concerns her. It always has, ever since she first spooned Farex into his gummy mouth and prayed that it would help him to grow strong. Such a skinny little thing he'd been, a child of bones as light as a bird's, of cloud-pale skin, of deep blue shadows beneath his eyes, con-cavities beneath his ribs. Not a fussy eater, no; he'd swallow whatever she gave him, but it never seemed enough to bulk him out. Tubular his bones were when he was a child, and hol-low – goodness no sooner poured into him than it ran straight out. Still peaky now, although no longer quite so thin.

In truth, there's not a lot to think about tonight, in the

matter of meals tomorrow. The planning has been done, was done a week ago, as the thinking for the week ahead is now in progress. For dinner when Stephen comes there will be tomato soup, and corned beef hash with potatoes and boiled carrots, followed by peaches and evaporated milk. Corned beef, being tinned, is one of those foods that keep from week to week but fresh meat isn't safe to store for very long.

Coralie is looking forward to tomorrow afternoon. The shops are interesting at this time of the year, brave with gold and green and scarlet, with cheerful tins of Quality Street and bumper packs and things you wouldn't see otherwise: chestnuts, Turkish Delight, tangerines like precious gems in their wrappings of blue tissue. There's a feeling of brightness and excitement, even though it's cold and the days are full of rain.

Is it raining now? Hard to say, when the windows are shut and the curtains drawn and Coralie secure within her walls in the lee of Didcot Power Station. Above her, less than half a mile away, colossal towers of steam rise up into the darkness of the night but here, in this squat brick house, the lamps are lit, the cat's asleep and the television is chattering in the corner of the room. There'll be no need to pull aside an edge of curtain and peer into the outside world until the morning. And, when the morning comes, so too will her son, her peely-wally boy, her clever boy, her Stephen.

Saturday

Country clothes, weekend clothes, moss-green and fawn-flecked tweed, leather buttons like carved conkers, checked cotton shirts and cavalry twill. Stephen's brogues were neatly polished. That Saturday morning, before he left for Didcot, he walked round to the corner shop to buy the milk he had forgotten the night before and, although it was not likely he would encounter anyone he knew in the network of streets where he lived just off Western Avenue, it was not inconceivable, and therefore he was correctly dressed. If he were to see anyone from the Institute he probably wouldn't acknowledge them in any case: an early lesson on the course he took as a new recruit warned against hailing any colleague met by chance lest that colleague was working under cover. 'Only think what damage you might do to a tricky operation if you were to cry "Good morning, Jim" to an operative who at that moment was calling himself Jack.' Nevertheless, acknowledged or not, if Stephen is to be recognised, it must be for what he is: a man off to the country for the weekend. By the same token, from Monday to Friday, he is equally appropriately dressed in a three-piece suit and tie. These are the cuirass, the greaves and gauntlets of the modern man.

Stephen thought of Jamie Greenwood, also in his country clothes, somewhere in a field that morning. What exactly is a shooting jacket? Is it a garment that has pockets for dead animals and guns? Waterproofed, presumably – or blood-proofed

– against the seepage from the rabbit's wounds and the torn flesh of the pheasant. His images of Greenwood are necessarily indistinct for he has not yet seen the man himself, either in the flesh or in a photograph. But he is easy to imagine. Stephen has seen many young men just like him, at Oxford and at the Institute. Tall men with loud voices who inhabit their clothes as if they were bespoke and never bought from ordinary shops. Or, indeed, as if they had inherited them, as if clothes were valuable possessions, to be bequeathed by fathers to sons and worn by those sons with pride. Second-hand clothes, in Stephen's childhood, were a source of shame. Cast-offs and hand-me-downs, smelling of mildew and desperation, piled in depressing heaps on trestle tables in church halls at jumble sales, picked over by sad-eyed women old before their time. It had come as a surprise when he first heard a boy boast of owning his grandfather's dinner jacket. However hard the times were when Stephen was growing up, his mother had insisted on new clothes. Before he went to Oxford she took a day off work so that they could shop together for the evening dress that Coralie believed her son would wear on a regular basis. In the gents' department of Elliston & Cavell she had examined the rows of shiny jackets and trousers with a single stripe, fingering the satiny lapels, shocked at their cost but nonetheless determined that Stephen should be suitably caparisoned at this new stage of his life.

He remembered their worry over ties. Red silk or black? In the end she had chosen for him: black and velvet, secured around the neck by an elastic band, as the alternative – a perplexingly thin strip of fabric – could not by any stretch of their imaginations be envisaged as a bow. When, at home, he had tried the new tie on, he had thought it was perhaps a little large. Above it, his face looked round and pale; the face of a kitten in a noose, suspended in cruel jest before it's drowned.

Coralie had taken that day of shopping seriously. She carried a list, based partly on the recommendations made in a helpful letter from a second-year student at Stephen's college, and partly on her own notion of what an up-and-coming man should have. A kettle, sheets and towels and coffee cups were obvious; cut-glass ashtrays, a decanter and a leather desk-set not.

Addicted to lists she was, his mother, then and even more so now. She'd be composing one this very moment. She had a special pad for them, with each sheet headed 'Shopping', and an illustration of cottage loaves and wheat sheaves at the foot.

Harpic
Whiskas
Raspberry jam
Sardines
Trifle sponges

Domestic litanies, the rosary beads of Coralie's week.

Later today, after dinner – after lunch? – Coralie will tear this new list from her pad and read it aloud to Stephen. Then she'll tuck it carefully into her handbag and prepare for their expedition to the shops. Now that her arthritis has made it hard for her to leave the house, that expedition will be one of the few she makes this week. Coralie can just about reach the bus stop on her own but even that short walk will tire her, and anyway she isn't fit to carry any weight. Her condition has worsened steeply over the past year and she is increasingly dependent on her son. Without perhaps intending to, they have fallen into a routine: Stephen will drive down on Saturdays and, since he is there, and the drive not inconsiderable, he might as well stay the night.

And so, that Saturday, as usual, Stephen rings his mother's front-door bell. It was his own front door for many years, and he keeps a key, but he doesn't like to use it. She takes a while to open the door; in greeting they do not touch or kiss. Lunch is almost on the table, as he knew it would be; the soup in its saucepan ready; the meat and the vegetables in the oven staying warm.

Coralie is fretting about turkey. Christmas falls on a Saturday this year and Stephen doesn't get off work until the day before. That's Christmas Eve, of course. The shops will be extra busy that day and there is a risk they may run out of what she needs. If she could, she would do the necessary shopping at least two days before. But, as it is, she has a problem on her hands. She doesn't own a freezer, having made do until now with the ice-making compartment of her fridge. And, although for most of the year that's perfectly adequate, it's obviously too small for a large bird. If she and Stephen were to buy the turkey next Saturday, would it keep in the cupboard that she uses as a larder until Christmas Day? What does he think? Because otherwise it would take up almost all the space that there is in the fridge and then what was she supposed to do with the other things she needs to store? It's awkward, isn't it? Some people do say that you can keep a turkey safely in the garden shed or in a coal bunker but Coralie is doubtful: what about the foxes and the rats? If only the weather forecast were reliable. Because, if you knew there'd be a cold snap, you'd not be taking that

24

much of a gamble on the larder. But it can be peculiarly warm round Christmas, all of a sudden and to everyone's surprise. You get primroses and violets some years, as well as snowdrops. Wouldn't it be unpleasant to have your turkey nibbled at and gnawed away by a nasty rat? The boot of a car – now that's a place which must be rat-proof, fox-proof and reasonably cold? Or possibly not if the sun were to shine unseasonably upon it. And would Stephen mind having the turkey in his car for a week? Of course he doesn't use it all that often, does he? Or should she just bite the bullet and buy a proper freezer? A snag is that there's nowhere really sensible to put one. The kitchen's cramped enough already. You could perhaps squeeze one of those chest types in the toilet, underneath the coat-pegs, but it might be a bit difficult lifting things out, if they were heavy things – like a turkey is. Would she be able to reach them, if they were at the bottom? And besides, she doesn't really hold with frozen food, although she does love those Martians in the advertisement for mashed potatoes. Though that's not precisely frozen, it's freeze-dried. They make her laugh every time she sees it, with their chortling away at the stupidity of humans! *For mash get Smash.* A very useful standby, she has found. But, going back to freezers, does it seem a good idea to buy one just for Christmas? They're expensive, aren't they? Does he think they will want ham?

'Well, ham is nice,' says Stephen. 'But you can buy that in a packet. Can a turkey be reserved? If so, it could be collected from the butcher's any time on Christmas Eve.'

Mother and son sit facing each other across the kitchen table; the same table they have sat at for the whole of Stephen's life. It's made of pine, thickly knotted, and long ago it split along

25

one edge; in the fissures there are crumbs of food. Mrs Donaldson used to dislodge them as best as she could with a blunt knife-blade but lately she has left them to accumulate: layers of sediment, bread and cake and spilled meat juices decomposing slowly into an undifferentiated sludge. After dinner she reminds Stephen that he must fetch the Christmas decorations from the loft.

Monday

After a sudden snow storm from the west, Monday morning is cold and dreary; the pavements are slippery, the coats of the crowd crushed together in the trains reek of frying and wet dog, but Stephen is on his way to work with a lift of the heart, in spite of feeling a bit queasy. Monday mornings are good mornings now; they bring new hope and an end to the barren wastes of the weekend that are devoid of Helen. Mondays used to weigh leadenly on him, but ever since one morning in October they have been as welcome as a lovers' reunion.

Stephen had heard tales of the Cube, of course, but had never seen it. 'What have I done?' he had asked Louise, when she told him he was wanted there. 'Nothing, you silly boy,' she said. 'It's one of "those" operations and it's time you were assigned one.'

The cellars of the Institute form a warren that extends beyond its above-ground boundaries, and beneath the street. To get there Stephen took a lift. Its door opened onto a lobby in which an armed and uniformed guard was sitting at a desk. 'ID?' he asked, politely.

Stephen showed the guard his badge. 'The Cube?' he said.

'Through the double doors, take the passage on the left, not the one that leads to the garage. Follow the painted arrows.'

Windowless corridors, chill and faintly clammy. Behind a

second set of double doors, Stephen found a tall man leaning against the wall, and a young woman, laughing. She was pretty, wearing a pink cardigan that looked as if it would be very soft to touch. 'Donaldson?' asked the man. 'Good. Rollo Buckingham. And this is Binks. Binks is going to lock us up together.'

'And throw away the key,' Binks teased. The two men followed her though a door that she unlocked and into a room where the Cube stood, in the centre. The Cube is exactly what the name suggests. The size of a large shipping crate, matte-grey, walls smooth and unmarked except for an entrance cut into one side. Binks undid its combination lock and the heavy door swung open. 'It gets stuck sometimes,' she said.

There was a table, chairs, and a bright light inside the Cube, cramped space enough for six. 'Bit of a squash', said Rollo, 'when it's full.' They stepped in through the door and it shut tight behind them. 'Grab a pew,' said Rollo. Stephen wondered if there was an inlet for fresh air. The interior walls were completely covered in leathery grey material, slightly wrinkled, like a dinosaur's skin.

Rollo took a packet of Marlboro from the breast pocket of his jacket, shrugged the jacket off, opened the packet and offered it to Stephen. Stephen shook his head. Rollo tapped out a cigarette for himself. His lighter was shiny gold, like the links that held together the beautiful cuffs of his white shirt. 'Before I say anything,' he said, 'I need you to sign this.'

He removed a sheet of paper from a file he had dropped onto the table. The paper was stamped TOP SECRET. He skimmed it across to Stephen who, glancing at it quickly, saw that it was headed by the code-word PHOENIX and held nothing but a typed list of departments and initials. He put his signature against his own. He didn't have time to decipher the other nine names on the list apart from the Director's.

'Right,' said Rollo, through his cloud of smoke. 'Now, I cannot emphasise too strongly that security is paramount. When I asked your group-controller to nominate a listener for this case she recommended you. She says that you will be discreet. I did rather expect her to take it on herself but she explained that she is working at full stretch and couldn't guarantee the sort of commitment that this investigation might in due course require. Potentially full-time. She said that you had capacity to spare and would do it very well.'

'I can only do my best,' said Stephen. Rollo smiled then, with a flash of warmth. 'The thing is,' he said, 'I'm afraid I cannot give you the usual background briefing. This case is complicated and extremely secret. The original source of the intelligence is ultra-delicate. No one who is not on this list is authorised to know anything about it. All I can really say at this point is that we are investigating a question of loyalty. Or should I say, disloyalty rather. Internally.'

'What do you mean? A traitor?'

'Well, that's perhaps too categorical a word.'

'But, are you talking about someone in here, someone in the Institute?'

'Yes.'

'Christ almighty! What's his name? Or is it actually a woman?'

'No, the subject of interest is a man. Look, please don't ask me any questions. Our view is that this particular investigation absolutely must proceed without prejudice or preconception. Otherwise it's just not fair. I'm aware that usually a listener

29

gets a whole dossier of facts – history, dates, personality traits and description – as well as details of the intelligence case, in advance of taking on a new investigation but just for once I'm asking you to do without. Begin with a clean slate and fill in the details for yourself, gradually, as they emerge. Discover him through what you hear. Because that way we will have a truer picture. Or at least that's what I hope.'

'But that won't work! I'll be completely in the dark!'

'Yes, but not for long. We have level Bravo Plus – telephone intercept and eavesdropping – orange-label naturally – so that's coverage for twenty-four hours a day. You're going to be with him every minute that he spends at home. You'll soon get to know him as well as you know your closest friend.'

'What about when he's at work?'

'Separate coverage,' Rollo said. 'For entirely obvious reasons.'

'Hang on, they're not that obvious to me.'

Rollo sighed. 'I've already said that I can't discuss the details. It must be obvious to you that we can't deploy the same techniques in here that we can outside. Ergo, there have to be different operations at his home and when he is at work. And at this point the latter is no concern of yours.'

'What if I already know him? If I've worked with him before?'

'I've considered that. He has nothing to do with your group of listeners. And so there's no particular reason why you should know him out of all the hundreds of people working in this building. But, if by chance you find you do, please inform me soonest. Meanwhile, please don't try to find out anything about him other than what emerges from the stuff you're hearing. I'm sorry to repeat myself but it's very important. We must not load the dice. Just note down every move he makes, every-one he sees, anything he says that strikes you as unusual. Note everything, in other words. We won't know what we are look-ing for until we've found it.'

'All right. I'll give it a go,' said Stephen.

Now, on this Monday morning, he must take Friday's report up to the seventh floor, where Rollo Buckingham has his office. It's too soon, though: Buckingham probably won't get in until ten o'clock, and the tapes from the weekend won't be sorted until lunchtime at the earliest. Stephen whiles away the spare time by reading through the weekly bulletin, copies of which are circu-lated to each department. Every member of the Institute must certify they've read it by putting their initials on the cover-sheet; by such means the Executive ensures that no one can plead ignorance of new rules. They intersperse their admonitory mes-sages with snippets of Institute news, the canteen menus, and the weather for the week ahead. The news is necessarily pruned of sensitive intelligence and tends to be mystifyingly anodyne. *A planned bomb attack was foiled in County Antrim. Two East German diplomats have been declared personae non gratae and will leave the country. The special of the day is chicken curry. Tomorrow there will be no more snow but it may rain.*

The current bulletin contains an updated list of pubs and restaurants in which hostile operatives have been spotted and which are consequently out of bounds to Institute staff. Some of the pubs are close to the Institute – The Fox and Grapes, The Queen's Head – but others are unfamiliar to Stephen. The Windsor Castle, The Sherlock Holmes, The Eight Bells – he had better write them down.

He wonders if these faceless officials of foreign powers are similarly forbidden to visit places frequented by members of the Institute. Or would they conversely be exhorted to drink in them as often as they could? How would the different factions recognise each other, unless against all the rules, they were talking shop? Stephen knows enough to know that spies do not loudly advertise themselves but are mostly shabby little men whom no one notices in the quiet corners of rundown cafés. He was shown photographs on his training course for new recruits. Now, imagining opposing ranks of operatives facing each other across the patterned carpet of a busy saloon bar, Stephen is reminded of the model soldiers with which he used to play for hours on end, when he was a boy.

While he is carefully inscribing names onto a blank page of his diary – Le Caprice, J. Sheekey, Porters English Restaurant – Charlotte comes lolloping up. 'Morning, petal,' she says. 'I'm on coffee duty this week. Do you want a cup? Twelve o'clock for Rafiq's birthday – you hadn't forgotten, had you? Delivery's held up today, glory be and hallelujah; Muriel's delayed by last night's weather – snow on the tracks in Kent apparently, though there was barely a flake in my neck of the woods – and won't be in till later. We might not get any morning tapes. Hurray! We can really go to town at lunchtime! Did you have a nice weekend? The blizzard didn't get you? I did think about you last night, wondering if you might be having a tough time driving back; it was ghastly around Croydon, I heard, but maybe it was better in the west. You are a jammy dodger, escaping the old smoke like that; I wish I could. I dream of a little cottage, miles from anywhere, surrounded by green fields. With a river. No, a stream. A stream running through the garden;

I'd have heliotrope and roses, honeysuckle . . . but what do I actually have, as a matter of fact, excuse me? A window box in Crouch End! Never mind. One day. One day my prince will come and I'll be out of that door before you know it, leaving my headphones behind me. But then you'd miss me, wouldn't you, Stevie-love?'

'Indeed, I would,' Stephen agrees. Charlotte scoops up his coffee mug and moves on to the next desk, where silent Harriet, who never says much more than please and thank you and hello, is already plugged into her machine. Stephen watches Charlotte mouthing 'Coffee?' at her in an exaggerated way, as if Harriet were deaf and an inept lip-reader. Harriet just shakes her head with a tight little nervous gesture.

No product that Monday morning means that Stephen has nothing to do. If she had not been late, Muriel, who is the clerk and registrar of the listeners, would have sorted through the Friday p.m.–a.m. tapes and the weekend's recordings too, logged them individually into her black book, labelled them with the code-words that correspond to the numbering system used by the furtive couriers, sealed the tapes in envelopes and then, very slowly, as she is near retirement age and has a problem with her hip, she would have deposited them envelope by envelope into each listener's tray. Without Muriel, there is no one who can correctly manage the bags of tapes that the couriers deliver twice a day. No one else can understand the arcane system.

Muriel's lateness is a blow to Stephen. A weekend is too long to be away from Helen, who has become essential. He has felt a real connection to other targets and their families; he is still close to poor old VULCAN, to Mrs ODIN, to OBERON,

33

a young Jamaican militant – they are like friends to him. But there's something about Helen that makes her very different. With her, and only with her, he feels no need to pretend, he is at ease in his own skin, he begins to like himself. She gives him back his truthfulness and when he thinks of her he thinks in poetry, not ordinary humdrum words. Her beautiful voice speaks poems to him, and her piano playing, and the sweetness of her nature. My mother wore a yellow dress; gentle, gently, gentleness. She's a listener, just like Stephen. She permits her friends to chatter on about their own concerns and she never interrupts or tries to hurry them. Even when she's racing against time, with an engagement to keep or work to finish, she shows no signs of impatience. She never tells her callers that she is in a rush. Gentle, gently, gentleness. Only she and Stephen know that if the caller doesn't shut up soon she'll have to fly across the city to her next appointment in half the time she'd planned.

That worries him. He hates it when he knows that she'll be making an arduous journey on her own. If he could, he'd summon Pegasus for her, whistling for the white-winged horse to sweep down from the skies and carry beloved Helen where she wants to go, at the speed of light. As it is, he can only wish she were more extravagant with taxis. It has crossed his mind to book her a mini-cab in advance, when he knows that she will be going out at night, and the forecast is for fog and mist. If only he could pay for it without needing to give a name. He can see her running down the stairs and out of her front door, dressed in something long and silky, that liquefaction of her clothes, smelling sweet, a silver girl in high-heeled sandals, already late and wishing she did not have to travel alone through the dark and frosty streets, and finding then a driver waiting, a taxi, warm and lit. If only he could be sure she would get in it. If only she were more often on her own. If only. He keeps her diary in his head and, whenever she is going out, he thinks of her and begs her to stay safe.

Charlotte holds her tray of coffee cups high on one bent hand, the other hand on her hip, pretending she's a waitress. 'Oh good, coffee,' Louise says. 'Perfect timing Charlotte – it's morning prayers!' It is Louise's custom to gather her flock about her every Monday morning to review the week that's past and discuss the one ahead. It's a time for concerns to be aired and problems shared, she says. 'A problem shared is a problem halved.' It's also when coffee and washing-up rotas are decided, milk money collected, applications for leave considered, reminders issued and arrangements made. The Christmas party is on today's agenda.

They pull up their chairs around Louise's desk at one end of the long room: Stephen, Charlotte, Damian, Harriet, Solly, Greta, Christophine; all the Group III listeners. Along the corridor, in rooms equipped like this one, the listeners of Groups I and II are also gathering. Ivan, Vladimir, Magda, Adam, Thaddeus, Rafiq, Mohammed, Werner, Carla, Natalia, Imran, Ana, Tomás, Edouard, Aoife, Martin. Into their headphones today and every day will pour a flood of Arabic and Farsi, accented English, Russian, Polish, German, Serbo-Croatian, Spanish, a dozen other languages; the languages of people in distress, at war, in conflict; anxious words captured onto spools of tape, where putative death and destruction may unfold. Their targets know that their telephone calls are intercepted and so whatever clues they give are inadvertent. They speak only when they must. But one unguarded reference is enough. Experts in drawing inferences, the listeners of Groups I and II are forever conferring in hushed voices, typing frenetically and rushing their time-critical reports to the operatives and analysts who await them on the seventh floor, in rooms that are starkly lit and shrill with urgency and drama. In contrast the domestic worlds of the Group III listeners can feel a little dreary, although there are occasional excitements.

Rollo Buckingham's office, although on that same seventh floor, is for the moment calm. It is also dimly lit; the neon lighting overhead has been switched off and all that remains is one old-fashioned lamp that casts a small gold circle on the abutting desks of the two men in the room. The other man looks just like Rollo, except that he is very dark, while Rollo has barley-coloured hair. Stephen has not been told the other's name. This morning both men are at their desks; Rollo has his feet on his and his chair tilted at a dangerous angle. He is on the telephone but he puts the receiver down as soon as he sees Stephen at the open door.

'What-ho,' says Stephen.

'Good morning,' Rollo says.

Stephen holds out the top copy of his report, keeping the carbon for himself. They need a copy each so that they can communicate with the least number of spoken words. If they must have a protracted or detailed discussion, they sequester themselves in the Cube, but that's not practical on a daily basis. Most of the time they confine themselves to pointing at words or speaking in generalities, as everybody must in a place which cannot be guaranteed as safe from outside technical attack and where no one should be able accidentally to overhear an operational secret. Stephen has no idea whether the nameless man is on the PHOENIX list. Certainly he shows no interest in Stephen's frequent visits to his colleague.

While Rollo reads, Stephen, standing beside him at his desk, not invited to sit down, gazes at his golden head. Why does Rollo Buckingham make him feel like that whining schoolboy with his satchel, creeping like a snail? Rollo is about the same age as he is, possibly a little younger; he probably went to the same university – if indeed he got that far; it could be that he was in the Army – Stephen has not asked. Out of Eton, into Sandhurst, Stephen thinks; a short-service commission in a glamorous regiment, which, if it is the case, would make Rollo less well-educated than Stephen is, less well-qualified. It's absurd to feel subordinate to Rollo. Stephen irritates himself by doing so. He pictures Rollo in the full-dress uniform of the Blues and Royals: a flower of England's youth. He will certainly possess a shooting jacket.

It does not take Rollo long to read through the report:

Subject of interest arrived home at 19.33. Stated he had been working late and further delayed by faulty bicycle chain. Made one telephone call: to father. Arrangements made previously for Friday 10–Sunday 12 confirmed., (cf. tape dated 2 December). Subject (and wife) plan to arrive at Harcourt Mill by dinnertime. Watched television. Went to bed circa 23.00.

One incoming telephone call at 17.54, unanswered (no one present in subject's premises). Nothing further to report.

'What did he do on Friday morning?'

'I don't know. We haven't had those tapes yet. Nor the week-end's either.'

'Why not?'

'Technical hitch.'

Rollo sighs and rubs his temples roughly. He wears a gold signet ring on the little finger of his left hand. 'Are you sure there's nothing else?'

'Yes, of course I am.'

'Well, but this is turning into a something of a headache. So far you've given me nothing that I couldn't have worked out by myself. Are you absolutely sure that you couldn't have missed anything that day?'

Stephen struggles to conceal the impatience that he feels although Rollo is in fact still looking down at the report. 'Of course I am,' he says again.

'You see, there may have been . . .' Rollo begins to say but Stephen interrupts. 'Look, I'm pretty sure that I'm not missing things even though I don't know what you are expecting. Anyway, how do you know that he's not doing whatever he's doing when he is at work? I really should be part of the workplace coverage because I can't otherwise give you the whole picture.'

'We've discussed that before. It's just not possible, I'm afraid.'

'But you do have him covered *here*?'

Rollo frowns furiously at Stephen. Apparently oblivious to the conversation, his dark-haired colleague continues to leaf through the *Financial Times*. 'As I have already said, separate coverage; different arrangements altogether. It's contact out of working hours that I'm expecting. So, anyway. Please keep paying close attention. We have less than a month before the investigation comes up for its first review and if there is nothing conclusive then the Director will almost certainly decide to revoke the licence.'

This is the first that Stephen has heard about a deadline. That it may be imminent comes as a serious shock. How could he bear to be torn away from her so prematurely? He had supposed, and now instantly he sees how unthinking he has been, that this case would run for years on end, as others often did. After all, ODIN's telephone has been permanently tapped since 1967. Stephen inherited him from his predecessor and expects to keep him until he gets promoted or retires or ODIN dies. As long as a snippet or two of intelligence emerges now and again, the quarterly extension will merely be rubber-stamped. The Jamaican revolutionary, OBERON, is Stephen's exact contemporary; they will grow old together, like an elephant and his mahout. But now he realises that PHOENIX must be different. He's an insider, he's a colleague, he wears the badge of the Institute, he may even be here on this seventh floor. He could actually be in the next-door room. It's an ugly thing to suspect a man of treachery and those who do will surely need to prove or to negate their chill suspicions soon. He can see why Rollo and his sub-director want a resolution fast.

All right then, Stephen will provide one. He is not prepared to part with Helen for the sake of narrow-minded and prosaic truth. He had thought that time was on his side but now he knows it's not and so he must move fast. And besides, if PHOENIX is a traitor – and there must be some good reason why he is under surveillance – he must obviously be caught. A man who seems to be a loyal friend, a loving husband, but in fact is something other – a whited sepulchre, a snake in the grass – cannot remain at large.

'Well,' he says, slowly, diffidently, 'um there is one thing – I mean about his working late on Thursday evening. I didn't pay all that much attention to it at the time but now I come to think of it, he didn't really sound convincing when he tried to explain that lateness to his wife.'

'That could be important. Please keep listening very carefully.'

'I will,' says Stephen. 'I will do my very best to get you what you need.'

Rollo nods in acknowledgement, smiles his thin-lipped cavalry officer's smile and picks up his cup of pale, milkless tea – a proper cup, blue-patterned, with a matching saucer; not a mug like the ones that are used by everybody else.

Rafiq's birthday drinks don't go quite according to plan because yesterday two Iranians blew themselves up in a car in Connaught Square, apparently with their own malfunctioning bomb. The Group I listeners are on high alert, with operatives and strategists breathing down their necks and Muriel's lateness has made the situation worse. Even so, Rafiq finds time to buy his round. This is what the listeners do, on birthdays. They gather in the Institute's bar, a dark, low-ceilinged room on the top floor of the building, next to the canteen. It is always full. As in every other room, the windows are shrouded by full-length curtains that are seldom washed. Cecil, the barman, is missing an arm and will not be rushed. Queues build up at lunchtimes. There are many regulars: men and women who come here every day and often stay on after work to drink their way through their undifferentiated years. They come from various departments of the Institute and are not allowed to talk about their work although, of course, they do, in ways that are lightly camouflaged. What else have they in common? Few of them would ever think of meeting outside the Institute. When they leave the bar, most of them go home to the suburbs of London where, if they are fortunate, their wives have dinner ready, or where they live alone. A few of them were heroes once – in wartime. About the things that they did then, they are reticent. There are some secrets still – not many – that are worth the keeping.

Rafiq's large order – nineteen drinks – takes Cecil a long time to fulfil and the regulars grow restive; they only have an hour in which to anaesthetise themselves against the afternoon. Pints of Young's, gin and tonics, gin and limes, Britvic orange for Rafiq and Mohammed; Harriet asks for crème de menthe. Stephen drinks bitter because it is expected of a man, even though he does not really like its assertive taste. He'd rather have lager, or the gin that he can smell in Charlotte's glass. The scent of it is medicinal and clean; a drink that smells like that must surely do you good. And the tonic, fizzing against a cube of ice. Juniper and quinine, lemon, spruce, clean and cold in this steamy place, which is loud with people, dark and full of smoke.

The Group I listeners do not stay long after they have sung to Rafiq and presented him with a cigarette lighter and a birth-day card, but the others, with nothing imperative to call them back, buy each other more drinks and spin the lunch hour out. Stephen switches to brandy. It scours his mouth and numbs it slightly; he feels the mixture of liquids swirling through his guts, his veins; his head is like a hot-air balloon, swelling steadily, straining to lift off. What will Helen be doing now, at

41

one o'clock on Monday? Does she have her lunch in school? Does she sit at a refectory table amid laughing children, eating the food that school children eat: roly-poly pudding, shepherd's pie? Dinner is what it's called, in schools. Or does she favour a break at lunchtime, a walk and some fresh air? Why does he not know? There's so much he does not know about her yet. On reflection he decides that she is more likely to go out than to stay in school; she is a woman who would need time away from noise and chatter, to collect her thoughts, to breathe, to be quiet for a while. Probably she makes good use of her time to do a little shopping. He sees her in her yellow dress, with a basket on her arm, strolling through a market where the stallholders all know her, love her and call her by her name. When she stops to buy a cauliflower, the greengrocer gives her a peach. She bites into its sweet ripeness and she smiles; she is garmented in light from her own beauty.

'I'm starving,' Charlotte complains. 'Come on, guys, shall we go for lunch?'

'There'll be nothing left by now,' says Damian. 'Or if there is, it'll be the swill that no one wants. Let's go out and get a sandwich.'

'Ooh yes. Yes let's. Prawn mayonnaise! Ooh yum. I do need something to line my little tummy. You coming, Steve?'

But there's Louise, who stopped after two drinks and went sensibly to the canteen with Harriet, and is back now and beckoning from the door because it's late and the tapes have come. And behind her Muriel, irate, because she has battled her way through ice and snow and missed the birthday drinks to register the tapes in record time, only to find most of the listeners absent.

'We'll have to make do with crisps,' says Charlotte, sadly. She buys six packets from slow Cecil and that afternoon the long room reeks of vinegar and grease and bitter-breath.

The tension is apparent before either of them speaks. Stephen can feel it in the air and hear in the silence, in the over-careful way the front door closes, in the sound of something liquid filling a single glass instead of two.

It's almost eleven o'clock on Sunday night. The only words that PHOENIX says in the first half-hour after their return from the weekend at Harcourt Mill are: 'It's bloody freezing in this flat. Did you forget to set the timer?' A while later Helen asks: 'Do you want anything to eat? I could do scrambled eggs?' Her voice is tentative and small.

'No, thank you,' Jamie replies, and Stephen knows his mouth is set in a straight, unyielding line. He speaks each of the three words with unnatural precision, the final consonant of the second word enunciated clearly, as if Helen were a foreigner with rudimentary English. His accent, always patrician, slides further up the scale. He informs his wife he's tired, he's going to bed; he has a busy day tomorrow and an early start. Stephen listens to him cleaning his teeth, spitting loudly, flushing the toilet, shutting the bedroom door. A gas boiler hisses in the background. It stops and there is quiet. Then the quiet is broken by a new sound: the sound of a woman crying.

Stephen does not hesitate. He seizes the telephone and dials Rollo's extension. Rollo is still in the office, thank goodness; Stephen does not want time for sober second thoughts. Breathlessly he pours out his invented story: 'I'm doing Sunday's tapes. The ones that were delayed today. The early evening tapes. We should have picked him up at his father's house. We've missed it, I think. Well, we've missed something. You were suggesting that, I think, this morning. It was yesterday night.'

'Slow down,' says Rollo. 'I'm getting confused. What are you talking about? But please be very careful. Remember that you are on the telephone.'

'Yes, yes, I'm not going to say anything. I simply thought you ought to know immediately that there are two hours unaccounted for last night. You remember where he was for the weekend? So, okay, then his wife came home at 20.53, but she was on her own. He didn't get back until 22.48.'

'Stop right there. I'm coming downstairs to listen.'

'There's nothing to hear, she was alone, she didn't speak, and besides I'm still working through the tape. He didn't say anything either, when he eventually returned. He just told her that he wasn't hungry and that in the morning he had an early start. Did he?'

'I don't know. What happened in the morning?'

'I won't know that until tomorrow.'

'Oh yes, of course, Come to think of it, you've been pretty quick off the mark with Sunday evening.'

'I'm giving it priority,' says Stephen. 'As always and as you know. Although this does mean I'll have to work late if I'm to have a snowflake's of catching up on the rest of my caseload. I'll be on the late-list yet again.'

'Don't worry about that. I'll write Security a note to say I've asked you to work overtime; I think you get paid for extra hours, at your grade? Or do you get time off in lieu? Keep a note of the times, in any case, won't you? But, back to the point. Didn't she give any indication of what he might be doing?'

'No. She didn't speak. I told you.'

'Maybe she got a lift with someone else and he stayed on at his parents' a bit longer? Or he was offered a lift and she chose to drive herself. There's only one car, I'm sure.'

'I don't think she drives.'

'My guess is that there'll be an explanation later. At least, I damn well hope there is. Because there's nothing I can do, if not. I couldn't have got cover over the weekend.'

'I know. It's rotten luck. But you could be right. There may be a completely innocent reason why he should send his wife ahead of him and come home by himself so late on a Sunday night.'

'Everyone was late last night. The roads were bloody awful, with the snow.'

'Not in Buckinghamshire, they weren't. We must have been lucky, and escaped the worst.'

'Look, I've got to go,' says Rollo. 'I'm meeting someone, sorry. Please catch me up ASAP, tomorrow.'

'Wilco. Have a nice evening, Rollo.'

Stephen's heart is still pounding when he puts the receiver down. Bastard, bastard, bastard, he says, beneath his breath. He feels so impotent. Helen was weeping and there was nothing he could do. She went to bed around midnight, still sorrowful. She probably lay awake the whole night long, still crying, probably, but stifling her sobs so as not to wake her bastard of a husband. Tears on her pillow. Longing for someone she could turn to, a friend in her hour of need. But what was Stephen doing last night at that same time? He was snoring on his sofa after a slow drive back to London, having had to stop every few miles to clear his windscreen, the wipers on his Datsun having

45

failed, having drunk all but a hand span of the Bell's he bought on Friday. What good was he to Helen? He was no friend to her at all.

Helen would not have been the only woman who cried herself to sleep on Sunday night, as Stephen knows. Indeed she was not the only woman who cried in Stephen's hearing. On Sunday evening, ODIN's wife, at her wits' end, telephoned her son in Canada, a rare occurrence, and sobbed so hard that she could barely squeeze her words out. Stephen had listened to them both: the helpless mother and her son, helpless also, because so far away. Oh Mum, he kept on saying: oh Mum. For really there was nothing else that he could say to console her for the sleepless nights, the repeated fits and the sheer, unending misery of it all. After a few heart-rending minutes Mrs ODIN had pulled herself together, recollected the cost of a transatlantic call, and brought the conversation to a hurried end, still sniffing. To spare her feelings Stephen merely noted the fact of the call and not its contents.

Did the ODINS' son, Emmanuel, feel wracked by guilt when he put the telephone down, in the hall of his house in Calgary, 4,000 miles away from the small flat on the Peabody Estate in Vauxhall where he was born and lived until he was old enough to find his own way out? Stephen saw that upbringing in his mind, more or less contemporary with his own: Emmanuel trying to shape a normal boyhood for himself in a household necessarily centred round an invalid sister, and any time left over given not to him but to a cause. Had he suspected even then that the cause was lost? Had he resented the poor pale thing pinioned to a wheelchair or had he loved her without question? His own sister, after all; that must count for something.

Deepening the melancholy of the afternoon was a telephone call that VULCAN made to the General Secretary of the Communist Party about an article he disagreed with in Saturday's *Morning Star*. His rambling points were hard to follow. The younger man had humoured the elder and jollied him along while dismissing out of hand the things he said. It is VULCAN's role as father-figure to the Secretary and advisor to others of the hierarchy that justifies the strategists' continuing interest in him, but that call suggested he might not be taken seriously much longer. To Stephen's ear there was also a worrying deterioration in the old man's health. These December days without heating must be taking their toll on him. VULCAN does not complain but Stephen is aware that until the boiler is mended he has no other source of warmth than a kettle and some blankets. That Sunday he sounded very tired, and underlying his usual pneumatic wheeze was a liquid, gurgling sound. This Stephen reported.

By the time he got back to his flat on Monday evening, Stephen was enveloped in sadness that clung like winter mist and would not be dispelled. He sought distractions – food, *The Hitchhiker's Guide to the Galaxy* on television, the rest of the bottle of whisky – but they only worsened the sick headache he had had since lunchtime. On top of beer and brandy, more alcohol, canned laughter and the kebab he had bought from the van next to the station churned into a nauseating mess. He could feel it coagulating in his stomach: a swill of murky liquid, seasoned with hopelessness, lumpy with globules of undigested fat.

Beneath it is something else, nagging like an incipient infection, an abscessed tooth, like the intermittent shrilling that he suffers in his ears. This feeling of anxiety is different. Is its cause the untruth he told Rollo? Or the unhappiness of Helen? Yes, he thinks, it must be that, and his powerlessness to help her.

A million women weeping in the night, and their children too. Stephen needs no reminding of the inconsolable tears of children that soak through their pillows and pool in the hollows of their ears. In his own bed that night his feet were cold and his nose too, and clammy, like a dog's. He slid a hand down his pyjama trousers to touch himself interrogatively but there was no immediate response and he was too lonely to provoke one. In the silence of the night he said Helen's name out loud, to interrupt that silence, to hear her name, for the companionship of a human voice.

Tuesday

On Tuesday morning the routine work of the Group III listeners is suspended because, in the middle of the night before, Department Four got wind of an impending IRA attack. Details are missing; the target is unknown. The Department's operatives will not divulge the source of the intelligence but the listeners can guess: somewhere, in a London pub perhaps, or the back room of a terraced house in a small provincial town, someone will have overheard a hint or careless word and in a panic called for an urgent meeting with his go-between, a man whose real name he will never know but whom for at least a year or two he is obliged to trust. There's nothing else that he can do, even though he knows the man with the alias is feigning friendship; he's long since sold the pass and the men who think that they're his real friends would kill him if they knew.

All the domestic listeners are required to help their colleagues in Group II to comb through the past three days of take from every relevant telephone line and eavesdropping device in search of further leads. The operation is codenamed CUCHULAINN. Charlotte, Damian and Harriet, who have worked on these targets in the past, are dispatched to secret places; Stephen, Solly, Greta and Christophine are asked to scan through dozens of tapes, listening for hesitations, strange turns of phrase, unexplained commands and half-voiced things. Any other day, Stephen would have welcomed this dramatic change from his usual caseload. Too much of his time is drowsily spent keeping half an ear on the maunderings of old men and hapless ideologues. But this morning his sole concern is Helen and it is painful to be made to put the PHOENIX tapes on hold. However, there's no choice. Today there is a job to do where, as Louise declares, the stakes could be life or death.

Helen's voice is like the sound of the sea or a river nearby, like a soft wind breathing on fresh leaves in spring – there, always, in the background of his hearing, there like the almost-silent beat of his own heart. Hush, he tells her, I will listen later, when I can. She will understand the need for this delay. Meanwhile, the work is difficult but also quite absorbing. Stephen does not know these people; their accents and their patterns of speech are new. How can he tell if that person whispering anxiously about a wedding is using a crude code or is in fact the best man of the groom? Long experience helps: in any voice, in any language, the practised ear can hear the sounds of tension.

Christophine finds it hard to tune her ear to Ulster voices and when she hears something that she can't make out, she pauses her tape and asks Stephen for his help. Christophine, somewhat reserved, an elegant woman with a blue gleam to her skin and traces in her voice of the French that is her mother tongue, doesn't often pay much heed to Stephen. That she should do so now makes him glow with pleasure. When he moves her headphones to his ears, they are still warm. Leaning in to share the headphones, he breathes in the scent she wears. Her smile is lovely when she thanks him.

All through the day the long room is alive with excited operatives and strategists dashing in and out in pursuit of news. Outside, in this city and beyond, trackers will be trailing suspects, inconspicuous in drab clothing, experts at blend-ing into any scene. All new recruits to the Institute receive some basic training in surveillance, mainly intended to teach them counter-measures. Stephen still recalls the main pre-cepts: don't keep turning round to look behind you. Don't keep dodging pointlessly in and out of doors. His instructor had been the Institute's head tracker and it was obvious why he held that post. In the classroom he was indistinguishable from all the other middle-aged white men who largely con-stituted the staff of the Institute; in the side-streets of Cam-den, where the students went for practical demonstrations, he was equally camouflaged. He was a man whom no one would notice, or afterwards be able to describe, a chameleon, a crea-ture virtually invisible in any habitat.

The new recruits were told to pretend that they were on their way to a meeting with an informer whose very life would hang on their ability to shake off any tail. Allotted two hours of an afternoon, they wandered separately through streets and into shops and pubs, trying to seem casual but purposeful, trying vainly to avoid a glance over their shoulders. Each one had arrived at the designated meeting point to find their pretend informer in handcuffs, and a team of trackers with a complete list of their movements.

Although he performed no better than the other students, Stephen had been captivated by this aspect of the course. So much of the course had otherwise consisted of injunctions about security and paperwork. There had been whole days on the correct procedures for handling files, registering docu-ments, minuting meetings, locking cabinets, deflecting intru-sive questions, adding extra years to pensions, and the rainbow of official forms: blue for authority to search the central index, green for action on a file, violet for mandatory notification of any suspect contact.

Three weeks into the course, Stephen was beginning to feel he had made a grave mistake. He hadn't objected to knowing so little about the Institute in advance of joining; that was understandable – you couldn't expect to discover its secrets before you had signed up. But, even after he had been officially inducted and had sworn an oath to keep all he was about to learn strictly to himself in perpetuity, nothing was vouchsafed that would not have been in keeping with the protocols of the dullest government department. After the enticing first contact by letter – a letter with no heading other than a PO Box address, delivered by hand to his pigeonhole in college – after the first interview, at the Randolph Hotel, the second in the Oxford and Cambridge Club, the third with a panel of three men in an anonymous building near Hyde Park, the listening tests, the verbal dexterity tests, the questions – have you ever had sex with a man, or had the urge to? – was this the anticlimactic finish? A future pushing paper in an insignificant little outpost and nothing to look forward to but an index-linked and enhanced pension? All work and no play at all. It was not for that that he had answered the seductive letter of invitation and the later questions about his sexuality, drug-taking and political affiliations; his life to that point had already been quite dull enough.

The final week of the training course came just in time to stop him handing in his resignation. It was as if the instructors had concealed till then the true nature of the work in order to elicit a deep gasp of amazement when at last they raised the curtain. Mobile surveillance, static surveillance, eaves-dropping, concealment devices, hidden cameras, invisible writing, radio communications, the best ways of steaming open letters, the discreet delivery of documents via dustbins or in the pages of newspapers dropped on benches, signals, ciphers and code-breaking, lock-picking, clandestine searches, informer recruitment, informer handling and case histories. Above all, case histories. Real, true-life stories. Real photographs of real people, real voices saved on tape, real objects, real traitors.

Five days full of hypnotising anecdote and information flourished before the dazzled students by a cast of instructors who tacitly implied that they had personally witnessed every one of these encounters, successfully employed these methods, upheld the nation's safety, as in due course their pupils, if properly attentive, would also go on to do. And yet these magicians looked so ordinary, dull even: grey men, balding and overweight men, and one middle-aged woman with a tight bonnet of blonde hair. The sense that they were people in disguise thrilled Stephen. As they were, so was he: a man beneath whose unremarkable surface lay an extraordinary capacity for action and an extraordinary knowledge of arcane and vital things.

In the last hour of the training course the instructors all at once retracted, suddenly at pains to emphasise that this, a fraction of the Institute's procedures, was all they were permitted to divulge. We have taught you what you need to know for the purposes of security, they said; better to know less than more. Half-truths are more dangerous than lies. Those who were to be operatives in the field would have further specialist training; for everybody else an outline was enough. Stephen had been very disappointed. He felt that having promised to bare all, the instructors had lowered too soon the curtain they had lifted – but they had at least allowed a glimpse into the world of secret tradecraft, and even in the long room the things that he had briefly seen might conceivably be useful.

For the whole of Tuesday the listeners sift through hours of speech, looking for essential nuggets. Speech, or rather, spoken words and half-words, mumbles, words in broken strings and fragments, sometimes making sense in context, sometimes not. Few targets speak in sentences, consecutive and fully thought-out in advance, subject, verb and object marshalled, the ending foreseen before the first word is pronounced. No one does; especially not on the telephone. Everyone abandons words midway, trails off, uses hesitating words to shape the thought that was unformed when they began to speak, and studs their talk with sounds that have their origins in another form of language, the one that speaks with hands and eyes, through gesture, movement and expression, that can't exist on any page or be transcribed, the one that is the ground of true communication. Want of this visual lexicon can make conversations overheard on telephones difficult to decrypt. There are simple conversations obviously – between people who have never met, and are speaking merely to trade information, and between people who meet each other often. Telephone calls are expensive, to be kept to the point and made only when needs must, but when meeting face-to-face is just not possible and messages are complex, there's no alternative. Therefore another kind of call: longer, more intimate, more softly voiced, punctuated by sighing breaths and wordless sounds, and silences sometimes. And listeners become interpreters of silence.

It's harder still to make good sense of the product of an eavesdropping device. Talk in offices and homes goes on against myriad sounds, and a speaker only needs to turn away from the implanted microphone or to stray beyond the compass of its reach for words to change to babble. In any case, even when the words themselves are clear, the flow will stutter. Spoken thoughts are constantly diverted, by distractions, televisions, babies, doorbells, other people. It often strikes Stephen how carelessly people interrupt each other and finish off each other's sentences as if the yet unspoken words were totally foreknown. And how often they are wrong, anticipating one conclusion when the speaker intended quite another. Dialogue in life is nothing like dialogue in transcript. There are times when Stephen thinks himself to be only person in the world who truly listens. And monologue the one true form of speech. A man speaking to himself in an empty room.

But there are exceptions, he has noticed. When two people are alone together in a car, they do sometimes speak with rare and concentrated intensity, and they also listen. He hasn't overheard many such conversations; his are not the kind of targets who demand a level of surveillance so intense that their cars need to be bugged, but he has helped out his colleagues when they are extra-busy. For some reason he remembers one of these times especially: a man, a South African, suspected of gun-running. He was Solly's case. An entrapment operation was in progress, it had reached a critical stage; the man had to be watched every minute of the night and day. Solly, having to cover the telephones and the home, had delegated the car to Stephen.

Most days the target made short journeys on his own, with

the radio on. There had been hours of Radio 3 to scan. But then, after an exasperating time when the target failed to rise to any bait that he was offered and the trackers kept on losing him, he casually mentioned to a friend that he was driving to Dover the next day. The operatives exulted: a fresh trap was sprung.

The easiest way to eavesdrop in real-time on a conversation in a moving car is to follow the car at a distance of no more than a mile. For the first and so far only time in his career, Stephen found himself in the back of a Ford Transit, with a relay microphone and a radio link to the mobile trackers. They were past Dartford before there was anything to hear. The target's wife was driving, their baby daughter in the back seat, fussing loudly. Only when she eventually dropped off to sleep did the target speak. Nothing that he said had any bearing on the case; to Solly's embarrassment it transpired that the reason for the journey was to collect the suspect's sister from the port. While the child slept and the woman focused on the road, the man described his sister as if he needed to recreate her after absence, to make her real by remembering, to explain her to the sister-in-law she had not yet met. Two sets of road sounds, the car's and the van's, and the man talking: his sister, her sweetness as a child, how she had looked out for him at school, the fraught relationship with their father, her first serious boyfriend, the horror of her injury by fire. He spoke of scarring but he did not say where she was scarred. Miri. Her name was Miri; she had been married but the marriage did not last. She had liked unusual foods when she was small: black coffee, anchovies, those sour dried plums you buy in Chinese shops. She kept terrapins and a cat.

To this day Stephen remembers Miri. He heard her voice on the journey back but by then the baby was noisily awake again and the talk was all of family news and travel. Of course he never saw her but he does sometimes wish he knew where she had gone and what she's doing now.

For that particular couple, the suspected gun-runner and his wife, uninterrupted time with each other must have been precious; they would have made the most of any journey when their child was quiet. But it wasn't that which explained the intensity and coherence of that hour, to Stephen's mind. No, it had more to do with the intimacy of two people in a private space, sitting side-by-side, the one's attention mainly elsewhere, the other freed from eye-contact and licensed to confide. Licensed to stay silent also, by the passing road. A small space and the listener's gaze averted, as in the confessionals of Stephen's early youth. Bless me, Father, for I have sinned. The child with his head bowed before the grille, the man's face turned away; a list of faults in thoughts and words, of things the child has left undone, the forgiving murmur of the adult.

It has been a long time since Stephen thought of making his confession and, if there ever were a time when he could have disburdened himself in a car, it was also long ago. His regular passenger these days is his mother. And yet, on that short trip to Dover, he felt some share in the couple's closeness. In step with the suspect's wife, he made sounds of listening and assent; he asked questions. And he wondered if there was another factor at work then – that of destination. The most ordinary of journeys has a beginning and an end – East Acton to Didcot, Walthamstow to Dover. Does the promise of a full stop encourage the telling of a story, does narrative need boundaries? The start defined and the finish in sight: 'The End' in ornate writing on a hand-drawn scroll as it appears above the closing credits of old films?

One of the people Stephen is listening to today runs a taxi firm. It's his office that is wired and not his cars, although, for all that Stephen knows, there may be tracking devices in them too. The tapes pile up: Saturday evening, Sunday, Monday; the take from Monday night to Tuesday morning arrives in the late afternoon. By then Stephen is dizzy from hours of ringing telephones, radio messages, background chatter. Unfamiliar voices and unfamiliar places: Crossmaglen, Coalisland, Silverstream, Loughgall. How can he make sense of them when he does not know what he is looking for? It's a labyrinth, or maybe it's a nightmare party game: a player rings up for a cab, giving his or her current location and desired destination, the controller passes the request to one or more of the drivers on the road, the one who answers fastest wins the job. Round and round the directions go: Lisnadill, Craigavon, Donaghmore, and as they do they get more garbled: calling number three, the controller says, and number three's reply, through traffic noise, through static, through the fragile wiring of a secret listening device is impossible to hear. As in a bad dream, the player whose task it is to find the hidden key feels a rising sense of panic. These were messages sent yesterday and the day before; current then, in the present tense. Elsewhere, in undisclosed locations, Charlotte, Harriet and Damian will have their ears pressed to voices likewise speaking in the present or the future, whereas for those whom Stephen is struggling to understand, the future then is now the past. And in other unknown places unobtrusive men and women will be loitering in cars, at bus stops, at shop windows, in the ditches of country lanes, and all of them on the lookout for something they can only hope that they will recognise if it ever it comes. Stephen is not at all sure that he will. But, if he misses the crucial hint and an ambassador or an MP dies, if a bomb explodes beneath a policeman's car, a platoon of British soldiers is blown to smithereens of bone, it will be his fault. There will be an inquiry, the tapes that he is scanning now will be re-scanned, his culpable incompetence will be revealed and he, Stephen, Step hen Waddlecock, will have been responsible for the deaths of innocent men.

It's desperate. But looked at in another way, it's not. Stephen has been here before, albeit not very often; he has seen other emergencies come and go, in a small way he can claim to have played some part in their success. Or, at any rate, to have been uninvolved so far in any failure. The game goes on – the Chinese whispers, the misunderstandings and the misdirections, the disinformation, the bewildering time lags, the words half-heard, the pauses and the silence – and it seldom comes to a definitive conclusion.

Nor does it today. A few minutes before seven o'clock, by which time the listeners have been working flat out for hours, removing their headphones only to take instructions or when interrupted by operatives or Muriel, a go-between puts his head round the door of the long room to call CUCHULAINN off. A false alarm, he announces, breezily, that's how it goes, so often. He cannot go into details, obviously, but he can say that the informer seems to have got the wrong end of the stick. Easy to do, of course, blokes can't be expected to go marching round asking direct questions about bombs. Go-betweens can't arrange a meeting at the drop of a hat. Thanks most awfully, anyway. You've been absolutely brilliant today. Real stars.

The PHOENIX tapes are in Stephen's in-tray. He saw Muriel deliver them, on her slow, painstaking rounds, distributing her envelopes, stopping to talk to anyone who would take their headphones off for just a minute. Damian is the one she loves the best. Sunday midnight to Monday noon, Monday noon to midnight, Monday midnight to Tuesday morning: it has been a torment to leave those envelopes unopened through the exhausting hours of unremitting work. Rollo Buckingham has also been impatient: Stephen saw him striding into the long room in the morning but Louise saw him too and shooed him off. Attack warnings trump all but Alpha investigations, she will have reminded him. She will not have given him more detail – Rollo is an operative in Department Six, not Department Four; he has no need to know that information. Even in his distracted state, Stephen, watching this exchange from the far end of the room, noted the precise and beautiful cut of Rollo's suit. He wears his clothes so well. How is it that his jackets fall in a perfect line from shoulder to hem, the waistbands of his trousers neither gape nor pinch and his collars are forever crisp? It was some comfort to see him being dismissed so roundly.

Stephen breathes out deeply through his mouth. He will help the others to finish off the otiose reports and then he will join Helen. He will tell Louise that these PHOENIX tapes can't wait a minute longer and it is imperative therefore that he should stay on late.

But he hasn't taken Louise's care for the welfare of her team into account. This has been a very long day, a difficult day, and she wants them to be rewarded. She forbids more work. She brushes away Stephen's earnest protestations; she has squared things with Rollo, she assures him, he is to put all his tapes away until tomorrow. Meanwhile Charlotte and Damian come trailing back, a little wan and deflated. Harriet has sloped off.

'I'm ravenous,' says Charlotte. 'And cheesed off. Me and Cecilia were going to meet in the lunch hour to do our Christmas shopping. She's going away tomorrow. Now I'll have to do it on my own.' She does not need to explain Cecilia, they all know she is her flatmate.

'Never mind,' Louise says soothingly. 'I've got Resources to agree to an extra hour for lunch tomorrow *and* the overtime. Because it's nearly Christmas! So you'll have loads of time, Lottie, to buy even more expensive presents! Now then, it's late, I'm tired and I can't face going home and cooking. Anyone want to join me for a cheap and cheerful dinner?'

'Ooh,' Charlotte says, more happily, 'that is a great idea. I couldn't half murder an Indian!'

'Um, well, that would be super but I must just finish off . . .' Stephen begins before Louise interrupts him.

'But me no buts, sweetie, I've already told you I've squared it with your man upstairs. I told him you'd have the whole day to yourself tomorrow. If we leave now, we'll escape the late list.'

There's no escape. Under the circumstances Stephen cannot stay on behind his colleagues. Damian makes his excuses: he has a ticket for *Tristan and Isolde* and if he dashes will just make it before the curtain rises. Christophine has a family to feed and Solly a wife who will expect him but Greta, Charlotte and Louise, like Stephen, live alone; there will be no one waiting hungrily for their return. Together they lock away the tape-recorders, files and papers, check the cabinets, turn off the lights and leave the long room to walk through thin rain to an Indian restaurant Louise knows near Victoria. Gin is the thing to drink with Indian food, says Greta. She and the other women talk, and Stephen hears them without listening, his thoughts entirely on Helen. Where is she this evening, could she have escaped from PHOENIX, will she remember to eat? Chicken biryani and lamb dhansak; in the rosy glow of the little restaurant grease shines on Charlotte's lips.

Wednesday

The morning began badly. After a night of broken sleep and anxious dreams that were hard to tell apart from waking thoughts, Stephen had slept through the screech of his alarm clock and had to rush to get to work. In a dream that seemed to repeat itself with variations on a constant loop like a demonic piece of music, he had been a witness to successive acts of violence and each time found himself unable to make the necessary 999 call that would bring the outrage to a stop. A man in a mask was skewering a woman with a metal rod, a man held a gun to a baby's head and Stephen, standing right beside a telephone, could not force his index finger into the correct number on the dial. Or, having inserted a finger, could not rotate the dial. Or, although on a fully working telephone, accurately sequence the essential numbers. Or remember what the numbers were. His head was thick with fitful waking and yesterday evening's gin, his stomach gassy from the food he'd eaten. There were delays on the Central Line and his train was packed. Between Notting Hill Gate and Queensway he had felt a sudden upheaval in the gut, presaging an urgent need for evacuation. He had willed his bowels to settle. Having already emptied them at home, and with no breakfast since, he couldn't possible need to go again. Something squirted inside him and popped wetly, like an eructation of marsh gas in a bog. Mind over matter, he told himself, as his mother always used to say of childhood pains. Mind over matter. If you bid it to be gone, it will. It worked: he felt secure enough to change trains as usual at Bond Street.

Just out of that station, buried in one of London's deepest tunnels, the equally crowded train that Stephen had joined came to a lurching halt and all the lights went out. It stayed at a dark standstill for what felt like an eternity, the crammed-together passengers becoming restive, nervous, the blackness hot and thick as bearskin, Stephen's belly horribly and noisily protesting. To soil himself on the Underground, to sense his sphincter muscle loosen and the noxious stream spurt out, his shit splattering the stockinged legs of the woman in a green coat who was pressed against him, indelibly staining his own legs, squelching into his shoes: more stuff of nightmare. His fellow passengers cringing from the foetid stink in justifiable disgust.

Stephen was feeling very shaky by the time he reached the Institute. There were queues of people waiting for their badges to be checked and waiting for the lifts; he couldn't trust himself that long but careered up the six flights of stairs, clenching his buttocks and his stomach, praying that the toilets on the third-floor landing would be unoccupied. He has an only child's dislike of crapping within earshot of another. They were, and he flung himself into a cubicle, arriving in the nick of time. Splatterings above and below the white porcelain rim but nothing on his underpants, he noted with relief; he did his best to wipe up the mess so that no one else would see it. While he was scrubbing himself and the seat, someone entered the toilet but left it rapidly, repelled, Stephen supposed, by his revolting stench. He stayed sitting in the cubicle a while; it was quiet in there, and cool and light.

Now after this, after abstinence prolonged, at last, the lady of consolation. Helen. Helen who, like any other earthly creature, perforce must eat and then excrete. He remembers playground titters about poo and pee and bums and asking his mother if Jesus went to the toilet too, like normal people, like the Queen. In response she scolded him for being blasphemous. He remembers learning that word from her and savouring the slither of it on his tongue, its snaky sibilants and its thrilling sense of sin. Although he can smile now at the guilelessness of the child, he still believes that bodily functions can be problematic. There are things that women ought to do alone, their ceremonies and secret rites, which should not be seen by lovers.

Louise is waiting to grab him as soon as he appears at the door of the long room. 'You're late,' she says. 'We've some catching up to do for Department Four. It turns out that things were not as straightforward as we were led to hope. We won't get that extra hour for lunch today, I'm sorry to say, though they'll let us carry it over. But before we get on with our work, we need to have another little meeting about the Christmas party. I'm about to have a chat with Ana and Ivan and I propose to say that we'll be responsible for the food. It's so much less hassle than doing the drink. And besides, if we don't do the catering, we'll be at the mercy of Group II and there'll be nothing to eat but crisps.'

'And blinis,' Charlotte says, putting a lugubrious emphasis on the liquid 'l'. 'Actually I seem to recall that they were rather good.'

'But there weren't enough of them to soak up Edouard's punch.'

'Oh yeah, that's right. Edouard's toxic mixture! I'm surprised we can remember anything at all about last year, after we'd drunk that.'

Stephen, not listening, tries to edge away. 'I'm happy to do whatever I'm told,' he says. 'If you could maybe have the meeting without me? It's just that I'm so behind because of yesterday. I promised Buckingham. He'll flay me. Could I possibly do his tapes first and then CUCHULAINN?'

'Look,' says Louise. 'I don't know much about the PHOENIX thing but I do know that it's going nowhere. Sub-director Six's secretary told me in the lift that they're about to have a case conference any minute now. Sorry, I was meant to tell you. She's arranging it this week.'

'Excuse me,' Stephen protests, 'it is Sub-director Six's secretary who is ill-informed. We're on the verge of a breakthrough, as a matter of fact.' The level of his voice is rising, although he tries to keep it steady. Charlotte is looking at him with amused surprise; Louise is laughing too. 'Okay, okay,' she says, 'keep your hair on. We'll make the meeting snappy.'

But by the time all the Group III listeners are assembled and everyone has a cup of tea or coffee and a biscuit and the list has been drawn up of who is to bring sausage rolls and mince pies, the morning is half gone. 'We'll have to make the sandwiches in the kitchen here,' Louise declares. 'They go all dry and curly if you do them at home the night before and they sit around all day.'

Stephen, still not listening, thinks of Helen in the staff room of her school, enduring a correspondingly frustrating time. She is not a woman who fusses over sandwiches; she knows what is essential and what is not. At this moment her attention will be on the choir of children who, under her gentle tutelage, sing like angels, in the pure lancing treble of small children that arrows to the soul. If she could hear what he has to put up with, she would surely sympathise. 'I'll take charge of cheese and biscuits,' he announces, 'if that's all right by everybody else.'

And, finally, at long last, yesterday's three orange-label tapes, safe within their separate envelopes, waiting in his in-tray like the answer to a wish. Stephen slides the first into the machine, puts his headphones on and listens. Quiet until Monday morning, the day before yesterday: good morning, my beautiful Helen.

'Come back to bed,' the man was saying and the woman laughed but she said nothing and there came a sound that was gelatinous, like the sound of a sea creature being sundered from a rock. Suction and a sigh. It's disgusting and it takes a while to comprehend what's happening. 'Let go of me,' she says but she's still laughing. 'You know I can't. I can't be late.'

Stephen shivers with disgust and shock. She's not crying, she is laughing. Instead of leaving silently for work, she is letting her husband maul her, submitting to his kisses, soliciting them perhaps. Come back to bed? What does this imply? And how can it mean what it must mean, after the night before? What could have happened in the night between wife and husband? The answer can only be that the husband tricked the wife. He must have spun a web of lies to turn her disposition so fast from sadness to good cheer. If good cheer is what it was. Is there a note almost of hysteria in Helen's voice? Could her laughter be concealing horror? Stephen thinks of hostages who, having somehow raised the alarm, are compelled to tell the policeman at the door that all is well, for terror of the gunman invisible within who has their frightened children bound and gagged. A woman's eyes frantically signal fear while her mouth speaks words of reassurance. For a wild moment he wonders if Helen is signalling to him. But then that sense of impotence that sickened him when he heard her weeping in the night descends on him again.

He stops the tape. This is unbearable. He can't go on listening but he must go on listening, he can't go to her, he can't do anything, he is as helpless as a fledgling in a storm. The irrational and suppressed anxiety he has suffered all his life – that he is in some way incomplete, the wounded remnant of a thing that should be whole, returns now strengthened like a thug with a jack-hammer and threatens to undo him. But he can't just lay his head down on his desk and shut the world out, as he wants to do, for Charlotte will ask him what the matter is, and in any case analysts and strategists are waiting for today's reports, as is Rollo. He has to be resolute and switch the tape back on.

As always Helen leaves the flat before her husband; school days begin earlier than days at the Institute. After she has gone, Stephen is forced to listen to PHOENIX in the bathroom with the door wide open, splashing, gargling, pissing. Then he makes himself a pot of coffee, and rustles through the newspaper that is delivered to the door, before he leaves for work. He and Helen read the *Guardian* and so does Stephen, although he buys his copy at the station. He used to enjoy hearing the couple talk about the news that he himself had read the day before, and to find he often shared their views. But he dissociates himself from PHOENIX now; nothing that he says or thinks can be trustworthy or true.

Stephen notes the time that PHOENIX leaves: 09.27. There will be no more until Helen comes back home. The tape will go on whirring to its midday end, recording the sounds of the outside world but they will not mean anything at all.

The second of Monday's tapes is still sealed in its envelope. Now it seems more like a creature poised to bite than an object of desire. But Stephen knows that he must hear it before he reports to Rollo.

Monday evening. Helen is halfway through a piece that Stephen thinks could be by Chopin when PHOENIX returns early. She stops playing; Stephen listens to the man's tread on the wooden floor, the sound of his keys and outer clothing being deposited by the door. And Helen then exclaiming on an indrawn breath: 'How lovely!'

'I'm sorry about yesterday,' says Jamie. 'I was horribly bad-tempered.'

'It doesn't matter . . . I love you . . . You didn't need to buy me flowers.'

'But I thought you'd like them. And I thought we might go out for supper tonight, unless you . . .'

'Well, there is that quiche we bought at . . .'

'But that'll keep. Oh come on. Let's go out. I've had a hard day, now what I'd like is to look at my love by candlelight and thank my lucky stars.'

Helen doesn't say anything but she reaches towards Jamie, or perhaps Jamie holds out his arms to her. Stephen screws his eyes tight shut and blocks his ears to the sound of their embrace. To the breath, the kiss, the sound of curtains being drawn. To the sound the man makes: half groan, half sob. To the woman gasping yes. To Jamie singing while he runs a bath.

Helen must be in the bedroom getting dressed; Stephen can no longer hear her but he can see her at her mirror, widening her eyes and looking upwards as she paints her lashes. It's a clouded mirror; the reflection that it shows is soft and hazy.

Later Helen and Jamie, having had a glass of wine, and chattering, elated, leave and Stephen is alone. The scent that Helen wears is lingering on the air. There will be a trail of it above the staircase she runs down. She has wrapped a cashmere scarf around her neck; when she takes it off and hands it with her coat to the waiter in the restaurant, the fragrance will catch in his throat like a memory of love and when he thinks no one is watching, he will bury his face in the soft grey wool to breathe it in.

In the upstairs flat, someone has turned a television on too loud and the sound is registered. Stephen, in despondency, his head bowed, is still listening to the distorted noise when he senses a shadow falling across his desk. He looks up to see Rollo Buckingham in a dark-blue overcoat, a fine spray of raindrops still clinging to his shoulders, so that they seem silver-spangled. 'Is it raining?' Stephen says.

'Drizzling,' says Rollo. 'Look, I've booked the Cube. We need to talk and we can't do that in here. Meet me there in ten? I need to get a cup of coffee first; I'm gasping.'

'Yes, all right, but I have to tell you that I'm still on Monday evening . . . It's been manic in here, you know. Wouldn't it be better if we were to talk later when I've caught up with yesterday?'

'No, not really. I have to brief the trackers today.'

'All right,' Stephen says again, having no real choice. His heart sinks further at the prospect of incarceration in that suffocating cell. 'Hurry back,' Louise instructs. 'You're needed for CUCHULAINN.'

Louise does not know how that name is said, Stephen says to himself. He does, though; he heard it spoken by an Irish poet who was lecturing in Oxford. He remembers the man lingering over the lyrical sound. Water flowing over rock, the sound was – mountain water, cool and clear. Stephen must have been studying Yeats, he supposes now, to have been at that particular lecture; yes, it was Yeats, the soft Celtic light, the myth-making, the lines that still come back to him at times.

The lift, descending, stops at the first floor to admit three men, one of whom Stephen recognises as Sub-director Six. He is a tall man with a fine head of carefully combed white hair and a curiously girlish mouth. They are remote figures, at least to Stephen, these sub-directors, who make up the board of the Institute but, although Stephen is not known to him, this one nods in polite acknowledgement as he steps in.

'Basement?' one of his companions asks.

This cannot mean they're holding the case conference already, Stephen thinks, with a surge of panic. Louise had said that one was threatened but surely Rollo would have told him? Besides, listeners are not usually invited to take part. Could Rollo be springing a trap for him? Stephen has never had to argue a case with one of the sub-directors: when an investigation demands that level of attention, the group controller will usually represent the relevant listener. But perhaps PHOENIX is different? Louise knows nothing but its barest bones; she is not on the special list.

Although it is only a matter of seconds before the lift and its passengers reach the basement, Stephen's fear is rising fast. He cannot be locked into the Cube with Buckingham and these three men; he cannot make a coherent case for a continuing investigation, but he must. It is impossible to stop it now. He has had other cases which were brought to an early end when the operatives or strategists decided they were not productive, or when new information intervened. He has had to get accustomed to not knowing how a story ends. His caseload is like a ramshackle library, or the shelf of books that one might find in a lodging house or small seaside hotel. An entirely random collection: some books that come in a uniform edition, all the volumes lined up and complete, others torn and tattered, with unexpected gaps and pages missing. But this story, Helen's story, this is different. This is a story in which he himself belongs. He's not just a reader, he's a part of it; she means much more to him than anybody else he listens to and he cannot lose her now.

He only breathes again when they reach the basement and the sub-director and his myrmidons veer off toward the garage. Stephen, waved through by the security guard, finds Binks. Today she has on a short black skirt and a purple jumper. She gives no sign of recognising Stephen. When Rollo arrives he pats her on her bottom.

'Now look here,' Rollo says, without preamble, as soon as he and Stephen are locked in. 'Frankly, I'm getting a bit worried. Things aren't quite adding up. We've been running this for two months now and I'd like to hear what you think is actually going on.'

'Yes, but the thing is, as I keep telling you, I am shut out of half the case. I can tell you everything that you might want to know about the man – what it sounds like when he shits, what he eats, what time he goes to bed, how much he cares about the Test Match, but not what he does every hour of the working day. If you'd let me . . .'

'That's just not possible. I have made that clear before. Where we are is where we are. We have to do what we can with what we've got. So, what *have* we got, in your opinion?'

'Not a lot, I must admit. And if we'd been having this talk last week, I think I would have had to say: nothing at all. But things do look a bit different now. Although as yet as clear as mud. You know, there was that odd thing on Sunday evening? Did you get anything from your trackers after that?'

'No. You know there were no trackers on him during the weekend. And since then there's been some massive drama in Department Four which has hogged all available resources.'

'Yes, I know all about it. But it's a shame. Because that means there are still two hours unexplained.'

'What happened on Monday? Did the wife say anything?'

'No, well, she was evidently upset. I can't tell you what went on between them when he got back so late on Sunday night; she was in the bedroom.'

'Which is of course completely out of range?'

'Yes. But, judging from her tone on Monday morning, she was agitated. I guess he refused to tell her where he'd been. She may suspect he's having an affair. Could he be? Would that account for where he was that evening?'

'I suppose. But have you any evidence of that?'

'Basically, there's no real evidence of anything. Except, on Monday, when he got home, he tried to make amends. He must have been feeling guilty. He bought flowers.'

'Was she pleased?'

'Not really. I'd say that his doing something so out of character – I mean buying her a bunch of roses – merely deepened her suspicions. But she's a very nice woman. Well, she seems nice. She accepted the flowers with good grace and didn't say anything else about the night before and nor did he. They went out to dinner. A spur-of-the-moment plan. You didn't give me time to finish that tape so I can't say what happened when they got back. Probably, if it was late, they just went straight to bed. And, as I say . . .'

'The bedroom.'

'Absolutely.'

'Is there a telephone in there?'

'Yes. Beside the bed.'

'It's not really on, you know, bugging a chap's bedroom.'

'Well no, of course, it's not. But . . .'

All through this exchange Stephen has kept his eyes squarely fixed on Rollo's. Now he notes the look of speculation in them. But Rollo soon dismisses the thought.

'I doubt I'd get authorisation. It would need an extra clearance. Let's just get on with what we've got, at least for the time being. The question is: do you think that PHOENIX is up to something?'

'Yes. I do. But I don't yet know what that something is. I just have an instinct that he's not playing straight. There's something slippery, evasive; if I were his wife I would not be sure that I could trust him. I mean, she does come across as quite a trusting person, but I'm getting the feeling that things are not going well for them; there's a bit of distance, they don't really seem to talk.'

'That sounds about par for a married couple. Not that I would know.'

'Nor me. But my sense is that he is holding something back.'

'You mean, there's something he is keeping to himself?'

'That's exactly it.'

'And what do you think that something is?'

'Well, there you've got me. I can't tell. You know, it would really help if you could give me some idea of what it is you think he's doing. Whom he may be contacting, at least.'

'I can't do that, I'm sorry. But I can say that my other avenues of investigation are not really producing anything very useful either. My sub-director is gunning for a full case conference. He is concerned that by keeping our sights trained on PHOENIX we might be missing something else.'

'Do you want my advice, for what it's worth? I mean, you're the operative but one does develop a sort of sixth sense as a listener. And my sense is that he's getting quite wound up. He's jittery; he can't sit still. Sooner or later he'll get careless. And then, if there's anything, I'll know.'

'Good man,' says Rollo. 'I think that does make sense. I think I'll try for that extension. As they were always drumming into us on the Advanced Training Course, one should listen to the listener! Let's ring the bell for Binks to get us out.'

After Rollo has thanked Binks and said goodbye, he and Stephen stroll to the lift together. Waiting for it in the basement lobby with him, Stephen offhandedly, as if reminded for some reason of something unimportant, says, 'Oh by the way, do you have a photograph? I've been meaning to ask.'

'Of PHOENIX?'

'No, of his wife. Of Helen.'

Helen. It is the first time that Stephen has said her name out loud to another person. Rollo looks at him if he has gone mad.

'The wife?' he says. 'Of course not. Why the hell would you want a picture of the wife?'

That afternoon, that Wednesday, a sudden storm of hail whipping against the windows of the long room, the taste of dust, a scum of cold tea in the bottom of a mug, the hiss of the machines, and Stephen with fear still roiling in him. It had been simmering all day, since his miserable morning and his interview with Rollo. Meanwhile Helen and Jamie have returned from dinner, in even higher spirits than before. Helen has declined a nightcap. There has been some play on words about nightcaps and nightdresses but Stephen did not catch it. There will have been a trace of Helen's scent still in the air when she went to bed, and Jamie with her. Would she wear the same scent in the morning?

She awoke, then it was Tuesday, yesterday. Stephen was quickly catching up with her: she went to work; she never even noticed Stephen's absence. While she was at work there was not time to keep watch over her domestic realm, to listen to the birdsong and the rain. OBERON, on a whim, decided he would go home to Jamaica, see his children, catch some sun. He booked his flight in person at a travel agent's; Stephen has had to pay him more attention than he usually does in order to discover when he's leaving. There'll be no point keeping his telephone tapped while he is away. OBERON has been on the telephone, arguing with the mother of his sons. He wants to bring the elder of them back with him to London; there are good schools here, he tells the woman, but she protests. He is only nine years old, she pleads; if you take him I'll be very sad. The possibility that she might come to London too does not seem to have occurred to her or OBERON. Maybe there are other children, other men.

VULCAN's health is worsening. What a pity he can't go with OBERON to that village near Montego Bay: a couple of weeks of sunshine would do him the world of good. Stephen thinks of VULCAN in the raw damp of a Clydeside winter, coughing up his lungs in his unheated tenement flat. Thick strings of phlegm and mucus clagging in his mouth. Please God they are not streaked with blood. What would VULCAN make of Caribbean beaches, white sands and turquoise seas? Sea, to VULCAN, would be grey and surly, snapping at his feet on a rare day out. He'd enjoy a paddle in warm water, the small waves gently lapping round his old, thin ankle bones. But, of course, he's never met OBERON, has no idea he exists, wouldn't know him from Adam. The only link between the two of them is Stephen. It's a pity.

Once OBERON's travel plans have been established, there is work to do for the Group II listeners. Now it transpires that yesterday's alarm may not have been false, or at least not quite as false as everybody hoped. But the crucial source of information has gone missing. Department Four's operatives and go-betweens are still rushing in and out of Group II's room wearing worried faces; Stephen has been given three more tapes to scan. Yet again he is trying to keep his head above the flood of directions, instructions, requests and messages that swirl through that taxi firm in a town beside the border. There is a moment when he thinks he may have heard something significant. A man's voice, calling in, a voice rough with the unsaid, asks if the boss of the firm is in. The woman who fields the calls says he is not and can she take a message? The male caller hesitates. 'Just tell him I have the woodwork done.'

Harriet, asked by Stephen to listen to the call, does not know this particular subject of interest and cannot comment, except to say that it would be sensible to share it with Martin in Group II. Martin is much too busy to drop everything and come round to Stephen's desk. Stephen will have to wait until Martin has finished the report that he is writing now, or go to all the bother of flagging up the tape before removing it and taking it round himself. Strictly speaking, he can't do this in any case, as no tape is ever to be transferred from hand to hand without being checked and registered by Muriel. From time to time Security carries out spot-checks of Muriel's register to see that the rules are being kept. They arrive in pairs: one to look at the register, the other to tally what it says with the tapes that are at the specified desk. They perform other inspections too, at intervals and unannounced. There are penalties for anyone caught in breach of the rules, and some of them are harsh. You can be fined, you can be demoted, you can even be dismissed. Blinds must be drawn in every office that could possibly be overlooked, if only by someone with a telescope, before a single light goes on. Pockets, bags and briefcases can be searched at random as staff are leaving the building. Every cabinet door and every drawer in every desk is checked each night to make sure that all of them are either empty of material or correctly locked. Stephen, working late, has heard the steady tread of the inspectors making their slow rounds, opening office doors and closing them behind them, rattling the metal drawers, the keys they carry with them jangling like a convict's chains.

Martin eventually appears, has a quick listen and recalls that

78

the owner of the taxi firm has commissioned a crib from a local joiner. The unidentified and hesitant voice must belong to him. A crib? Yes, a doll's crib, Martin thinks; it's a present for his little girl at Christmas. A surprise. That would account for why the caller was reluctant to give details.

All afternoon, then, sped away, and it is not until he gets to the second of Tuesday's tapes that Stephen remembers Helen is going to a play. She comes home simply to put her school books down and change her clothes; she does not lay a finger on the piano or sing a single note. There'll be another night without her: after the theatre she is going on to dinner, she's going to get home late. It's desolating, another night alone.

Coralie was sitting at the table in her unused dining room and picking through the box of Christmas decorations that her son had fetched for her last Sunday from the loft. She had made an appointment with herself to do that this Wednesday afternoon. Every Sunday evening, after she has waved good-bye to Stephen, she lists the things that she must do during the coming week. There are things on the list she would not forget to do even if they were not written down, but she likes to write them in any case: they lengthen the list and make it look more purposeful. The house can seem quite empty of a Sunday evening. Coralie says each entry aloud as she makes it:

Monday. Pay milkman (eggs)
Tuesday. Change sheets on S. bed. Telephone Sheila
Wednesday. Sort out Christmas decorations
Thursday. Order taxi
Friday. Bank. Pay gas bill. Hair appointment (12.15)

The box is just a cardboard box that once transported Fyffes bananas. It's getting a bit battered now but it's holding up surprisingly well given the age of it and the fact that it spends eleven months of every year in the damp and cobwebby loft. At least, she supposes there are cobwebs; it's been some time since she dared mount the rickety loft ladder that folds into the access hatch and has to be pulled down with a special grappling hook. All sorts of things are up there: an ironing board, an old tin bath, a clothes horse, the Hoover she bought when she got a pay rise, in the days when Hoovers were a luxury, which had kept on going with the odd repair for years and years until suddenly one day there was a smell of burning rubber and a shower of sparks. The man in the shop had said it would be almost as expensive to repair as to replace, which was a pity. It's not as if those appliances were really cheap. There are a good many cardboard boxes, in case they're ever needed, probably even the box the Hoover came in. Stephen's playpen and his cot. He went straight from his cot to a proper bed; there was no sense having a child-sized bed when you would have to buy a bigger one before you knew it. Children grow so fast. Coralie smiles when she remembers Stephen standing in that cot, clutching the bars and shaking them, for all the world like a little monkey in his cage. And for quite some time the little monkey, entranced by the freedom of the bar-less bed, just wouldn't stay put in it after she had tucked him up. No sooner had she left the room then she would hear the patter of tiny feet skittering on the lino and a small voice calling from the top of the stairs. Mummy, Mummy, I'm thirsty. Mummy, Mummy, I can't sleep. Her uniform from the FANYs must be up there somewhere in the old suitcase. She'd looked so neat and tidy in it, Lance

Corporal Coralie Platt, that khaki skirt and belted jacket. His uniform as well? No, now she came to think of it, he must have taken it with him or she had thrown it out. Though would she have thrown away an army greatcoat? That wouldn't have been like her, not then, not now, a waste of good hardwearing wool – what were they called? – oh yes, the officers' variety, the British Warm. A nice name that, British Warm: toasty, bedsocks, Ovaltine, nicer than the British upper lip in all its stiffness or the proverbial cold shoulder. Epaulettes. That's what they were. He'd looked handsome in his coat, she had to say. She used to make her own clothes then; lots of women sewed and knitted, more than they do now. Rationing, of course – you had to learn to make and mend. Her old dummy for dressmaking must be in the loft, still shaped to her statistics when she was a girl. The vital ones: 34 and 24 and 37. A little creepy, actually, to think of that silent wire figure watching over all the jumble of a life. If jumble was the word. Which it wasn't, quite. It's just that you can never tell when a thing might come in useful. Stephen had wanted those old saucepans when he got his flat. Waste not, want not – another forgotten virtue.

Every Christmas decoration that Coralie has ever owned is in that box, some wrapped in tissue paper. The paper is getting a bit too creased and torn now to be properly protective, tissue isn't meant to be folded and re-folded but only used the once – soft layers freshly wrapping clothes in elegant boutiques – she must make a note to buy some more. Every year at this time she takes each little object out, inspects it, sets aside the ones that are destined for display, puts the rejects back, stows the box away for the time being underneath the spare-room bed. The chosen favourites are laid out on the dining table, like the pieces of a board game, ready to be hung or placed into position over the next few days. And then, on the sixth of January each year, Coralie will take each decoration down, gather them together, dust them with a damp cloth, wrap them up in paper if it's needful, lay them all back in their box. Every time she does this she has the sense that she is daring fate. To repeat a single action annually is to chance it being the last time; when she puts her trove away she can't help thinking she might never unpack it again. That's a daft thought, she admits, you could say the same about anything you regularly did: watching the news, brushing your hair, having a cup of tea, going to bed. The last time you close your eyes, the very last time you draw a breath. And of course you wouldn't know, you couldn't say: oh my last ever forkful of mashed potato; that's the last time I'll put food out for the cat. But one day, and that day somehow seeming sooner, it will be the case. Already she finds herself saying: 'That's the last time I'll ever need to buy a winter coat, this one will see me out.' To tell the truth, in some ways that's not a totally unwelcome thought; life can be rather tiring; it would be quite nice to be outlasted by the majority of your teeth. On the other hand, to think of Stephen having to unpack the Christmas box all on his own next time. It's like stocking up a freezer, one of the many reasons she hasn't been all that keen to have one – after a death do the bereaved just throw the food away? The homemade food, that is. There's nothing very personal about a bag of peas. But, a cheese and onion tart? A cottage pie? Wasteful just to put them in the bin and yet peculiar to eat them up when the cook is dead and buried. Coralie pictures the widower grimly chewing his way through his late wife's beef and onion casserole. Well, the extent of the grimness would depend, perhaps, on the dear departed's status as a cook. If she'd been a dab hand in the kitchen the widower might wipe away a tear or two while he commemorated the lightness of her pastry but . . . Either way, she wouldn't like to think of Stephen having to decide between eating or wasting something that his mum had left behind in a Tupperware container. Or sorting through the Christmas things, all by himself. Though would he? Or would he leave the box untouched to gather more dust in a loft unvisited, untenanted but for her ancient dummy? Whichever, either way, it did give her a little shiver of relief, when the time came round each year, the dark December afternoon, and she opened that box and found its contents safe. What's the word? Oh, yes, that's what it was: reprieve.

A bit of sheeting covers the contents, an old cot sheet as a matter of fact. The box is nowhere near full, although one item, housed in a square box of its own, takes up a fair amount of room. Coralie will leave that one till last. On top of it are a plastic bag of tinsel and the Christmas lights, disentangled on the feast of the Epiphany and carefully re-wound round their original cardboard packaging, which has a separate compartment for spare bulbs. There are globes of coloured glass so fragile each must be double-wrapped. A robin made with real feathers. A lace and plastic angel. A golden star. Crib figures also wrapped, painted plaster, a gift from Stephen's godparents the Christmas he was born. His first Christmas, how long ago that was. It had been his particular delight when he was a little boy to lay the baby Jesus in his manger last thing on Christmas Eve. Silent night, holy night; they would set the scene on the sideboard in the dining room earlier in the day, expectant mother, father, ox and ass, the sheep in a patient line out-side, the waiting shepherds, an attendant angel and the plaster baby, swaddled completely, secreted in a drawer beneath the serviettes. The deep and dreamless sleep. And then, when the stocking was hung and the boy in his nightclothes, the baby would be tenderly brought out. Naturally, the three kings and the orient camel would spend all of Christmas in the drawer, emerging only at the final moment. The ox's hind leg was broken, in consequence of Stephen disobeying the injunction not to touch.

Most precious are the things that Stephen made. The snow-man out of paper plates and doilies, the lumps of approximately modelled clay: remembrances of infant school, of early child-hood. When does it stop, all that excited creation of things for mother? There ought to be a warning with the final gluey collage: this is the last that you will ever receive. Oh yes, older children do make things and bring them home, but those are different – more elaborate, connected with their schoolwork, less spontaneous, associated with necessity not pleasure. Cor-alie has some of these things still – a flower pot of coiled clay, a wobbly stool – but they do not bring the same sweet and tear-ful memories with them. Stephen as a small boy, round-faced, trusting, the neat straight line of his blond fringe; when had he become a hollow thing regarding the world from behind his glasses, as likely as a man of straw to be blown off course by a strong wind? Well, even as a child he had been gifted with imagination. Coralie had often thought he ought to be a writer. And at the grammar school you had to choose by the time you were fourteen: Latin or woodwork, art or history, and for Ste-phen that really hadn't been a choice, as he was always clever.

Scholarly. So a complete end to any bits and pieces then. No more bags for clothes pegs, matchbox constructions, smudgy watercolours.

Delightful though the babyish artefacts might be, they could not now be brought out for display. Stephen wouldn't like it. Even though no one but he and his mother might see them, nevertheless, two decades on, he would think them out of place on the mantelpiece or the tree. Reluctantly Coralie laid them back in the banana box, and having set out everything else she planned to use this year, she lifted up the separate container.

This is the jewel of Coralie's collection, always stowed in its original packaging, with a strip of foam around it for extra buffering against accidental damage. A model carousel, hand-crafted out of wood and delicately painted; tiny prancing horses skewered on barley-sugar poles, beneath a sky-blue canopy and a scattering of silver stars. It works: if correctly wound, a little knob sets the horses circling and plays Brahms' Lullaby in tinkling notes. The horses are as new and fresh as they were the day that Spencer bought the carousel – in all the time that's passed since then they have not been put through their paces very often. Twice a year, on average, once on their liberation from their box, once on their return, the silent stars go by. The mechanism's fragile, the ornament too precious to run the risk of repeated winding. Strictly speaking, the carousel is probably not a Christmas ornament; it could perfectly well be left on show the whole year round. There are no angels or shepherds or babies on it, no snowmen, nor even donkeys. But it was given to Coralie at Christmas and in her mind it's a Christmas treat. Besides it wouldn't have lasted half so well if she had allowed it to stay out. As it is, each year she tests the workings nervously, her heart in her mouth in case they've given up the ghost. There's no reason why they should, being well protected from the damp by their multiple layers of packing, but then these things are mysterious; who can say what might mysteriously befall a thing that slumbers dreamlessly so long in the silent dark?

This year – reprieve, again. The knob has always been fiddly, it must be set just so, but Coralie is practiced and this time without a false start or a stutter, the horses begin to glide, the tune to peal out thinly and Coralie to cry. She knew she would. She always does. It's that tune and the memory of it, the memory of choosing the carousel with Spencer on the eve of their first married Christmas, the resonance of it through all those years. 'Little darling, goodnight . . .' It had been so cold that evening at the Christmas market: *stille Nacht, gute Nacht*, she had never known winter like it, those arctic winds that sliced right through you like a knife, the tips of your fingers even if you did have gloves turning numb and blue. She had felt it terribly, especially after Malta. But, her arm through Spencer's, the warmth of him beside her, and knowing it'd be snug enough at home in their married quarters and in bed that night and a whole day with nothing to do tomorrow. Must have been made before the war, Spencer had said of the carousel, poor bloody Huns had better things to do now than make little painted horses out of wood. Like staying alive and finding food; what wood there was was used for fuel. No, you won't get craftsmanship like that again, he said. That's why he had bought it, slightly to her surprise, him not being a sentimental man, nor given to buying presents and their not really having money to burn at that stage, newly wed. Nor did they later, come to that, or ever. The Christmas markets, what were they called, Weinachtsomething? – a poor shadow of the ones they used to have before the war, a vestige, everybody told them, but even so, in the bleak midwinter, a flicker of warmth, and there'd been hot red wine with spices, and chips and sausages and her breath frosting on the air, and Spencer in his greatcoat, laughing. And on one of the stalls with their meagre displays, the carousel. They hadn't any other Christmas things, the pair of them, well you don't, when you've been married a matter of months and a war is only just over. We'll get one new thing each year she'd said to him, and with each one we'll be reminded of where we were that Christmas. She hadn't said, but she had thought, that by their second married Christmas there could be a third person and they'd no longer be a couple but a family. That's what Coralie yearned for. Armfuls of babies and handsome Spencer and happily ever afterwards, amen.

But it doesn't work like that, now does it? Month after month, and the hot blood coming, that feel of it like nothing else, the sudden flow between your legs, sticky, hot, impossible to take for any other source of wetness. Month after month and year after year and Coralie, already past her prime then, older than her husband, crying in the toilet every time she got the curse. Worst were the times when it held off long enough for her to feel hopeful. A few days or weeks sometimes, a few times even longer. As each day went by her hopes would rise and with each day the plunge into black misery when the dreaded flow came would be proportionately deeper. Who knows, there may have been a baby there, or the first new bud of one, those times when she didn't bleed as she expected, poor little thing, one small hope of life flushed down the drain like a slug off a lettuce. Who would ever know the children who could have been? And are they there still, the thin, transparent wraiths of them, mourning the lives they never led?

Well, there did come a time, a long time later, after Berlin, after Gütersloh, after Catterick and Dhekelia, when no blood flowed, and Coralie supposed her change had come, although she was not a great deal over forty. As she had pretty much given up hope by then and, anyway, seldom spread her legs for the man who had been ardent once but lately had lost interest so it seemed – well, that happens too, after several years of marriage, especially if they bring with them a freight of disappointment and unspoken blame – it had not been an unreasonable assumption. Oh but the wonder of it, as the weeks wore on and the symptoms grew apparent. And the greater wonder of the babies.

A time of joy, a time of grief, for the little one who came into the world already tired and wizened and left it with a small sigh ten days later, having seen enough. Lullaby and good night, Henrietta, Stephen's sister, Stephen's twin: another waif to join her unborn children. Well, but, Stephen Spencer Donaldson. An August child, a harvest child, as gold and full of promise as a grain of corn. Old enough by his first Christmas to open wide his eyes and reach his hand out for the dancing horses on the carousel.

Hard it had been, very hard, not knowing whether to weep or sing, to celebrate or grieve. But, in the end, you know, there's no real choice: the babe that lives needs all the strength that you can muster if he is to thrive. Coralie remembers her worries of the first weeks, all the weighing and the measuring – will he grow plumper, longer, stronger or will he wither like his sister or, like the changeling child of nightmare, wane and fade away? The terror of all mothers – to wake and find your baby lying stiff and silent in his crib. A memory that still has power to send shudders through her decades later: lifting Stephen up one morning, he by now fifteen months old, and his eyes looking into hers completely blankly. Not a glimmer of recognition, a smile or a response. As if the child she'd laid to sleep had vanished in the dead of night, substituted by a stranger. Or as if an evil thing had slunk into his bedroom in the dark and sucked his soul from him.

But, fear and anguish notwithstanding, notwithstanding malign fate, the babe not only lived but flourished. In a manner of speaking, if flourish is a word that could apply to a child who was as narrow as a willow leaf, as thin as the stalk of a dandelion – he could suck his belly into such a hollow you would swear his spine showed through – and who causes to this day outpourings of anxiety in the matter of his diet. It was his mother's responsibility from his first minutes on the earth to feed and succour Stephen and, as far as she can tell, there is no other woman yet to take that burden from her shoulders.

Spoonfuls of mush ladled into a gummy mouth: Farex, creamed rice, creamed oats, creamed potato. Bottles of sweetened milk. Condensed milk on a rusk. Mashed bananas with brown sugar, extract of malt, sponge fingers and strawberry jam. Thank goodness Stephen comes home at weekends so that she can keep an eye on what he eats; she has a hunch that what he feeds himself is not what she would see as wholesome food, and besides, speaking for herself, meals for one are not the same. Although Stephen had been gone for years now, Coralie has never summoned up much interest in cooking for herself.

An egg on toast will do for her, or a can of soup.

Anyway, so her son survived but he came too late to stop his father straying. Off he went, into the night, like a tomcat on the prowl, Spencer Albert Donaldson. No, let's be fair; there are always two sides to a story. Maybe he'd had his fill of her, of the scrawny, tearful woman she'd become. The barren wife, already middle-aged while he was young. In bed he'd always been more keen than her, keen as mustard to begin with, she'd be quite bow-legged, but to be honest she could never see the point of it, or get the hang of it, perhaps. And as soon as they started to connect the deed with her need for a baby, that's when the rot set in. Funnily enough, it hadn't put her off as much as it had him. She'd even been the one to start things off, or at least to make it clear that she was willing, which she certainly would not have done before. But she had to admit there was something unromantic about urging a man to pump away while you lay stock-still beneath him, desperately trying to keep the seed in, encourage it upwards, having washed yourself with lemon juice, drunk nettle tea, hung mistletoe above your bed and monitored the moon.

He stuck around for a year or two. No, let's be truthful: he must have been there, in body at least, until Stephen was four or thereabouts; she can remember his fourth birthday, Spencer bought a bicycle, blue, with stabilisers. But he didn't stay long enough to teach his son to ride it. Coralie did that by herself, running along beside the child, one hand on the handlebars, trying to stop him swerving wildly or coasting down the hill. She had had to buy a spanner when Stephen eventually mastered the art and the stabilisers could come off. Long before that birthday Spencer had left the Army and was an engineer on Civvy Street; better money, he had thought, a more settled life, less wandering about from pillar to post. That's why they moved to Didcot, to be close to the Atomic, where Spencer got a job.

Spencer had gone by the time Stephen went to infant school, of that Coralie is sure. She can remember his first day; she was certainly on her own, the lump in her throat when she left him there, trying not to let him see her tears. How he had doted on that teacher! He kept in touch for a while, Spencer that is; he sent money every now and again, and birthday cards, but both dried up eventually. Someone told her he had emigrated to Australia. Whatever the case, she has not heard from him for a long, long time but she bears him in mind, especially on their wedding anniversary, Stephen's birthday and the anniversary of Henrietta's death. And maybe other times as well. He'd been much more upset by the little girl's death than she would have thought. It was as if the loss of his daughter overshadowed the childhood of his son, the baby's twin.

Stephen says that he doesn't remember his father. Coralie is not sure if that is true.

Thursday

That it is better not to look too closely in the mirror when you're shaving in the morning would be Stephen's general rule, but on this particular morning, naked in the chilly little bathroom, he inspects himself minutely. How odd it is that his face looks utterly familiar and yet at the same time alien. There are small markings and lines on it that he could swear he has never seen before and the expression is not exactly his. *Mon semblable,* he thinks, again; an alter ego or twin brother? He takes his glasses off and leans over the washbasin until his forehead touches its reflection. His eyes are somewhat bloodshot, as if he has been crying, which he hasn't, not last night. The line of dry skin along his lower lip is stained by Spanish red, and the wine has also left its dark tinge on his teeth. He stretches his lips and snarls. There is nothing wrong with his nose, except that the cartilaginous bridge of it is slightly crooked. There is nothing wrong with his eyes either, apart from the transitory redness; in fact only the other day Charlotte had told him they were nice. Maybe she was teasing. But they are positively blue, not puddle-water, winter-sky blue, like so many other people's, which are nearer grey. The eyelashes are long. He looks deeply into his dilated pupils. Will they reveal the new determination that he felt this morning when he woke? Is there anything essentially wrong with his appearance? In the winter his lips are always cracked. His hair is receding at the temples. His complexion is pale but his skin is clear apart from a spattering of freckles. Perhaps they're moles. There are a lot of them on his chest and shoulders too, and on his back, for all he knows. He straightens up and steps away to frame as much as he can of his whole self in the mirror.

Fairly narrow shoulders. A concavity between the breasts where flatness might arguably be desirable. A slight protrusion of the belly. The hair on his chest is sparse and sandy but it forms itself into a pleasingly straight line and darkens past his navel to a thicker cluster above his pubic bone. His cock is perfectly normal, as far as he can tell. He lifts it and lets it fall. The line of his groin, where it tapers downwards from his hips, is actually quite beautiful; the skin there smooth and milky. Beyond that point he cannot see in the mirror but he is sure his legs and feet are not remarkable in any way. He is reasonably tall.

So, is there something that he does not have? Is there something that he ought to change? He has never asked himself these questions in so direct a way before; there has been no need to: a man goes into the world completely clothed, not as a bare, forked animal, after all. Today he wants an answer.

He had spent another restless, sweaty night, his heart pounding and his dreams intermingling with his waking thoughts, eliding into meaningless confusion. At an hour long before first light he had given up the fight to stay asleep and had lain in the tangle of his sheets, reliving yesterday. He saw that he had started something which he must follow to its end. He had taken control of the PHOENIX case, although he hadn't meant to, or anyway not so soon, having believed there would be time to see how it played out. But there wasn't time – Rollo had constrained him to work against the clock. In any other investigation he wouldn't have cared, but there was another element here, and that element was love. Until this moment he had not allowed himself to analyse his feelings or define his hopes. He had been afraid to: both were so fragile, so vulnerable and precious. Examining his heart would have felt like wrenching the shell off a live turtle and stabbing the flesh within. Now, though, he must armour that heart, map out his strategies, accept the risks he would incur and take decisive action. The prize that he will win outweighs all caution and all danger. She is there, and he will claim her.

Ecce homo. Behold the man. Out loud Stephen speaks the words. I am a man and I know exactly what it is that I must do. There has been altogether too much wasted time. He is twenty-eight years old; already he is older than Keats was when he died. In five years' time he'll be as old as Christ when crucified. A man whose name was writ in water? Think of all that Keats had felt, had truly experienced and expressed, in his short span on earth. Time is not an infinite resource and Stephen can no longer squander it away.

But where to start? The obvious place is where *she* starts: from her flat in Battersea in the mornings. Stephen knows where Helen lives because he has heard her name the road and the mansion block. He knows what time she normally leaves for work. But even if he were to leave his own flat now, right this very minute, he would not make it to Battersea in time. Of course he has studied her part of London in the A-Z and is aware that there is no Underground station anywhere nearby. From East Acton he'd have to go to Victoria, take the overground to Battersea Park, and walk. Or catch a bus – but bus routes are a mystery to him, who still feels like a stranger in this city. He has seen how easily people like Damian and Charlotte, who were born here, move around. Envying their command of London's topography, he confines himself to the Tube, on which it is difficult to get lost, although he dislikes the blackness of the tunnels and the sense of being leagues below the surface. If ever one allowed one-self to think of the weight and depth of water above those lines that snake beneath the Thames, one would never make a sin-gle sub-riverine journey. That great mud-swollen mass of water, limb of a monstrous reptile extending through the city, stretched above the feeble little carriages shuttling below, poised to rup-ture the tenuous layers of brick that keep it from them, waiting to claim back those narrow tunnels and refill them with cold tides, the jetsam of ancient bones. But most of the time there's no alternative. Driving in London is even more nerve-racking. Stephen was never an enthusiastic driver; he had to take his driving test three times and did not acquire a car of his own until his mother gave him her old Datsun when arthritis made it hard for her to grip the steering wheel. The journey from Acton to Didcot is one thing, negotiating the labyrinth of London's roads quite another. London's drivers are so confident and brash, hurtl-ing into unbroken streams of traffic, flinging themselves round Hyde Park Corner. Do they not know how vulnerable they are in their flimsy shells of steel? And, worse, how frail the skull, the small soft bones, of the child who happens to step into the road without remembering to look left, right and left again, just as the car bears down at breakneck speed. It's another of Stephen's recurring dreams: the head pulped like a ripe peach; blood and bone and particles of brain spraying across his windscreen.

*

'You're looking a trifle flushed,' Louise said to Stephen as he arrived for work that Thursday morning. 'Are you quite well?'

'Diddums,' exclaimed Charlotte, who was perched on Louise's desk, swinging her legs to and fro.

'I have excruciating toothache,' Stephen said. 'It came on all of a sudden in the middle of the night.'

'Oh you poor love,' Louise cried sympathetically.

'Were you eating sweets in bed?' asked Solly.

'Louise, would you mind awfully if I left the office early, so that I can see my dentist?'

'No of course I wouldn't, petal. But I can't imagine you'll manage to get an appointment with your dentist today? Might it not be wiser to go straightaway to Casualty at St George's? They do teeth, I think.'

'My man keeps a slot free for urgent cases every afternoon.'

'Coo. You must let me have your dentist's name some time. To see mine, you'd probably have to wait a week, even if you were dying of the pain!'

'Even if you had an abscess? Have you an abscess, Stephen?'

'I do hope not. But it is frightfully painful, all the same.'

'Toothache is the worst,' Solly agreed. 'It's because the nerves run so close to the brain.'

'Worse than childbirth, my mum says,' interjected Charlotte.

'Poor you,' said Louise. 'I was meaning to ask if you would have lunch with me upstairs today; it's moussaka on the menu, something new, which makes a change! And we could take the extra hour that we're owed. But you won't feel much like eating, will you?'

'Not really,' Stephen said.

*

Without listening to the Wednesday 00.00–12.00 tape, without even unsealing it, knowing that the truth was unlikely to be helpful, Stephen wrote the following report:

15 December 1981:

00.33: Subject of interest and wife return to flat. From conversation it is evident that subject did not attend theatre as planned (Another Country, cf. reports dated 8 and 9 December). Instead he met wife and other members of party (J. and L. Cummins, q.v.) for dinner later, at a restaurant near theatre (Greenwich), name unknown. Subject's reason for missing play, for which he had a ticket, is unclear but appears to be connected to an unforeseen emergency at his place of work. Extract below verbatim:

Mrs PHOENIX: It's such a pity, it really is. You would have found it fascinating, I know. The way that it explored the causes of treacherous conduct: oppression, a sense of powerlessness, alienation, *Geworfenheit* – you know, Heidegger's word: being thrown without reason into an unreasonable world. There were such interesting ideas in it about loyalty, friendship and betrayal . . .

PHOENIX: I know. I was looking forward to it. And I gather from what Laura was saying that the play's sold out; last night was my only chance. I couldn't be more pissed off. But you know, darling, it really couldn't be helped. These things happen, I don't mean to sound self-important but there really was no one else who could have dealt with the situation . . .

Mrs PHOENIX: I know, I know, you don't have to say it again. I only hope it doesn't happen often or there'll be no point making any plans with you, I might as well go out on my own.

97

PHOENIX: Well, at least I did make it to the restaurant. That coq au vin was really memorable.

Nothing further to report.

Then, to be on the safe side, Stephen played the tape. There were no telephone calls at all. Helen and Jamie did come home well after midnight, at 00.47 to be precise. They were tired, they hardly spoke, she made a cup of tea, they went to bed. Obviously they had already discussed the play over dinner in the restaurant with the other couple; there was nothing left that needed to be said. They did not talk about the dinner they had had; people don't on the whole dissect or even describe the dishes they only finished eating an hour or so ago; at least not when it is almost one o'clock on a weekday morning. Nor did they mention the name of the restaurant. Why would they, when both of them knew it anyway? Jamie muttered something about the cost of the taxi and the absurdity of living out there in the sticks at Greenwich. That was all. Later that Wednesday morning husband and wife got up and went to work as usual.

Having filed the carbon copy of the report, Stephen placed the top copy in an envelope, sealed it, marked it *PERSONAL for RMEB/Dept Six BY HAND*, and took it up to the seventh floor. Rollo Buckingham was not in his office but the other man was, the nameless dark-haired colleague. He looked up enquiringly at Stephen hovering by the open door but neither spoke nor smiled.

'Rollo?' Stephen asked.

'Out. Back this afternoon.'

'Would you be most awfully kind and give him this as soon

as he gets in?' Stephen asked, handing over the envelope. 'It's urgent.'

The nameless man received the envelope with nothing but a nod.

Stephen spent the rest of the morning with his other targets. He listened to their talk of miners' strikes, of Solidarity, of shootings reported in Poland: Lech Walesa may have been detained; Margaret Thatcher has been voted the most unpopular prime minister in the history of Britain; mountainous waves thrust forward by the gales have broken through seawalls in Somerset. The weather is set to continue cold. ODIN's daughter is going to see a heart specialist on Friday; VULCAN's cough is splintering his chest. GOODFELLOW, an investigative journalist, is trying to have a meeting with an Argentine army officer for reasons that remain obscure to Stephen. He reported that. OBERON's strategist dropped in to check his travel itinerary; they'll switch that line off until he comes back from Jamaica at the end of January. Greta knows someone who lives near the Bristol Channel; she has had a foot of water in her kitchen. Louise has written names on scraps of paper and jumbled them into her hat; passing it around she invites each member of her group to pick one. 'If you pick yourself,' she says, 'fold the paper up and put it back.' This is the fairest way to deal with Christmas gifts, she thinks; better than everyone having to buy eight individual presents or thinking that they have to – not that *everyone* does – and she has imposed a strict financial limit. Stephen picked Christophine out of the hat.

When the others went up to the canteen at lunchtime, Stephen crept out to Shepherd Market. As he had permission to leave early, he would be expected to work throughout the break but he was hungry and he needed a drink. A sandwich was not enough. He quite often went to pubs in the area of the Institute, having found them to be safe retreats for drinkers on their own. Too late, when he had already ordered a double whisky and a sausage, he remembered that this particular pub, the closest to the Institute, had recently been put on the proscribed list. It didn't really matter; he wouldn't be there long. Security couldn't possibly patrol every banned place every day, and here at least he would not be spotted by anyone else from the Institute. He looked round to see if there were any identifiably hostile operatives in the bar but, as far as he could tell, the other drinkers were ordinary men like him, in working clothes, by themselves or in small groups. There were a few women, each with a male companion. No one showed any sign of interest in Stephen. He relaxed, hid himself behind the *Guardian* and drank a second whisky to numb the toothache he had almost convinced himself he had. The sausage came unaccompanied and foot-long. Pink innards poked through its brown skin. He cut it into segments and ate them one by one. He was back at his desk well before the other listeners returned.

The second tapes of Wednesday would not be ready for distribution until late afternoon. Stephen planned to leave at three and to come back afterwards, taking his chances with Security and the signing list. In the meantime he kept his headphones on and counted the minutes passing; they ticked by at snail's pace. The telephone on his desk flashed its red light at him but he did not answer it, in case it was Rollo Buckingham. Then, for fear that Rollo would come stalking in person to his desk, he took the A–Z into the toilet and locked himself into a cubicle. He had already looked at page 76 a hundred times but he wanted to be quite sure that he had memorised it. That took up half an hour. He made tea for himself and his colleagues. It was almost time.

'I'm off,' he said to Louise. 'But I'm coming back.'

'When is your appointment?'

'Three-thirty. It won't take long, I hope. I haven't finished today's take so I'll come back as soon as I can.'

'No, no don't. Especially don't if you have to have anything done. Where's this dentist anyway? Surely you won't have time to get there and back again in conditioned hours?'

'Harley Street,' Stephen said at random.

'Oh. Well, it's true that's not so far to go. How very posh, to have a dentist there! But even so, I don't think you ought to come back. I think you should go home. Have a stiff drink and recover! And that's an order, Steve!'

'But Rollo Buckingham –'

'I'll deal with Master B, don't worry!'

He hadn't reckoned on the rain or the early onset of the dark. There was daylight when he descended into the Underground but it was already shading to bruise-violet when he got onto the overground train, and by the time he crossed the river and arrived at Battersea Park station, dusk and rain were falling fast. He found the road and Helen's block of flats with ease but when he did, he realised that he did not know the number of the flat. He had assumed the mansion block would have one main central door but in fact there were five entrances, each with a brass panel of numbered doorbells next to it, and one was on a side-street. How could he tell which one to watch? This redbrick slab was more like a fortress than an ordinary block of flats: it extended from one side-street to the next and stood like a great bulwark against the lowlier buildings of Battersea behind it, keeping them from the green spaces of the park.

Stephen looked up at it, almost losing heart. The road between the mansion block and the park was wide, the pavements almost empty. There were iron railings along the border of the park, broken at wide intervals by gates leading onto paths, and the gate nearest the mansion block did not afford a clear line of sight to any of the doors. He thought of the tracker's lessons in surveillance: by standing here, in the gathering dark and the falling rain, on this pavement where no one else was waiting, by staring gormlessly at the building opposite, he was breaking every rule. But then he remembered the resolve that had begun to flow in his veins the day before. Stiffen the sinews, summon up the blood, he told himself, faint heart ne'er won fair lady. This first step was after all a simple one and danger-free; he only wanted to set eyes on her and nothing else.

Testing different vantage points he found that from one it was just possible to glimpse the entrance on the side-street while keeping the others in view, but it was obviously not sensible to loiter any longer on the pavement. A discreet position behind the black railings was the only option. He hurried down the pavement to the nearest gate and went into the park. It was not going to be easy to conceal himself at his chosen point. Between the circular path and the railings was an ample planted border, dense with holly and dark ivy and a tangle of thin branches, leafless now. Ivy crawled across the ground as well – grotesquely twisted and whiskery with thick white roots. Fortunately for Stephen there were some hedge plants that had kept their foliage: a small-leafed bushy thing – he thought maybe it was privet – and another, with larger, shiny-looking leaves rather disgustingly dappled with yellow, as if they were diseased. Thanking heaven for the camouflage of his dark coat, Stephen forced himself into a thicket of this speckled bush, ignoring the thorns and the pricks of holly.

The bush did not completely hide him. From where he stood he could see the mansion block quite clearly through the fret of leaves, and in the gathering dark was glad to note lights coming on above the doors. But the pavement in front of him, the road beyond, and the path behind were getting busier now. Cars drove past him frequently, obstructing his view. Children were starting to appear, a good sign, with mothers or perhaps with nannies, walking home from school. None of the women looked anywhere but straight ahead; some of the children darted quick glances to the side. Even in the depth of his pre-occupation it struck Stephen how sharp-eyed these children were, how full of curiosity and yet accepting of a man standing silently inside a hedge with rain seeping down his upturned collar. One small girl stopped and watched him solemnly, before giving him a little wave. He waved back, and put his finger to his lips in a gesture of complicity that made her smile, and without a word she ran off after her mother, who had paid no notice to the dawdling child.

His life had been empty of children since he was himself a child, and even then he was seldom in their company, except at school. Other people had younger brothers and sisters, nephews and nieces, little cousins. It must be a fine feeling, to hold a trusting child's hand in yours. He would like to be a father.

Apart from the children and their chaperones, there were

few pedestrians. Stephen reviewed all that he knew of Helen's daily routine. She went to school by bus, he was almost sure, and the school was somewhere near Sloane Street. He had not seen any bus stops on the road between the station and the mansion block, and certainly no buses passed him. Therefore she must make the last part of her journey on foot, coming in all likelihood from an easterly direction.

He waits. A young woman on her own is what he waits for. A woman with two children unlocks the second of the doors on the façade; an older woman, grey-haired, comes out of the third door with a dog. The rain has eased but now the dark is deep. It is impossible to distinguish features clearly or even to make out figures unless by the glow of street lamps or the entrance lights.

Older children are arriving now, in clusters or alone. Cyclists spin past. A dog-walker under an umbrella marches briskly towards the park gate; the dog stops to inspect the waiting man. Stephen listens to the sounds: footfall, the rustle of twigs and leaves beneath his feet, voices, wheels swishing on the wet surface of the road, raindrops weeping off wet leaves. Invisible in the black branches of a tree a bird sings out with sudden and startling clarity, as if it had forgotten this was a winter afternoon, as if it wished to pierce the dark, to try the power of song against it. From the river to the north, the cry of gulls. And then, on the tarmac path behind him, the sound of rapid footsteps, purposeful, heels tapping, someone walking fast. Stephen swivels round as best he can while at the same time burrowing deeper into the thicket; the path is a few yards away and he is reasonably well concealed from it, but it is essential that he is not seen. Because the woman coming closer must be Helen.

He knows the sound of Helen's footsteps. This woman walks as Helen walks: lightly, quickly, without flurry, as light on her slim feet as a gazelle. He should have known that she would walk home through the park. A woman like Helen would never choose a flinty, shit-smeared pavement, a loud exhaust-choked road, over a green path in a green shade, a soft way, a way through flowers and leaves. She walks in beauty, heralded by birdsong, she is silver, she is starlight in the night.

Stephen rages against the night. There are no lights on this stretch of the path. The woman is in a raincoat, pale-coloured, cream or fawn, a moth against the dark. She has a hat pulled down over her head, which hides her hair, and a scarf around her neck. She is carrying two bags; one slung across a shoulder, the other, seemingly heavy, in her hand. She is wearing boots. He strains his eyes but it is hard to see her clearly. He dare not make a movement to get closer – he scarcely dares to breathe lest his breath dislodge a leaf. It is vital that she should not be frightened by this watcher in the undergrowth, that she feels safe, that she *is* safe, that angels guard her so that she will not hurt her foot against a stone.

She walks past Stephen without a single glance. The whole world around her holds its breath to watch her go; the bright bird falls silent in salute. When she is gone a trace of her sweet scent lingers on the damp and heavy air.

His sixth sense is right. The woman leaves the main path to take the fork towards the gate and Stephen, safe from observation now, frantically pushes through branches of ivy as thick as a man's wrist to get closer to the railings. On the pavement she halts for a passing car and then she crosses the road. Stephen can hear the thudding of his heart. On the other side she turns right towards the side-street; he tears and tramples the shrubbery about him to keep pace. Now he can see her more distinctly in the lamplight as she walks straight up to the side door of the mansion block and stops to search in her shoulder bag for keys. She unlocks the door. It is overwhelming; he forgets to note the time.

Pale figure in the twilight, swansgleam, moonkiss, pale and slender as an evening lily. All that evening Stephen cradled her image in his heart, hidden like a treasure known only to its owner, like a medallion worn next to the skin, like an icon that cannot be exposed for adoration until the world is sleeping and the solitary worshipper is shielded by the night. He was almost afraid to bare it even to his mind's eye as he made his way home and once there did ordinary Thursday things. The thought of food was curiously distasteful, almost sacrilegious, as if he, like a man entrusted with a vision, should be fasting until dawn. But he was very thirsty and from the corner shop he bought an extra bottle of wine and a bottle of whisky.

His neighbourhood seemed strangely full of light. The pub, the betting shop and the funeral parlour glowed; even the chapel of rest next door to him had a low light showing through its curtains. He could hear the telephone ringing inside his flat while he was fitting his key into the lock but it stopped before he reached it. Unlikely to be his mother, on a Thursday. He supposed whoever it was would try again.

He was home much earlier than usual, having realised it would not be wise to defy Louise by returning to the office. The flat seemed different at that time. What do people do by themselves when it is dark but not yet evening, before they draw the curtains and hide themselves away, uncork the bottle of wine? He looked round the room, trying to see it as if for the first time, or as if through Helen's eyes. There was not much in it: a sofa, covered in a nubbled, brownish weave, that Coralie had found in a sale and thought would be hard-wearing, three chairs and a table at which he could eat, if he did not always do so standing up, or with his plate on his lap in front of the television. A bookshelf. The carpets and the curtains were there when he took the lease of the flat; they are rather tired now, and a little drab. He ought to think about replacements. A coat of paint would spruce things up. Or simply a spring clean. There is a veil of dust on every surface. Certainly he would not wish her to see his bedroom in its present state. Paint is flaking off the window frames; he finds fragments of it, yellowish-white, like broken bits of shell, scattered on the floor. It is a long time since he remembered to wash the sheets. The truth is that he does not mind their sour smell, their greyness: they smell of him, familiar and consoling, they bear the marks of his own body, like a shroud. He chose the bed himself; a double. A patch of damp has drawn its contours on a wall. If he were not accustomed to the mingled smells of damp and sweat, he might worry about the added taint of mould.

What is Helen doing now, this moment? He will do the same: he will have a cup of tea, watch the television news, listen to his newly bought Schubert *Impromptus*; he has to make up quickly for knowledge yet unlearned. How can he have lived so long in ignorance of music? Helen will be sifting through her music and flexing her fingers, stroking one soft hand against the other, entwining them, before she starts to play. She will sit quietly at the piano for a while, her head bowed and her hands clasped as if in prayer. If you press your index finger hard against some-body else's and rub the two together with the thumb and index finger of your free hand, you will not be able to tell which one is yours. Both the conjoined fingers will feel familiar and strange; moulded into one and borderless. Helen, I knew thee before the world began; in the silence of eternity we loved.

Later, on the television, Charles Ryder kisses Julia for the last time, before a fountain in a garden in the moonlight: do you remember the storm? Stephen in the shadows watching; Helen too. Sweet Helen, make me immortal with a kiss. Her soft lips yielding, rose petals and the taste of honey. Oh, it is hard to be alone on a night like this, and the west wind blow-ing and the lady as remote as if there were an ocean in between and yet only a few miles away in measurable distance. Can I get there by candlelight? Yes, and back again.

It is half past ten. Helen is alone in a bedroom full of flow-ers and flinging her window wide onto the night. Seizing the chance for which it has been waiting, the wind at once will come storming in to wrap her in its wild embrace. And the moon and stars, struggling vainly to be free of the confines of their orbits, can only look on jealously while their rival runs his fingers through her hair. But she will brush away the tres-passer and, leaning from the window, will look down at the dark expanse of parkland where, among the dead leaves and the roots of ivy, the small creatures of the night halt their rustlings to lift their beady eyes to her in adoration. Stephen opens a window too. The outside air is fraught with cold and city smell. Please, take a message to her, Stephen asks the wind.

Friday

On Wednesday night Helen was talking about young men on hunger strike, starving themselves for their quixotic cause. 'I just can't get them out of my mind,' she said. 'Those images, they haunt me.' They were having a conversation over dinner, she, PHOENIX and a third, another man. There had been a telephone call from a call-box at 18.55: PHOENIX to his wife asking if he could bring Michael home with him. They had bumped into each other at the traffic lights – not literally, of course – had been to have a quick drink, really good to see him after too long, now he's at a loose end, just broken up with that boyfriend whom we didn't care for, he'd love to see Helen, would she mind? No, of course not, she'd love to see him too. They could pick something up on the way back if they needed more for supper? No, no, she's going to make risotto; it will stretch.

When Jamie and the man called Michael arrived at the flat and Michael greeted Helen, Stephen recognised his voice. Out of context it was difficult to place. An actor familiar from film or television? Someone from the Institute? And then he remembered, and with that memory came a sharp reminder of a steep stone staircase, an archway open to the air, a wooden board with his own name inscribed on it in neat italics, other names, and that name: *M. W. R. Bennet-Gilmour*. Loud and confident voices shouting in the night, young men laughing loudly. Could they really have laughed that much, for so much of the time? Did they ever stop to listen to themselves? Did they ever cry? Their footsteps on the staircase as they ran up and down at speed, forever late, forever urgent, forever in a rush to get to pubs and theatres and parties. To the river, on summer mornings. Smell of sweat and games kit, smell of mud, of cold air, dampness, beer and marijuana.

Stephen sets the memory aside to concentrate on what the three are saying. Jamie, having not had time for lunch because things at work are hectic, says he's ravenous; Michael, are you starving too? Michael, lightly, says that's a word his mother did not let him use when he was a child if what he meant to say was he was hungry. She knew hunger, and she never forgot the things she saw in Poland during the war. And besides, there's no one more likely to be a language purist than someone who learned English later on in life.

'Jamie's mother's favourite adjective is "blood-stained",' Helen says.

'But everybody says things like that,' says Jamie. 'We say we're dying for a drink, could kill for a cigarette. Words are metaphors, you know.'

'I think they should be truthful,' Helen says. Stephen can hear the sound of cutlery, of metal against metal, as Helen is speaking; the three are in the kitchen area, at a little distance from the microphone – against the noise of cooking some of their words are lost. 'It's to die for,' Michael says of something Stephen did not catch, and the other two laugh. Later, when they are eating, he goes on:

'Everyone who survived the war has hang-ups about food. My mother, yes, of course. She knew that people really could kill for a crust of bread. But other people too, even those who didn't have such a hellish time.'

'Yes,' Helen agrees, 'my dad really used to hate it when we didn't finish the food we had on our plates. He'd eat our leftovers himself rather than see them go to waste.'

'It's to do with wanting to be safe, isn't it?' Michael says. 'You only feel safe when you know you won't go hungry, when there's always enough food.'

'My father told me about a man, in fact his oldest chum, they'd been in the Army together, young subalterns in the war, you know; anyway, they shared a house together, with some other men. And one day, they were looking for this bloke and he'd vanished; they couldn't find him anywhere, although they called and called for him. So, they were just about to leave, for the pub or whatever, without him, when somebody opened the airing cupboard, one of the ones that are actually the size of a small room, and there he was, hunched up on a slatted shelf, with a saucepan of potatoes. He'd hidden away to scoff them by himself.'

'Raw?'

'No, of course not. Boiled, I suppose.'

'Poor devil. He must have been mortified when they caught him.'

'My father found it comic,' Jamie says.

'I don't think that sort of thing is funny at all,' Helen demurs. 'I'll never forget, when I was a little girl, seeing an old woman sitting on a window ledge outside a shop, all by herself, eating a packet of butter. Rectangular and yellow, wrapped in silver foil. Her attention was completely focused on it; she was like a miser with her treasure, hungrily licking away. I thought it was the saddest thing I'd ever seen.'

'Why sad?'

'Because it was butter? Because she was old and on her own? Later I came to think that it was probably not butter but ice cream.'

'Did that change the memory? Did it no longer seem so sad? When you realised she was simply an old biddy giving herself a little treat?'

'No. Butter or ice cream, it didn't change the way she was huddled over it, in her shabby winter coat, shielding it as if it might be stolen from her. Anyway, even a young and happy woman eating ice cream on her own would make me feel sad.'

'That's silly!'

'Seagulls steal ice cream from children at the seaside.'

'It's a primal urge. The fear of starving is our oldest fear.'

'Is that why hungers strikes are so disturbing? Because they show that for believers there is something even more important than that basic need?'

'I can't get them out of my mind. Those images . . .'

The talk goes on. Stephen, invisible fourth at the table, today's man at the day-before-yesterday's meal, listens carefully to every word. Bobby Sands, victims, heroes, the beauty of the hero, Bobby Sands the image of Christ, and Che Guevara, dying for a cause. To care enough about a cause to give your life for it? Any cause, you name it. *Pro patria mori?* Not us, not any more, no thank you.

'To starve to death. Ah, how terrible. Would you know that the end was coming, or would you be unconscious long before you reached that stage?'

'Like a prisoner on Death Row. Isn't that the cruellest thing, to let a man know in advance the moment of his death? The key turning in the lock of the cell door at exactly ten to seven.'

'And the saddest thing, the condemned man's final meal.'

'Steak and pizza, usually. And a Coke. Not what I'd choose. What would you choose, Helen?'

'How could anybody want to eat, on the eve of death?'

It takes as long to listen as the exchange itself took, protracted over drinks, risotto, cheese, more wine, and coffee, going on till nearly midnight. It was considerate of Michael Bennet-Gilmour to leave before the clock struck twelve, Stephen thinks, before this tape ran out and the new one began, with the inevitable hiatus. But, while Helen and Jamie are still talking, he is interrupted anyway, by Rollo Buckingham materialising through the long room's permanent haze of cigarette smoke with yesterday's report sheet in his hand.

'Cube?' says Stephen, forlornly.

'Haven't time. I've been in Wales all morning and I must get back tonight.'

'Wales?'

'Wales,' Rollo says, impatiently. Naturally Rollo has other cases to investigate, about which Stephen does not know. In Stephen's imagination Rollo thinks of nobody but PHOENIX. But in fact he knows the opposite is true: Rollo is a busy man; the Institute is at as great a risk of penetration as an ancient beam of wood is from the worm. Rollo does not have time for small talk now, or ever.

'To get to the point,' he says, 'let's be very careful what we say, although as everyone in here is wearing headphones, we're as safe as anywhere, I guess.'

He does not say, because he does not have to, that walls have ears, or may do, even in the Institute, in spite of all the measures

113

that are taken to sweep them clean. It's a mantra of Security's, constantly repeated, emblazoned on posters on noticeboards everywhere.

Now Rollo waves the report sheet in Stephen's face. 'It doesn't make sense,' he says. A chilly wave of fear ripples all through Stephen but he keeps his head.

'What doesn't make sense?'

'Well, in the first place, how did the wife know he wasn't going to turn up at the theatre? Did he ring her at home?'

Stephen pauses to consider. Buckingham could easily obtain a log of telephone calls; he cannot take the risk.

'No,' he answers truthfully. 'But there is a possibility that he called his friend John Cummins. The wife was home only very briefly after work; it takes a long time to get to Greenwich. Anyway we don't know that she did know, before the play began.'

'But if that were the case how would he know when to meet for dinner? Or where to go?'

'Yes, he must have telephoned Cummins. From a call-box. Or he could have guessed the time the play would end and waited for the others outside the theatre.'

'And there was no explanation at all of why he missed the play?'

'Only the reason that you have there. That "unforseen emergency". Was there one on Tuesday evening? I thought that you'd be bound to know.'

Rollo ignores this hint. 'So, basically you are saying that for the second time this week the subject went AWOL for several hours and we can't account for a single one?'

'In essence that is right.'

'But how come? How come we only ever hear about it afterwards, that he isn't where you told me he would be?'

'Look here,' says Stephen, mustering injured pride. 'This is not an Alpha investigation. There's a time-lag of at least a day. As you very well know. That is why you have to deploy the trackers.'

'But I don't have the trackers. Or only on occasion. Not often enough. Beside, as it's obviously out of the question to let the whole team of trackers into the know on a case as sensitive as this one, there are restrictions. Ergo, there are only two trackers on the special list. And two people can't possibly track a suspect for twenty-four hours a day, and seven days a week. That is why we are relying on you. You are supposed to give us warning of his movements in advance.'

'I do! Whenever I can. It's not my fault if he keeps changing his plans at the eleventh hour.'

'It's absurd. We can't pin enough on him for Category Alpha and yet without a Category A we'll never get enough to nail him.'

'I could track him if you like. I mean, on an informal basis.'

Rollo laughs outright. 'You could track him? You?'

'I did rather well on my training course, you know.'

'No doubt. Of course you did. But this calls for specialists. You must be forgetting how delicate this is. I mean you wouldn't ask a tracker to do double-duty as a listener, would you? What's he doing now, I mean last night?'

'Actually it's the night before. Wednesday. I haven't got round to yesterday – a personal emergency cropped up. He's having supper quietly at home with his wife and another male. Forename Michael, surname unknown.' Instinct warns him not to say that he can identify this man himself. It's important to keep any hint of a personal connection away from Rollo.

Rollo looks alert. 'No more particulars? No clues? Does he have a Spanish accent?'

'He sounds quite English to me. I think he's an old friend of PHOENIX's; he certainly knows the wife. But I'm only halfway through the evening; you stopped me in the middle; that's the tape there on the machine.'

'May I have a listen?'

Stephen rewinds the tape back to the conversation over dinner and passes the headphones to Rollo who, having refused a seat, has been standing over him all this time. Rollo stretches the wires to his ears and listens attentively for a few minutes. Then he pulls the headphones off. 'What a lot of crap these people talk,' he says. 'All that balls-aching poppycock about death. What sort of girl is she? Heidegger, for crying out loud!' He flourishes yesterday's report and in the process crumples it. 'And that's another thing that doesn't make sense. That play. It's not about the root causes of treacherous conduct. It's about homosexuality at Eton. And I don't think it's sold out. I'm going to see it myself, on Monday, as a matter of fact.'

'Have a good weekend,' says Stephen. Rollo, foregoing a reciprocal exchange of courtesies, turns as if to leave but is struck by a sudden afterthought. 'I don't think I'm going to get the extension that we talked about on Wednesday,' he says. 'We've had that case conference. Sub-director Six already thinks that we are on a hiding to nothing. We're going to look like real charlies if we keep our sights on this one when the issue's somewhere else. Because of Christmas, the date of the review board's not yet fixed.'

It's like being shown the scaffold and told you'll have to mount it unless you can magic up some proof to save yourself. Stephen had believed he'd bought a stay of execution but Rollo has kicked away the stool beneath his feet; it seems that the seeds of doubt he has been sowing have not taken root. He desperately needs help. He is praying for it while he finds the place where he stopped the tape when Rollo interrupted him and, when he does, he hears Helen saying that the next few days are busy and they must be sure their diaries match. She is making him a gift; it as is though she wants to let him to know where she will be. She's giving him her present. Tomorrow evening they'll be at home; of course they will – Stephen saw her going there; it's *Brideshead*. On Friday the school term ends but she has to be back the next day for the children's carol service, which begins at ten o'clock in the morning. Yes, apparently it's always on a Saturday for the sake of all the mummies and daddies who can't take time off work. No, he doesn't have to come. There's George and Gina's party on Friday night. Yes, she has remembered that he has a work commitment then and will get to the party late. She'll make her own way there, or maybe she'll go with Allegra, who has been invited too. Don't forget you said you'd meet me after the carol service; you said we'd go to Harvey Nicks, we still have to do your brother and your father, for whom it is impossible to find a present, and you did say you would come with me: what *do* you give the man who has everything he wants? I loathe shopping, Jamie is in the middle of saying, when midnight comes and the recording stops.

Stephen whispers his heartfelt thanks to Helen. In some mysterious sense she knows that he is there. Spirits are connected in unearthly ways that no mortal can explain: it's only unimaginative literalists who think communication needs a physical link, as a telephone needs wires. Who knows how souls reach out through eternities of time and space?

He considers chasing after Rollo to inform him that PHOENIX has made a mysterious arrangement for tonight. But what's the point? At this short notice, Rollo won't be able to rustle up the trackers, will he? He remembers the look on Rollo's face when he offered to tail PHOENIX by himself and at once is quite sure of the next step he should take.

He opens the door onto noise and heat, in such abrupt and unexpected contrast to the darkness of the street that he reels back and has to take a deep breath before threading his way in through the crowd. It hadn't occurred to him that this pub would be so busy, but it should have done: it's ten past six on the last Friday before Christmas Eve; men are jostling each other to get to the bar and spilling beer from overflowing glasses held at shoulder-height. There's something feverish about the hubbub; it's a night of possible misrule. Scanning faces through the swirling smoke, like someone looking for a friend, Stephen can't immediately see anyone who stands out, but perhaps it's early yet. There's no one obviously alone or in a clandestine couple. It's a long shot, he's aware of that, but it *could* pay off. There are four pubs in the vicinity of the Institute and PHOENIX might conceivably be in one.

Stephen had decided to begin with the pub that is furthest from the Institute and has long been on the proscribed list. Like a hunter – no, more like a naturalist – he must think himself into the mentality of his quarry. And like an expert naturalist, he has made a careful study not only of his subject's mind but also of his habits; his quest is based on more than random guesswork. PHOENIX is indolent: when he is at home he sprawls around while his exploited wife cooks and cleans and irons his expensive cotton shirts. Why would he go haring round the wilds of outer London, the back of beyond, when he could make an assignation on his doorstep, without effort? PHOENIX is cocksure; rules don't apply to him. PHOENIX is possessive. He won't abandon his beautiful wife to the company of other men for long; he'll want to claim her at the party as soon as he possibly can. And most crucially, PHOENIX is professional. If he's seeing someone whom he shouldn't be seeing – a representative of an unfriendly government, for instance – he will do so in an environment in which both he and that hostile operative can feel safe. Operatives are mortally afraid of being caught red-handed in breach of protocols, and consequently being expelled. Who can blame them? No one in his right mind would run the risk of forfeiting a cushy post in London for a desk job in a dismal bunker in Berlin. Or Budapest. Or Bucharest. Wherever. With no escaping from it. Once he's been identified and his cover blown, he's done for. So there's no point whatsoever in inviting one to meet you in the middle of Clapham Common at the dead of night. Or the toilets at Victoria station. Meetings must be held in places where, if challenged, the official can explain his presence. Theatres. Restaurants. Pubs like this. Which is why this and many other pubs are out of bounds to staff of the Institute. Because they are opposition haunts. Logically it follows that PHOENIX will have a use for them as well.

It would help if Stephen knew where George and Gina's

party was, and when it would begin. As it is, the window of time is rather too wide, although there are reasonable parameters. Unless PHOENIX left work early, he would have been in the Institute until about five-thirty. And it could have been later, if he's an operative or a strategist, for long working hours are a source of pride to them. And surely he'll want to get to the party before nine o'clock? A maximum of three hours then: a long shot, yes, but worth a chance. Luck, in Stephen's view, plays an underestimated part in life.

The second pub on his round seems to have been taken over for a private function and is heaving with people wearing tinsel necklaces and paper crowns. No one could hear himself speak in there, let alone hold a surreptitious meeting. The third is less crowded but the few couples in the bar consist of men with women. In books and films, enemy agents are often glamorous and female but Stephen knows that this is seldom the case in real life.

Nevertheless it is not impossible that PHOENIX is meeting a woman. Stephen had tentatively planted that idea in Rollo's mind already, without believing it himself. Now he stops to wonder. Jamie Greenwood wouldn't be the first adulterer to deceive his wife with lies about staying late at work.

It certainly makes Stephen think. What is it that he really wants? Where is he trying to get to, what is he trying to do? Yesterday morning he had stood before a looking glass and pledged himself to follow this endeavour to its end. He had identified the first moves he must make and now he's making them, but he had left the actual ending out of focus. He was afraid of dooming it by spelling it out precisely, even to himself. When he was a child he thought that imaginary things could come true if you wished for them hard enough, and he still believes in the potency of will. But now that he's a man, he also knows that you cannot map your future out on the smallest of all scales because something unforeseen or omitted from the grid will trip you up. You are less at risk of disappointment if you leave your goals in outline instead of packing them with detail. His goal in this journey is union with the woman he loves, but he hasn't tried to define it yet in the drearily practical terms that the outside world would understand: Helen to him is grail and mystic rose, the core of the flame, eternally companion of his soul. But this evening, standing in the doorway of a pub, he begins to see that he may have to plot the conclusion in advance, if it is to be the right one.

Where has he got to now? Well, in all honesty he can't convince himself that PHOENIX is having an affair, much as it would ease his way ahead. Although he'd be happy to believe the marriage was breaking down, he knows from what he hears on tape that PHOENIX is smugly and infuriatingly uxorious. Likewise he must admit there's no real proof – as yet – that PHOENIX is the mole that Rollo Buckingham is seeking. But. But he's too good to be true; there's something disingenuous about him. And. And there must be very solid grounds for Buckingham's suspicion for otherwise he would not have had the licence to investigate the man. The system works; those licences are not lightly won. And, this evening, it is an undeniable fact that PHOENIX has told his wife he's working late. On a Friday evening? The last before Christmas Eve? Who makes a work appointment then, when they could be at a party?

Treachery cuts far deeper than adultery: could even the most loving wife forgive a man who led a double life, deceiving her *and* betraying his country? Stephen is quite sure that Helen has no idea her husband's playing false. When she is told, her whole world will be devastated. But he, Stephen, will be there beside her, to hold her hand, to explain to her, to support her through the trial and comfort her. PHOENIX will get Life. There used to be the death penalty for treason.

Stephen orders whisky, and drinks it leaning casually against the bar from where he can observe the room and overhear the tone, if not the words, of the many conversations that are going on around him. This pub has a less masculine air than the one in which he began the hunt. Of the four couples he can see, three are evidently lovers. One pair is openly kissing, between deep pulls on their cigarettes. None of the men has the confident, patrician look that Stephen expects of Greenwood, and no one looks especially furtive. Three of the couples, or more relevantly the male halves, are audible, when he strains to hear them. There is an empty place next to the fourth.

Having bought another drink, Stephen wanders nonchalantly over to the unused stool and sits. The girl is pretty. As he watches, she leans closer to the man and whispers something; the man smiles at her and tenderly strokes a straying lock of hair back off her forehead. Such casual gestures of intimacy as this – they wrench at Stephen's heart.

A little while later the man stands up, about to go for refills. Halfway to the bar he turns and calls back to the girl: 'Do you want ice this time?' His accent is unmistakably Australian.

Stephen finishes his second whisky while he considers what to do. It's only half past seven. One more pub to go. Is this an utter waste of time, a wild goose chase? On the last Friday before Christmas Eve he should have other things to do. He *could* have had other things, he is not without friends, Damian asked this afternoon if he'd like to go and see a film. Stephen had fibbed and said he couldn't because he had to meet his old friend Giles. Damian is impressed by that connection. So in effect he's cooked his goose; it's Friday night and he has nowhere else to go.

The last pub then. Why not? It's the one nearest the Institute, the one he ate his lunch in yesterday when he had his toothache. As it is the nearest, it is also the least likely place for Greenwood to choose. But in any case, what is there to lose?

This pub, to his surprise, is almost empty. Perhaps by now the early evening drinkers have gone home. It's an old-fashioned pub and feels like a place of calm. He can't tell if the fittings are genuinely old or made to seem so, but either way they're comfortable: high-backed settles, bentwood chairs, a gas fire, stools drawn up beside the bar. On one wall there's a glass case of stuffed animals: a fox, one forepaw raised; in the waxen undergrowth a pair of cowering rabbits.

Stephen's thirsty now; whisky's too acerbic. He asks for a pint of Guinness. He likes its creaminess and that unliquid-seeming head, so white against the blackness and defined, as if there were two substances, both held together in a single glass. He likes the care the barman takes with pouring, and the time it takes to settle; the froth against the mouth.

He chooses a stool at the far end of the bar. Opposite him, at a table near the door, three men and two women are in lively conversation. A couple, wearing overcoats, is sitting side-by-side on one of the settles; they are in late middle age and have the air of being married. There is another solitary man at a small round table, with a pint of beer and an unlit pipe resting in an ashtray. He is reading the *Daily Telegraph* and paying no attention to anyone around him. At the first sight of him Stephen's hopes did rise but with a closer look he sees that the man is in his forties, much older then than Jamie Greenwood.

Too bad. Now that he is here, he might as well enjoy his evening. It's warm in here and cold outside. By now it's well past eight. God only knows what PHOENIX is doing or where he is. Helen will be arriving at the party; he can see heads turning as she comes into the room, dressed in something silvery; it will be as if the darkness that was there before had been dispelled. O Helen, thou art fairer than the evening air, clad in the beauty of a thousand stars.

Strange that she should be a friend of Michael Bennet-Gilmour's. Not that Bennet-Gilmour had been a friend of his; he was merely a man who shared his staircase for a year. Bennet-Gilmour probably wouldn't remember Stephen, who would have been beneath his notice, although to give him his due, he had always been polite. Unlike some of the rowdier boys who treated the staircase, the college, the town, the world as if they owned them by ancestral right. To boys like those, boys like Stephen barely existed.

And that was so unfair. When Stephen was at school, the demarcation lines had been blurrier and mutable: the pinched eleven-year-old with knock-knees and buck teeth could metamorphose into a star, as Giles Dix had done in their Upper Sixth year.

Giles is on his mind because of the excuse he made to Damian. He and Giles had been friends of a sort at school: Donaldson and Dix – with surnames sharing an initial they had adjacent desks. When they were new boys they had other things in common: they both wore glasses and played chess, and Giles was the son of elderly parents, or parents who seemed old compared to other people's, as Stephen's mother did. Even at infant school Stephen had felt embarrassed by his mother's age. And fearful. Sometimes she was taken for his granny. Grannies had a tendency to die. Giles, though, was not an only child; he had an older brother and a sister.

As Giles and his family had only just moved to the area, he knew no one when he joined the grammar school. But Stephen had arrived there with a cohort from Moorland Juniors and no hope of shedding the burdens the other boys had long ago laid on him. Step hen. Step hen Duckson. Runty, four-eyed, mouth-breathing Stephen who lived in a council house and had no dad and didn't learn until far too late to pretend he didn't know the answers. Step hen who was the best at reading in his class and the worst at games. Who could never get over the vaulting horse in gym and was never picked for any team. Whose head was once pushed down into a toilet bowl, which had not been flushed. Who always mooched around the playground by himself. Step hen, Stephen Waddlecock, Stephen cleverclogs, poor Waddles.

Clever, though, is useful. Clever can win you prizes, scholarships and a place at Oxford. It armours you. It gives you a place to hide. It can be a mask. It admits you into other worlds and gives you words for weapons. Cleverness is helpful to a solitary child.

Giles was clever too. Waddlecock and Willy. Together they had passed exams while staying on the edge of things, at the back of the classroom, in the long grass on the boundary of the playing fields, until Giles, with practically no warning, became the singer in a band. Stephen had known that Giles was good at music, he'd been a choirboy, his voice stayed high and pure long after Stephen's own had broken. But the band was something that had happened at weekends when the two boys seldom met. For Stephen it was safer to despise rock music than to dare the heat, the sweat, the pulse of it, and he had not paid any attention to Giles's talk of guitars and gigs, resenting this divergent interest. They were taking the entrance exam for Oxford: he wanted Giles to speak of Donne and Keats. But Giles quoted the Velvet Underground instead and failed the exam, perhaps on purpose. And Giles now has another name and it, like his sharp cheekbones, his thin-lipped mouth, his flame-streaked hair, is famous.

Giles is proof that a man can change, as a caterpillar changes to a butterfly, or a frog becomes a prince. That pallid little boy is now the man whose face looks down at Stephen from a million billboards and assures him every time he sees it that transformation does not only happen in fairy tales and myths. But it does need a helping hand from chance. In Stephen's opinion Giles's voice is nothing special, and without the make-up he'd still look like the stick insect he was, but he did have luck and determination. It was Giles's determination that kept him on the hard circuit of clubs and pubs where he could get a hearing and it was luck that led the right A&R man into the pub in Kensal Green on a night when Giles and his band just happened to be playing.

No one is sole author of his life. Stephen, looking back, sees his own divided into chapters – before school, junior school, secondary school – in which his younger self was swept along by the tide of other people's actions. Children have no power to steer themselves. Reminded by Bennet-Gilmour, reminder of his three years at university, he remembers how sure he was in the beginning that that particular chapter would contain an open door, the door that would magically yield to a secret password and give onto a new and better world. Three years seemed like a long time in prospect at eighteen but in reality it wasn't long enough. The seventy-two weeks that are all you get of stone staircases, linenfold panelling, low-lying mist on mown grass, girls in silk and rainbow colours – they don't give you time to turn yourself from the boy you were into the man you want to be. But they do show you where the doors are and how to forge the keys.

Stephen had watched and listened closely. Who told the long-limbed boys, the Greenwoods and the Bennet-Gilmours of this world, the Buckinghams, that asparagus is eaten with the fingers not a fork? Were they taught at school to tell their Château Lafite from their Château Latour when he, who has actually read some Heidegger, had only ever seen those names in books? Stephen observed buttonholes on the sleeves of jackets, links in place of buttons on shirt cuffs, bow ties that were actually tied, not pre-formed with elastic. He noted clipped consonants and drawled vowels, and changed his own to match them. In his new voice he didn't do much talking but instead, in lecture rooms and libraries, he listened and he read and the words of poets filtered deep into his mind.

He was not alone. There were dozens of young men like him, some in his own college. He went to lectures with them, to cinemas and pubs and, occasionally, to parties. They were friends, or passed for friends, during that time at least. Like Stephen they'd been top of the class at school and thought that they'd secured the passage to a future more expansive than the past they'd left behind. A future that would have in it success, careers and love. Hard work was important to them; that's the reason they were there, spending all their days and half their nights in laboratories and libraries, aiming for the high degrees.

There were also girls in lecture rooms and libraries of course. Most of them were like the boys by whom they were outnumbered – unobtrusive, studious and shy. The fortunate among them – boys and girls – recognised in each other the beauty of their souls and cleaved like twins thereafter. The rest looked on in hunger, from their own obscurity, with no choice but to wait, and hope that the wait would not be too agonisingly prolonged.

Girls in libraries. He can see them still; he even counted a few of them as friends. But they were not the sort of girls who floated through his dreams – those were girls with silver bangles jangling on their wrists, and swathes of shiny hair. Distracted girls, fresh from their lovers' beds, willow-slim and silk-skinned, in their tight tight jeans and flimsy layers of finest cotton, their small breasts showing through. Painted toenails, mouths like newly unfurled petals, drifts of rose-scent, lilac and patchouli; one long golden hair left lying on the scratched wood of a desk.

One girl in particular, whom he had encountered on his way out of a seminar on a summer afternoon. She'd been trying ineffectually to pin a poster on the English Faculty notice board and had dropped the others she was holding into a fan that spread across the floor. He'd stopped to pick them up. 'You're sweet to stop,' she'd said. 'Could you possibly very kindly help me to put the others up?'

For an enchanted hour he had followed her around the sunlit town, pasting posters onto walls at her command, her image on them as Titania. He was still trying to summon up the nerve to ask if she would care to have a drink with him when the last poster had gone up and she said she had to dash. Hey, but if you're not doing anything next week, why don't you come and do our front-of-house? What that meant he did not know but he went anyway, and carried chairs for the three nights of the play's run, and on the last night was invited to a party.

Now, on this December night, he looks back to it again, that summer – the air so still and soft, and heavy, as if heat had lent it weight. The night of the party, a bed of scented flowers beneath the window of the room, and the pulse of music echoing off the high quadrangle walls. The room so full it was hard to get in through the door, and dense with sound, and he knowing no one but another quiet boy who had also been roped in and yet, for once, no shame in being a stranger. When the press of bodies opened to make way for him, it enfolded him and told him he belonged there. At its centre, in the heart of the maze, the girl whom he would always think of as Titania, flushed and laughing in her wisps of silk, that evening's star.

She saw him and she smiled, and when he made his way through the crowd to her, she reached up to kiss him on the cheek. 'Thank you for all your help,' she said. She was small; he could have lifted her in his arms as easily as if she were a child. When she turned aside he saw the smooth crown of her head. He reached out his hand to hold her back but someone else had caught her up and spirited her away into a throng of dancers. And she was gone. It was the end of term: like migratory birds the students were departing to spend the summer somewhere else.

The next day he roamed the streets of Oxford in search of

Midsummer Night's Dream posters that were not yet overlaid. There was one undamaged on a board beside the Covered Market, which he carefully peeled off and kept; he has it still. Perhaps he could have found her, if he'd tried. But he let her go. He won't do that again. He is older now, a grown man: there's another chapter opening. But there won't always be new chapters; he knows now that stories end.

For a while he's lost in thoughts and memories. The pub is warm and quiet, the man behind the bar feels no need to talk, Stephen's almost in a trance in this safe haven. When he shakes himself awake he finds his glass is empty and the group at the table by the door has left. He might as well have another drink before he has to face the night and the journey home. But first he needs to pee and anyway the bartender is nowhere to be seen.

When Stephen comes back from the gents', the other solitary man is waiting at the still-deserted bar. He smiles at Stephen. His pipe is lit now and the smile is partially occluded by a cloud of smoke. 'It's cold tonight,' he says.

'It is,' Stephen agrees.

'I better had been on my way but I am putting off the moment.'

'And so am I.'

'But where is that barman then? Ah, he comes. Maybe you would care to join me? What's your choice of poison?'

'I was drinking Guinness,' Stephen says. 'But please, let me . . .'

'No, no. My shout. I myself am fond of an Irish pint from time to time but in general I do favour the local ale. London Pride! Unbeaten, for my money.'

He is a shortish man with a faintly melancholy look and thinning hair that is still more blond than grey. His lips are the same colour as his skin. There is something Nordic about him, or Slavic perhaps, but to Stephen his accent is unplaceable: a slight gurgle on the 'l', an elongated 'a', the suggestion of a diphthong on the 'e', – a liquid sound – a trace of mid-Atlantic maybe, and something else from somewhere more remote. After ordering the drinks he moves along the bar to offer Stephen a handshake. 'Alberic,' he says.

'Are you visiting London?' Stephen asks.

'No! I am a denizen, I live here! Since four years I have lived here and I am sorry you mistake me for a tourist!'

'I do apologise. It isn't that I took you for a tourist; it's simply that you don't sound exactly like a native, although I must say that your English is extremely good.'

'It is,' says Alberic. 'I study. I am especially hot on slang. I find it good to listen to the radio; it improves my accent but better by far is normal conversation. Like we are having now. Londoners are friendly. By chewing fat with normal people I hear the real language, do you know what I mean? There is not an excessive quantity of slang on the radio except, I guess, for Radio 1, but I have to tell you I am not a groupie of pop music.'

'Nor me. Actually, I'm thinking of learning the piano.'

Alberic looks delighted. He adores the piano! Only last week he had the great good fortune to hear Horowitz playing the Chopin *Fantaisie Impromptu*, fantastic really, but even more than the piano he adores the cello. That marvellous instrument that is the heart's voice and comes closest to the human form, he says, outlining with his hands a shapely woman.

'Another?' Stephen asks, indicating his empty glass.

Alberic consults his watch. 'One shouldn't. But, listen to the rain!'

Both men turn their heads towards the door. He's right: in the hush that falls as they stop talking, Stephen hears the rattle of heavy rain against the windows. 'We'd be better staying here until it stops,' he says to Alberic.

'I'm of your mind. One for the road then, thank you, but any more beer and I'll be pissing up all night so I'll take a brandy, if I may.'

Stephen orders the brandy and a Southern Comfort for himself; a drink that's new to him but sounds right, on this winter evening. It's beginning to seem dream-like, a sleepy, underwater feeling. It's good to be here in this warm place, with this companionable stranger. Alberic, returning to the question of accents, asks Stephen about his. 'Ordinary RP,' he says. 'Not very interesting, I'm afraid. Received Pronunciation.'

'Is that the same as Oxford English?'

'Well, yes, I suppose it is. Well, I was up myself, as a matter of fact.'

'Up?'

'At Oxford.'

'I could tell you were a varsity man. It was your clothing that showed me, even before you spoke. But is that perhaps your old school tie you wear? Is it true that that some gentlemen wear their old school socks?'

Two doubles later and the two men are still talking when the bartender calls time. Alberic is in import–export; he has an office up the road. He also has a wife and a teenage daughter but they are on an extended visit back to family at home. His wife's mother is unwell. It can get a little lonesome of a night.

Stephen, using a form of words approved by Security, tells him in response to his enquiry that he works in a government department that deals in defence statistics and research. 'Far too dull to talk about, I can assure you.'

'That, old boy, I simply don't believe. A clever young man like you who received his education at the University of Oxford? You're pulling my leg. I won't believe that you would jam yourself into a routine job!'

Having to pretend that you are duller than you are: that was not what Stephen had expected when he joined the Institute. No, far from it. He had thought that he was entering a new world, a world which offered him the chance to make himself into the man that he was always meant to be: correctly dressed, well-bred, a man of the world, a man of action and a scholar. Indeed he has become that man, or like enough, and that is how his colleagues see him, clad in his suits and cut-glass accent. As soon as he knew he'd got the job, he went to Ede and Ravenscroft with an advance against his salary. But it's ironic: an occupation that should confer glamour and mystique on him makes him more invisible to outsiders than he was before. A dull man in a dull job? Yes, and the job really is dull most of the time, but when it's not, when it involves action that the outside world sees as exciting, he's forbidden to say anything about it. He didn't want to be a listener, he assumed he'd be an operative, and no one has satisfactorily explained why he is not. 'We need your capabilities,' Sub-director Personnel had said. 'The initial selection tests you took show unusual verbal skill. You may apply to the Board for promotion in due course. When you have served at least four years at your current grade.'

Fuck him. Oh it is hard to be relegated to the shadows when

you should be in the limelight. How dare anyone decide that he, Stephen Donaldson, was less capable than Rollo Buckingham? He has applied to be promoted, twice. And twice been told to re-apply when, perhaps, there may be a vacant post. Meanwhile that wingèd chariot is rushing up behind him at a furious lick; he will be thirty before he knows it, he can feel the cold air whistling on his neck. He winks at Alberic. 'Well, you know what government work is like,' he says. 'Hush-hush.'

'Time, gentlemen, please,' the man behind the bar reminds them. Alberic knocks out his pipe into an ashtray and puts on the coat he had draped carefully over the back of a chair. 'Once more into the breach, old man,' he says, making for the door.

Buttoning his own coat up, Stephen follows him outside. The rain is falling still, cold and sharp as surgeon's steel. In the shelter of the doorway, Alberic comes to a sudden halt.

'Look,' he says. 'I have an idea. Piano music. Of which the two of us are lovers. I happen to have a spare ticket for a concert, I think at the Festival Hall, next Tuesday; it was for my old Dutch but of course now she had to leave for home. If you could join me for the evening, I would be deeply honoured. For if not, that ticket will go to waste.'

About to make an excuse or at least to ask what concert, Stephen stops. Why not? Alberic is charming. 'That would be nice,' he says.

'Super! Just tell me your phone number. I'll remember it, don't bother to find your card or a piece of paper, for in this rain the ink will run.' For the second time he holds his hand out to shake Stephen's.

Saturday

Later that Friday night a blizzard swept in from the west. That night eleven people died when a bomb exploded in a pub in Wolverhampton, not far from a Territorial Army training base. Four of the dead were soldiers; the others were civilians unconnected to the base. One of them had been celebrating her engagement. There were serious injuries to people who survived.

As he didn't listen to the radio news on Saturday morning, Stephen did not know about the bomb until he saw a news vendor's billboard at the station. He had left his flat before first light to get to Battersea in time for the second stage of his reconnaissance. He had made his plans. He is methodical and he is well trained, although this morning he has a pounding headache. Perhaps he's coming down with flu.

The cold caught him by surprise. It was so intense that it had body to it; it filled his mouth and probed the nerve-endings of his teeth. When he got off the train at Battersea the snow had turned to sleet. Realistically, even in the half-light, he could not expect to hide for very long within the shrubbery of the park, nor loiter inconspicuously on the street: a solitary figure in the freezing rain. No, his intention was to be strolling past Helen's mansion block at exactly the same time as she was leaving for the carol concert. She had said that it began at 10.00. She normally allows three-quarters of an hour for the journey from home to school. She is the music teacher; obviously she will have to be there well before the event is due to start. She is conscientious; she will want to get to the school by 9.15. It was now just after 7.30. He had about an hour to kill, but found a convenient workmen's café near the station. If he can be outside the mansion block by 8.25, he will see Helen again.

He was right, and he was lucky. The first time he walked up the street past the entrance there was no one there at all. At the far end of the street he stopped and, for the benefit of anyone who might be spying on him from a window, pretended to consult the A–Z. His umbrella would afford him some protection from busybodies twitching their lace curtains. He turned back down the street and as he was approaching it on the opposite side he saw that the main door of the mansion block was opening.

Three people emerged and walked down the shallow flight of steps together. One was the lovely woman in the pale coat; the other two were men. A man of average height in a hooded yellow waterproof; a much taller man in a green waxed jacket, bare-headed, his thick hair almost black. Stephen knew him instantly as the man who shared a room with Rollo Buckingham, and the shock of that recognition stopped his breath.

It was more than ever crucial now that he should not be seen. He couldn't stand there on the pavement staring, but neither could he swivel on his heel and stride off in the opposite direction. There was nothing for it but to tilt his umbrella at an angle like a shield and march right past the three of them, with his head bent and his face averted. When he reached the corner of the street he dared a backwards glance; both men were unlocking bicycles that had been chained to the railings by the flats. Helen was standing near them, struggling to put up a red umbrella. Dangerous though he knew it was, Stephen was desperate for a closer look. He ducked into the portal of the next block, where it could seem that he was ringing a doorbell.

It was an inspired move. Raised above the level of the street, sheltered by the roofed portal and in a feigned attitude of waiting, Stephen could observe all three as they reached the corner. The two men were wheeling their bikes. At the corner Helen gave a little wave, crossed the main road and went towards the gate into the park. One or other of the men called after her but a passing lorry drowned their voices out. Both then swung their legs over their crossbars and rode off side-by-side in the direction of Albert Bridge.

Stephen watched Helen walk away from him. He was in no condition to follow her or anybody else through the wintry park. The thunderbolt was having a serious effect, now that the immediate risk of being caught was past. He needed to wait a while until his nerves were steady.

How could he have failed to identify PHOENIX weeks ago? He must have seen him in that room a dozen times or more. It is true that he only delivers reports by hand when they may be urgent and that when he does, he often finds Rollo there alone, but even so, how could he have been so blinkered and obtuse?

Could he be going mad? The horror of that thought is an icy tidal wave crashing down upon him. But no, of course he's not, he is as sane as he has ever been, and in full possession of his wits. The wave recedes a little. And then it dawns on Stephen that he has never heard the dark man speak. Or, if he has, then nothing more than a few clipped and muttered words. In all these weeks he has been silent to the point of rudeness, rarely acknowledging Stephen with anything more forthcoming than a nod.

But that does not explain the other staggering fact. Rollo Buckingham is conducting an investigation in the very room he shares with that investigation's target. Can that actually be true? It seems absurdly cavalier. And yet, now that Stephen comes to think of it, nothing is ever said in that room or in any other that would give away the game. Generalities are permissible; specifics are forbidden; no names, no pack drill; we are all too well aware that careless talk costs lives. He recalls Rollo's furious expression when he thought that Stephen was about to blurt out some details. No wonder then that Rollo is so insistent on the Cube. Christ almighty, this is a stroke of genius on Rollo's part. What better way to hide this most delicate investigation and to lull the suspect into a false sense of safety than by investigating him under his own nose? Not in a million years would Jamie Greenwood dream that Rollo had any idea what he was up to.

The sleet had thickened once again to snow. An old man with a dog was walking towards the doorway in which Stephen was sheltering; it was time to go. Feeling a bit safer now, he decided to take a closer look at the entrance to Helen's block: it could be that there were names beside the doorbells on their polished plaque of brass. He'd like to know which flat is hers and in fact may need to, if he is ever to tail PHOENIX or carry out any other investigations of his own.

He examined the building from the street. At its west gable there was a high wooden gate in the wall, which must lead to a yard or narrow garden. Opposite the block was the brick slab of the next; behind both blocks were ordinary terraced houses. The street was not very long. Like others in this part of London, its name echoed an imperialist past: Soudan, Khartoum, Kandahar and Khyber; shades of Englishmen fresh off the playing fields of Eton, ruling single-handed over tracts of land that were a hundred times the size of their home counties; imposing their own codes on alien frontiers. What were those late Victorian builders dreaming of, when they gave their new streets those exotic names? Peshawar? Maybe, Stephen thought, through the fog of his fear and his thumping headache, these were actually the sites of battles. Dead men then, those young Etonians, in their foreign fields that are no longer England? Street names like war memorials, in a city that is not the one the young men knew, in a country that has no idea where it's going and is caught like a dog with its head in railings, railings just like the ones that fence off the park before him, a bulldog facing backwards, sick with sentiment and nostalgia. If Jamie Greenwood had been born half a century earlier he'd have been one of those young rulers. And what are they doing now, these men, the Buckinghams and Greenwoods who were born too late? They're still fighting their tribal wars against the VULCANS and the ODINS, the trade unionists, the miners, the Irish and the foreigners, the whole mishmash whose voices, aspirations and lost causes fill Stephen's waking hours.

To Stephen's disappointment there were no names against any of the doorbells. He carefully inspected the side elevation of the building to see if he could tell how the flats were laid out but, as it was evident from the doorbells that a few were subdivided, it was not possible to ascertain which windows belonged where on any floor. He could hear the passing traffic from the Greenwoods', which must mean their sitting room faced the main road and the park. That was good to know. He was right to think of Helen gazing out at grass and trees, green thoughts in a green shade, oasis in the city. Whenever she opened her windows she would scent the salt breath of the distant river. There were seventeen flats in this section of the block, including subdivisions. There was an entry phone. As no one had ever mentioned a lift or many stairs, it was a reasonable assumption that Helen's flat was on the first or second floor. Stephen knew that it couldn't be on the ground floor or in the basement because, if it were, there'd be a different quality of sound.

The main door did not yield when Stephen pushed it, and its large brass knob was purely ornamental. That came as no surprise; he'd seen that Helen used a key. He crouched down to the level of the letterbox plate, and pushed it open to peer inside. It was dark in there, and hard to make out anything but the foot of a flight of stairs. And the lower half of someone running down them.

Stephen dropped the letterbox plate quickly and stepped backwards but there was no time to retreat; the person on the other side was already opening the door. It was a young woman with short brown hair, wearing a navy quilted jacket and green wellington boots. Seeing Stephen hovering on the doorstep, she nodded to him politely and stood aside, holding the door open. 'Er, thanks,' Stephen mumbled, sidling past her, his wet umbrella still unfurled. Now he was inside, and the door was swinging shut behind him.

How could that silly girl be sure he was neither a burglar nor a rapist? Were all of Helen's neighbours so careless of her safety? The sooner he could get her away from here the better. Meanwhile it was deeply thrilling to be in the place where Helen lived. For the time being he shut his mind to the carnal reality of PHOENIX and to the disturbing solidity that gave to images that before were clouded. That reality would have to be confronted – the man is Helen's lover, Helen's husband – but Stephen had not the strength to face it now.

The entrance hall was clean and tidy. There were the doors to flats 38 and 39, numbered pigeonholes, and an old-fashioned lift of the kind with double folding grilles. The stairs were carpeted, the hall floor made of patterned tiles. For the moment it was quiet.

Stephen quickly checked the contents of the pigeonholes. There must be a porter or a caretaker in this mansion block: in other buildings that Stephen had seen old letters and bills and unwanted papers piled up in dusty drifts, but here the mail had all been sorted. Nothing bore the Greenwood name. Their mail, of course, must have been read before it got to them, thought Stephen, recalling his one training visit to that branch of Technical where two women sat with their trays of letters and a steaming kettle.

He dragged open the sliding metal gate into the lift. Six floors. It did not go to a basement. It was exactly like a cage. He closed it again; if anyone should summon it, he would have more than enough warning from the creak of metal. He'd take the stairs and make his way up slowly.

On the first landing there were three flats: 40a and 40b, and 41. There was a window that looked out over the side-street and across to the opposite block. The pattern was the same on every floor, except that on some there were the two original flats, and at the top of the building there were four. All of them had identical front doors. Ordinary wooden doors, unremarkable, except that one belonged to Helen. He rubbed his fingers over every handle as he passed, hedging his bets; her fingers would have been on one. From behind a door on the third floor he heard a baby crying and stopped to listen: is it a visiting baby or a new one? Had he heard a child here before? A dog, yes; there was a dog that barked sometimes but it was making no noise now. Was there the scent of Helen? On each landing he sniffed the air but it was difficult to tell, in a place where there were smells of breakfasts – coffee, bacon – and the smell of snow. But least he knew that he was stepping where she stepped, his hand was on the banisters that her hand touched every day, he was breathing where she breathed. Oh Helen.

In the time that he was there, he saw no one else. Could he have stayed there on the stairs and waited? But waited for what? Imagine if Helen were to come back home and find him sitting on the second flight, barring the way to her front door . . . No, this was not the right time yet. He wouldn't know what to say to her; not yet. If he made a move too soon, he would scare her off. He'd rather sever his right hand than cause her to be frightened. When the time comes he will approach her gently, as he would a shy, wild creature – a kitten or a fawn – step by slow and careful step, holding out a coaxing hand until he gains her trust. That time will surely not be long; not now that he is making such good progress; he must enforce patience on himself.

But what instead should he do now? It's Saturday; it's snowing; his mother will be expecting him to take her to the shops. Helen will still be at the carol service – perhaps he might slip in at the back, seeming like a father who is late? Except he doesn't know exactly where it's being held. What is PHOENIX doing now? It's surprising that he left the flat so early when he doesn't have to be at Harvey Nicks until about eleven. Maybe even eleven-thirty. Who was the other man? A neighbour? Wouldn't the service be followed by coffee or something? Mince pies. Harvey Nicks. It took him a moment to work out what Helen meant when she said that. It's funny, the familiar terms that people use, almost a sort of code. Outsiders try to adopt them but often get them wrong – like Alberic, with his quaint use of words. Stephen squirms when Charlotte chatters on about H. A. Rods, but for all he knows that's what everyone who's in the know calls it. He can't take the risk of being seen this morning in Harvey Nichols himself, now that he has recognised Jamie Greenwood. He really must stay hidden from now on. So anyway. There's nothing he can do here any more; he might as well go home and get the car and drive to Didcot where his mother waits.

Coralie is thanking heavens for the cold. Who would have thought it: snow so thick it was settling in and there still a week to go till Christmas? It means that the blessed turkey – which, to be on the safe side, really must be bought today – will live quite happily in the boot of the car all week. And the Brussels sprouts. Unless there is a sudden thaw? But she'll cross that bridge when she gets to it – there's no point fretting over things that might not happen when there's quite enough already to occupy one's thoughts. She'd like to get her watch mended this afternoon if possible; it stopped working on Wednesday and it's hard to do without. There's a little man in that arcade off Duke Street. In the supermarket car park she is checking through her list. 'Sausagemeat,' she reads. 'Parsnips. Tin-foil. The milkman will bring the extra butter. Icing sugar. Mistletoe.

It used to grow in plenty in the apple trees in the garden when I was a girl. No one would have dreamt you'd have to buy it.'

Each year the sad unberried twig tied with green ribbon to the hanging lampshade in the hall. 'Perhaps this time you needn't bother,' Stephen says.

'Oh well, you never know. Have you done your shopping, Ste?'

Shopping. He hasn't thought about it really. Now he does. 'I'll do it in London,' he says. 'At Harvey Nicks.'

'At where? Who've you got to buy for then?'

'Christophine,' he says, 'and . . .'

Coralie isn't listening. Her mind is on her own uncompleted tasks and slowly, painfully, she is manoeuvring herself out of the passenger seat of her son's car. 'That's an unusual name,' is all she says.

Coralie believes that it is rude to ask intrusive questions. If Stephen wants to tell her something, let him. They've never poked about in each other's lives; she has respected her son's privacy from the time that he was little. 'What did you do at school today?' 'Nothing.' It doesn't do to badger a child; you can tell by looking at his face whether or not he's happy. But, was he? Well, what's the use of asking that sort of question now?

Later, after *The Two Ronnies*, Coralie and Stephen watch the news. 'Terrible shame,' she says, seeing the pictures of the wrecked pub, the twisted bits of things that must have been furniture, the stains at which it is better not to look. 'I'm glad you didn't choose the Army.'

'Was that ever on the cards?'

'Well, you did use to be in the cadets. Although of course

you didn't have a choice. Compulsory it was for all of you, I seem to recall, except the orchestra. Have I got that right?'

It is not until he sees the pictures that Stephen comprehends the scale of the devastation caused by last night's bomb. There will be pandemonium at the Institute. Perhaps he should have reported for work today; the Group II listeners will need all the reinforcements they can get. He can feel their sense of shock and fear from here. The hours they spent last week searching for leads, for evidence; now look at what has happened, and nobody was warned. It makes you wonder why you do the job. Come to think of it, the telephone in his flat was ringing again this morning, after he went in to get his car keys. He could hear it from where he was, outside. It could have been Louise. No one knows where he is now; they'll not be able to reach him here in Didcot. But then a sudden thought: why not go in to the office tomorrow, using the emergency as pretext? He's not keeping pace with Helen; he's falling behind. It worries him that he doesn't know what she is doing tonight. On second thoughts, he probably wouldn't be able to get hold of the new tapes on a Sunday – although you never know, and the crisis could be quite exciting, so he might as well be there. At the very least it would please Charlotte and Louise.

Thursday's tapes had not been helpful: whatever Greenwood had been saying about Saturday was lost in the moment of change-over and by the time the new tape was running there was nothing to hear but the ordinary sounds of washing up and going to bed. There had been nothing significant on Thursday either. Nothing significant in the context of the case, that is, although for Stephen there had been a world of difference between listening to Helen that evening and listening to her the day before. Then he had seen her only in his mind's eye but from Thursday on he knew her in the living flesh. He had actually watched her walk to her front door that afternoon and so, when he listened to her the next day, he could visualise her entering her flat, taking off that pale coat, hanging it on its hook and easing off her long black boots. Slender legs in silken stockings; those perfect narrow feet, which one day he would kiss. Later she told Greenwood she had been caught in the rain and was frozen to the bone. He turned the heating up. Stephen screwed his eyes shut to keep that picture out. Charles Ryder wished the woman he loved a broken heart and in uniform prayed in the chapel of Brideshead, the sanctuary lamp still burning. Helen and her husband went to bed when the programme ended.

'I couldn't have borne that,' his mother is saying. 'I still could not.'

He looks across at her, where she is sitting in her armchair. He has been paying no attention to her monologue, his mind exclusively on Helen; he's at a loss to know exactly what it is she couldn't bear. She's so much smaller than she used to be. How is it possible that a grown person can shrink so suddenly by several inches? She's stooped; her arthritic hands are twisted, the fingers knobbled and bent like roots of ginger, the skin stretched thinly over her joints is shiny red. Her feet are afflicted too. For the time being she can get about alone – she takes a taxi into town once a week to get her hair done and to pick up a little shopping – but soon she's going to find it hard to walk. 'What are you on about, Mum?' he asks. But she's moved on: the news is of the miners' vote to strike and her mind is on more imminent things. 'Do you suppose we should have got more sprouts, in case?' she asks.

'Mum, you're not exactly feeding the five thousand.'

'I know that. But it would be dreadful if there weren't enough.'

Stephen can foresee it clearly. His mother and himself. This year, like last year and like next. His mother getting up at five to put the turkey in the oven, because it's certain death if it doesn't cook for a minimum of half the day. And the table that they only ever use on this occasion, decked with crackers and paper serviettes. Napkins. Mr Fisher, who used to be the chief accountant when Coralie worked at the Council, and who has been coming to them every year for ever, as he has no family of his own. He never married. In all these years he's never changed; he must have been born ponderous and boring. And lonely. His unvarying gift of handkerchiefs for Stephen. Coralie's unvarying gift of woollen gloves for him. The three of them around the table, toasting the season in sweet sherry. The 'Well, it comes but once a year,' that his mother will say when Stephen opens a bottle of wine and the scandalised delight that will greet the opening of a second. 'Isn't this nice,' his mum will say but he will know that on this Christmas Day, as on every Christmas Day, and on every one of his birthdays, she will feel an absence. He knows, because he feels it too. What would it have been like, if she had lived, if he had had a sister? A twin sister. In the womb I knew you. *Mon semblable, ma sœur.* There would have been a girl who knew him as she knew herself, and who understood him as no one else has done – or no one yet. Sometimes he thinks she *does* know him, this ghost girl, that she's a presence, not an absence, like the tremble in the air of heat haze or the slight breath stirred by a passing bird in flight.

Sunday

When he woke on Sunday morning to find that snow had already covered roofs and levelled roads and pavements, Stephen, foreseeing problems on the Great West Road, had again been in two minds about going to the Institute. But, looking out of his mother's kitchen window at the little scrap of garden made beautiful by whiteness, untouched but for the tracery of a bird's claw prints, he came to his decision. This is no time for drifting. You might dream of walking into that pure whiteness, lying down, drawing the coverlet of snow above your head and letting go, but you know you will not do it. Soon the prowling cats will come, and the hungry foxes, for the hunt goes on, and the unbold and the vacillators, they will be the losers. The empty page on which the dove has written now awaits the fox.

'You must need your head examined,' his mother said, when he told her what he was going to do. Coralie has an imprecise idea of her son's occupation. Her impression is that he works on defence policies and strategies, which comes to much the same as responsibility for the nuclear deterrent. This being obviously a secret matter, she knows better than to ask for details. She was a FANY, don't forget: there were things she heard during the war that she will go to her grave without revealing. Careless talk costs lives, as they used to say. And Stephen's father – well, what he was doing in Berlin with the Engineers was so clandestine that he used to joke he'd have to kill her if she overheard him sleep-talk. He didn't sleep-talk as a matter of fact. He didn't even snore. A quiet sleeper, Spencer; he would lie there on his back beside her, like a fallen pine-log, his eyelids not quite shut and a tiny sliver of the whites still showing, as if he were a corpse. The Cold War. It didn't get much colder than that December in Berlin.

She waved Stephen off at the front door. It was early; she was still bundled in her quilted dressing gown with the tea-stains down the front. In spite of the cold that instantly sucked out whatever warmth there was in the small house, she waited at the open door and watched until he turned the corner and was out of sight. This is her unvarying habit and every time he leaves her Stephen has the same thought: this might be the last time that I see her.

The main entrance to the Institute, always manned on week-days, was locked behind bars on Sunday morning. Stephen found a small side-entrance, rang a discreet bell and waited. At length, to the sound of stout bolts grating, the door was opened by a guard. He looked dubious. 'I don't have your name down here, on this duty roster.'

'Well, I'm volunteering for special duty. Could I have a quick look at that list to see if my supervisor's on it?'

'No, sir, you cannot. What's your supervisor's name?'

The guard ran his finger down the list looking for Louise, and Stephen, practised at reading upside-down, saw that her name was there. He looked for Rollo Buckingham and Jamie Greenwood too. Annoyingly, there were two pages of names, pinned together, and Louise's was on the first. The guard left Stephen on the doorstep and went inside, presumably to telephone Louise. When he came back he nodded Stephen through, having checked the spelling of his name and written it down on a separate piece of paper of his own.

Stephen climbed slowly up the stairs and on an impulse halted at the landing of the first floor, the domain of the Director and his private staff. As there was already something transgressive about being in this building on a Sunday, he pushed through the double doors, impelled by a desire to see this corridor of power that ordinarily he had no cause to visit. There was nobody about and no sound from behind the office doors but Stephen felt at once that this was a place apart. It looked different – every other corridor in the building was carpeted with grey tiles but here the floor was covered in continuous blue pile and the doors were varnished wood, not plastic. The air was different too. Elsewhere it smelled of stale smoke, damp clothes, dust, teleprinter ink and instant coffee but here it was cleaner, although strongly tinged with something indefinably metallic.

As there was no one there, Stephen penetrated further in. It's odd, he thought, to be spending so much time in empty stairwells, on deserted landings, looking at closed doors. If it goes on like this, he'll start feeling like a ghost. He tried the handle of one door gently and, to his surprise, it gave. He pulled it closed it again; of course these offices are left unlocked, he realised – cleaners go into them at night, security guards patrol them. As in every office in the building, the surfaces will have been swept clean of personal belongings or anything which might identify the occupants. He could go into any one of them himself, sit on the chairs, leave a fingerprint on the shiny surface of a board-room table, his spoor on the chill, exclusive air.

Emboldened, he opened the nearest door the whole way and looked into a large room, empty in accordance with instructions, except for a desk, a telephone, a table, chairs and a wooden coat-stand, on which hung an overcoat; a man's one, full-length and charcoal grey. Stephen lifted the coat from its peg. It felt warm and inviting to the touch. Its label showed that it was made by Aquascutum. He slipped his arms into the sleeves and shrugged it on. Sliding his hands into the silk-lined pockets he found in one a cotton handkerchief and a bus ticket, in the other a tightly folded scrap of paper. He took it out. Its edges were rubbed; it had been in that pocket for some time. Unfolding it he read the three words written on it: I LOVE YOU. He folded it up again and put it back.

In this other man's coat, he felt like another man. It was tempting to keep it on. But he was no thief. He did up all the buttons, undid them all again and took it off. It smelled faintly of its rightful wearer, and now it would also bear a secret trace of him.

Leaving the first floor, he paused for a second on the stairs. Louise would be expecting him but he did not want to lose this temporary sense of sole possession and the power to be in spaces where he could not normally belong. He'd take his time and she'd suppose he'd met someone by the lifts and stopped to chat. Or that the lift was stuck. Like the needle of a compass inexorably drawn to magnetic north, Stephen continued to climb upwards to the seventh floor.

Most of the doors on the seventh floor had been left open to reveal unremarkable rooms, fitted with the same grey metal and plastic furnishings, strip lights and carpet tiles that were ubiquitous except in the Director's precincts. From the far end of the corridor came voices. Rollo Buckingham's room was empty: there were just the two desks face-to-face. Rollo's held his special lamp, his ashtray, his teacup and saucer. On the other desk – Greenwood's desk – was a mug: white bone-china on which was printed a facsimile of a page from a nineteenth-century edition of *The Times*. 'Accouchement of Her Majesty', it said. Stephen picked it up. It had been rinsed but not washed, and the interior was deeply stained. Greenwood's mug. The lips that touched that china rim kissed Helen's mouth. To hold that object in his hand gave Stephen a shiver of revulsion, as if it were a shard of human bone.

The top two drawers of the desk were locked; the bottom two were not. Stephen pulled them open, one after the other. The first contained a clothes brush, a London A–Z, a broken bicycle light, a packet of peanuts and a paperback copy of Samuel Beckett's *Molloy*. The other had nothing in it but a rolled-up pair of socks. Stephen skimmed hurriedly through the novel, searching for markings, underlinings or any other sign that Greenwood had been using it as the basis for a code but, although the book had evidently been read, he could see nothing untoward. It would take more time to examine the street atlas thoroughly. He slipped it into his jacket pocket.

He had not been paying attention to the voices he had heard at the other end of the corridor. They had seemed safely distant. But now the undifferentiated sound was breaking up and, startlingly, Rollo Buckingham's voice rose out of it and called: 'Shall you be here in the morning, Marlow?' Another male voice that Stephen did not recognise said something not quite audible in reply, a door banged shut and Stephen heard no more.

But there were footsteps coming closer, scuffing along the carpet tiles in the corridor outside. Stephen shut the desk drawers as quickly and as quietly as he could and turned to face the door that he had left slightly ajar behind him. If it were to be pushed open, if Greenwood were to walk straight in, what would Stephen do? There was nowhere he could hide. Of course Greenwood was coming, it was his own office; could Stephen escape by saying that he had been hoping to find Rollo? On a Sunday morning? Icicles were spiking through his veins. Nightmare choices flickered through his brain and he was on the point of falling to the floor as if in a dead faint – or quite possibly a real one – when he sensed that whoever it was who was approaching was not going to stop. He stood trans-fixed and shaking, catching a passing flash of movement and dark clothing through the partly open door, hearing through the rasp of his own ragged, panicky breath the man's footsteps carrying on towards the lift.

Downstairs, on the third floor, in the long room, Louise was at her desk, with her headphones on. She did not hear Stephen coming in. Damian was also there, and Harriet and Christo-phine. They were intent, bent over their machines, in a quiet as deep as the quiet of a cloister; the sibilance of the running tapes an undertone like the wind's sigh in a grove of trees, or the constant sea. For a moment they seemed to him heroic, the four of them, on that Sunday morning, in their dedication and complete absorption.

He touched Louise's shoulder. She looked up, and Stephen saw the lines of tiredness round her eyes. He fought the urge to fall to his knees beside her and bury his head in her lap; he would have given a great deal for that solace and protection. Although somehow he had got himself out of Greenwood's office and to his own, the past minutes were a blank.

'Hello, love,' Louise said. 'It was nice of you to come.'

There were piles of tapes waiting for attention. 'They're worried this might be the beginning of a new campaign,' Louise explained. 'And, what with the threat from Abu Nidal and the Iranian level at its highest ever, we've every reason to be fearful. We're tasked to look for clues to the identities of perpetrators and to future targets. Actionable intelligence and corroborative evidence, in other words.'

The requirement was familiar. Too often the intelligence that streamed through tangled wires or disaffected voices into the files of the Institute just stayed there, too difficult or too dangerous to use. To compromise a source would be to sacrifice it. In they poured – the suspicions, the allegations of treachery, the subversions – to be processed, analysed and stored away, unless some evidence to buttress them could be found by other means. There were exceptions, in extremes of life and death. But even then, not always. Calculations must be made: does the preservation of an especially fecund source outweigh the loss of an unimportant life; how many lives would have to be endangered to justify the loss of an irreplaceable source; how much is one life worth, in any case?

Which is why the listeners are useful. Tapping telephones is routine, as those with things to hide will know, and the innocent believe. A telephone call that confirms the thing some frightened man has mumbled to an equally nervous go-between in a car parked off the road, or a pub out of the way, is what the analysts need. But it's not that simple. What if the frightened man was lying in the first place? Or thought he told the truth but had it wrong? When a need to believe is strong enough, any act of the imagination or construct made of words can easily be proved.

Gratefully Stephen sank into the hubbub of the taxi firm – the incomprehensible radio chunter, the pick-ups and the destinations – shelter from his own obsessions. This time he also had the owner's home telephone line, largely taken up by his wife and her extended family. It was soon quite clear that if anyone there had foreknowledge of the bombing, they were keeping it strictly to themselves. Stephen scanned through the take from the night of the explosion and heard no reference to it at all. What a gulf there was between the world of the Institute and the world outside. In that world people were talking about Christmas and the weather; in this, behind the blast-proof walls and the protective blinds, no remark was innocent; no words were to be taken at face-value until they had been forensically examined.

The five listeners worked without a break until the early evening. Then Louise removed her headphones and stood up. She scrunched her eyebrows together between thumb and finger, corrugating her forehead in an endearing gesture Stephen had observed before. 'I'm tired,' she said.

Damian pulled a corner of a blind aside to look out of the window. 'There's a lot of snow,' he said.

'Bother,' said Harriet. 'The trains will be a nightmare. And it's Sunday. They're always bad on Sundays, anyway.'

'You can stay here if you like,' Louise said. 'In the Annexe. I asked the housekeepers for a bed.'

'No, I can't, my contact lenses. Don't you want the bed?'

'I've got to go round to my mum's. I always go to her on Sunday evenings. Come hell or high water, she depends on that. Damian? Stevie? Do you want to stay the night instead of trudging home through all that snow?'

The two men looked at each other. 'The buses'll be running,' Damian said.

'I'll stay if no one else wants to,' said Stephen.

'Have you slept in the Annexe before? It's a bit spartan but you'll be used to that, having been to boarding school. Don't they always say that Eton prepares you perfectly for prison life? At least they give you sheets here, though you may have to make the bed. Right, so I'll tell the guards that you'll be staying.'

As soon as the others had left, Stephen regretted this decision. What was he doing here, imprisoned in the long room? After the gut-wrenching fright he had had on the seventh floor this morning, he didn't dare go anywhere else. He was tired and he was hungry and his ears were ringing. It was infuriating to know that Friday's tapes were bundled in a bag somewhere in the building, waiting, when he could have spent this extra time on them and kept in closer touch with Helen. Muriel had not been at work today but a stand-in registrar had processed the essential tapes. Perhaps, if that registrar had taken in the whole delivery, he would have left the rest, including PHOENIX, in Muriel's room for her to sort on Monday. It just might be worth a look.

Stephen locked the long room temporarily, in case of prowling guards. Muriel's office, a cubbyhole wedged between this room and Group II's, was fully lined with cabinets. In the long room, all the combination locks were set to the same code, periodically decided by Louise. Was it possible that Muriel used it too? He tried the nearest lock. To his surprise it opened.

The cabinet was packed with folders. He knew what they were; he'd seen them before: they were the investigative records, stored in alphabetical order, each one labelled with a coded case-name and a number. The number cross-referred to the number of the main file, kept centrally in the Institute's underground repository. The function of these subsidiary files was technical: they held the operational plans, the specifications of intercept devices and the licences for each investigation, past and current. Together they constituted a comprehensive record of the Institute's eavesdropping methods.

These folders were for case-names from A to F. Stephen closed the cabinet, re-locked it and unlocked the next. G to O. The third must be the one he needed. It did hold cases P to Z. But there was no folder there for PHOENIX.

He should have guessed that such a secret folder would not be kept in a cabinet accessible in theory to everyone in Group III. In practice Muriel's room was out of bounds. She controlled all the paperwork as well as the tapes, and kept the pending files and minute-sheets; if you wanted to consult a record you were supposed to ask her. Listeners were only allowed to store current papers and up to two weeks' worth of duplicate report sheets in their own cabinets, with their indexed casebooks. As a rule they had no access to the technical records.

Dear old Muriel, with her powdery face and perpetual wreath of sweet perfume. Who outside the walls of the Institute would ever think that this ageing lady in her tailored skirts and rows of pearls was the custodian of so many secrets? But perhaps she did not read the documents she filed? Why would she, when she cared only for their safety, not their contents? She seemed to be as incurious about the cases as she was keen on gossip; she and Charlotte were forever chattering. Muriel might as well be stamping library books as registering secret tapes, although it had to be admitted that in her own slow way she was impressively efficient. She must have a separate system for the especially sensitive investigations. Where would she put those?

Stephen unlocked each of the five remaining cabinets in turn. Three held pending files, by date. He could find no tapes. The last cabinet contained Muriel's registers and a large safe-box. Absurdly, it was not secured to the cabinet itself. But it was locked and the code was not the same as the one used for the cabinets.

Wouldn't it be simple to walk out with this box? Not out of the main door, on a weekday, when he might be stopped. But tonight, when he was booked into the Annexe? To reach the Annexe you used a door at the end of a passage on the ground floor. But the Annexe, which was actually an ordinary house, a relic of the time when the alleyway behind the Institute was residential, had a front door of its own to make it inconspicuous to passers-by. Even though you couldn't get in without a key, you must be able to get out.

Stephen hesitated. He was sure the PHOENIX file must be in that box. He wanted very much to know the details of the licence, the background to the case and how the technicians had got access to the flat. And there might be other useful papers in it. Then he came to his rightful senses. At least he now knew where to find the box. If Muriel had set her own code for the lock, it was bound to be her date of birth. That would be easy to work out. And if she had used a different date, he could probably take the box to a locksmith – it had no outward sign of provenance.

He was on the point of sliding it back into the cabinet when he heard the jangle of keys that warned of an approaching guard. She was a woman, whom he did not think he had seen before. She stopped at the door and gave him an enquiring look. 'Special duty,' he said. 'In the room next door. I need access to a file.'

She nodded. 'Right you are, sir. Can I take your name please? For the list?'

Unwillingly he gave it. He knew that he could not give a false one in case this guard chose to cross-check other lists.

Back in the long room, he worked for another three hours and finished the tapes that he had been allocated. By now it was very late. But he had bought the time he wanted: he'd be well ahead of everyone else tomorrow. He locked up properly and went downstairs. The woman guard was on her own at the side door. 'Is there a key to the Annexe?' Stephen asked her.

'There is. But you'd be better to use the internal passage. It can be dodgy out there in the alley. All sorts of shady people use it. The fire escape especially; you'd be surprised.'

'I need to go and get something to eat.'

'Well, off you go then. I'll be here when you get back, whatever time, and I'll sign you in.'

It was very cold and very dark. Past eleven on a Sunday night. The pubs had long since closed. He should have thought of that; he was dying for some whisky. He tramped over blackened snow to Piccadilly Circus where there was a Wimpy that he hoped might still be open.

Pallid faces in the harsh light, behind the counter, at the tables. The few people who were in the Wimpy could have been survivors of disaster. Their pallor was the pallor of blown pieces of scrap paper, of those deprived of sunlight, of dwellers in subterranean places; in their eyes the look of those who have witnessed things they wish they could forget and know they never will. I did not know death had undone so many, Stephen said below his breath.

The soft white bread and the thin brown disc of fatty meat coagulated in his mouth, coating his tongue and palette with the bloom of grease that also hung like vapour on the air. Near him was a young man, a boy really, alone – they were all alone, these refugees from the winter night, the starveling boys with nowhere else to go – but this one looked more solitary than the rest. His skin had the same unhealthy waxen sheen but it was pocked with angry red infected pustules. He ate hunched over his food, his forearms flat on the formica table-top, encircling the polystyrene housing of the meal as sea walls guard a harbour or a hungry dog a bone. He crammed the burger and chips into his mouth so fast that he barely had time to swallow, let alone taste the food or chew it. Stephen, watching him, tried to slow his own pace down but found he gobbled anyway; everyone was shovelling food into themselves as if it were essential but disgusting, like a barium meal.

Sated, in a way, Stephen went back to the Institute. He cut through Shepherd Market where there were still a couple of doughty prostitutes standing in their doorways, defying the lack of trade and the freezing night. 'Looking for someone, love?' the first asked him, and for longer than a heartbeat he thought of answering: yes.

Later, in a cell-like bedroom in the Annexe, he questioned this decision too. It was so bleak in there, and comfortless. What would it be like to spend the night beside a warm and yielding body, to be lying in someone's arms, not on this cold and narrow bed, with his face pressed to a pillow that smelled of strangers' unwashed heads? To cup a hand around a breast and feel a nipple rise, a breast that fits the hand exactly, as an acorn fits its shell, a bone its smooth white socket. Lay your sleeping head, my love, human on my faithless arm: foot against foot, thigh against thigh, mouth against mouth; reflected in each other's eyes, cradled in each other's thoughts. Ah no, that's the whole point: he is not faithless; when a woman lays her head upon his shoulder, he will have earned her trust.

He remembered a time in college. There had been a celebration, of victories on the river maybe – the rowdy boys and their ringing voices. Stephen had kept to his room, making no sound that might betray his presence. It was safer to stay out of sight. Up and down the stone staircase: the clattering shoes, the laughter, and a voice more boisterous than the others shouting, Have you met my girl? And later, when the revellers had swept out into the night, a shocking glimpse through a bathroom door of a naked woman stretched unmoving on the floor. He had stood stock still by the door, afraid of her, afraid she was a corpse, until he forced himself to go in and he saw the bright pink vinyl that made her skin, the horrible gaping O that was her mouth, the conical red tips of her inflated breasts.

Yes, a man might as well fuck a blow-up doll as a woman he did not love. A woman who didn't love him. Making love, that's entirely different. But. But it is hard to tell apart the hunger of the body and the hunger of the heart. Millions are crying out for love. The world is shuddering to the silent howl of the lonely and the unconsoled. Here he lay, as cold as a corpse himself, between the stiff white sheets that he had spread upon this single bed, and he was crying too. But. But nobody ever said it would be effortless, the search for love. Love, like elemental gold, is rare and precious; a man must fight for it as Lancelot fought for Guinevere or Galahad the Grail.

Monday

Muriel was complaining that she had got up at four o'clock to be sure of catching the first train and getting to work in time, knowing all too well there would be much to do and she'd be required, but then she'd had to wait a whole hour on the platform in the perishing cold because the train was cancelled and so she might as well have aimed for the later train in any case. And on top of that, there were terrible delays along the line, apparently caused by frozen points, whatever they might be, and the train was so full she had had to stand until at last a nice young man had noticed her and offered her his seat. 'Chivalry is not quite dead,' she said, 'although it probably is dying.' And now there are all these Department Four chaps stamping around and kicking up a fuss and no one with a minute to spare to make a cup of coffee.

'We were busy yesterday,' Louise told her. 'I was in all day, with Damian and Christophine, and Harriet came in later, and Stevie here, and I must say that, although it was a bit chaotic, we managed to get through a heap of tapes and I honestly feel we should be giving ourselves a big pat on our backs this morning. But I do think that we are being tasked to find the proverbial needle – and I'm not at all convinced that it's in any of these haystacks. Not in the ones that we've been given, anyway.'

'Charlotte wasn't here, then?'

'No, her baby niece had that op on Friday. You know, that's

why she had to go off early. She'd promised her sister that she'd stay the weekend so that she could take care of the other little one. A dreadful time for them, poor things, her sister and her brother-in-law.'

'So how did it go, the operation? Poor wee mite.'

'I don't know, Charlotte's not in yet, but I expect she'll be here soon. If the worst had come to the worst, she'd have called in to say she couldn't make it. Yes. It *was* busy. Just like a week-day really. I even saw a couple of Department Six chaps rushing in and out.'

'Really? What were they doing here?'

'No idea. Another operation, I suppose. Or it could be they were that short-staffed in Department Four. Gracious! It's like a madhouse! I'm just hoping against hope that we can have the party. I've two dozen mini-quiches sitting in my fridge!'

Louise left the room to put the kettle on and Muriel, grumbling about the likely mayhem caused by locum registrars, set off to find her ledgers. Stephen, who had been hovering beside the women, seized his chance. 'Look, Muriel,' he said, 'the Department Six men were in the office yesterday because they're also on high alert. It's about something that even Louise is not totally cleared to know. I appreciate that the other stuff has priority but this is also desperately important, so if there is any way that you could really kindly find the latest PHOENIX tape, Department Six and I would be grateful to you for life.'

'You boys think I'm superhuman,' Muriel said, but she'd see what she could do.

Stephen could have sworn that he had spent the whole night lying sleepless in his cell in the Annexe, but he must have slept, for morning came as a surprise and he knew that he'd been dreaming. He'd been on a mountainside, alone. A steep and very high mountain, snow-bound and, scattered on the snow, the bodies of dead climbers, their bones picked white by carrion birds beneath their ropes and furs.

It had been very cold in the little room. He could hear other people rising in the rooms nearby and although he had a pressing need to relieve himself, he was shy of encountering these strangers. Even worse, though, would be meeting someone he knew: how disquieting to see a colleague in pyjamas. He himself had no pyjamas, not having anticipated staying for the night. His mouth, uncleaned since the night before last, tasted bitter and disgusting.

Breakfast would have been a sensible idea but Stephen could not stomach the thought. He'd go out later, buy himself a toothbrush and a razor. Right now he craved Helen's voice. There were only four days till Christmas; it was unbearable not to know where she would be or what she would be doing.

Muriel, half an hour later, clutching a pile of envelopes, stopped at Charlotte's desk. Stephen, listening to nothing on his headphones, could not hear what they were saying but guessed that they must be talking about the baby. He hadn't known that Charlotte's niece was ill; he hadn't even known she had a niece. It was rather hurtful to think that when his colleagues talked to each other about such things they excluded him. Perhaps Charlotte had only confided in the women. Men were not supposed to care about sick babies. But, actually, he *did* care: it was very sad to think of a tiny baby on an operating table. He thought of the child who had waved to him through the railings of the park – that solemn little girl. In the one photograph that he had seen of his dead twin, she too had been grave-faced; wide eyes staring from a small triangular face, beneath a suprisingly thick fringe of hair. Charlotte, he was glad to see, looked tired but not tearful; the baby must be alive.

There were five sealed envelopes: the tapes from Friday, Saturday and from Sunday morning. 'You owe me a very large gin and tonic at lunchtime,' Muriel said, when at last she got to Stephen's desk. 'I really had to ferret around to find these tapes in the bag.'

Stephen, rising to his feet to take the envelopes from Muriel, wondered for a moment about giving her a kiss. Might she expect some manifest display of gratitude? In a situation like this, Charlotte would certainly have thrown her arms around the woman; she was constantly bestowing little hugs and squeezes on her colleagues. He saw himself lunging towards Muriel, his lips aiming for her powdered cheek, the awkwardness of it if she were to recoil and his trajectory had to be absurdly halted. Instead he merely thanked her. It didn't matter anyway, nothing mattered now; he had the tapes he wanted.

The tapes he wanted? No, the tapes he needed, as a drowning man needs air to fill his lungs in place of cold saltwater. Helen unheard since Friday, left behind in last week, the days of her calendar and his never yet in synchrony, their lives for ever out of step. His tomorrow hidden behind a tear-off tab; it used to be a source of pleasure, that Advent ritual – opening a new window every morning, daily coming closer to the window in the centre of the scene, the breathless wait for Christmas Eve – but it is torture now, when Helen's tomorrow will not be his till Thursday. Unless he can compel their days to mesh. Until he can compel their days to mesh. But when? But how? And how much longer can he survive in his isolation chamber, like a hermit in a doorless circle of stone wall?

For now, it's Helen's Friday. A routine workday morning, the last of the school term. It used to be enough for Stephen to know her as a blinded prisoner serving a life sentence behind glass might know a lover: by her voice alone. An inflection or a tone, a way she has with words that is all her own, the way she laughs on a small intake of breath, the way she sings when she's alone, have been the signposts that he trusted. It's not so strange to trust like that. Newborn babies trust their mothers from the moment of their birth for they've been cradled by their voices, by their heartbeats, for nine months. (Do unborn twins sing to each other in the womb?) Besides, Helen is not the only one whom Stephen intimately knows by sound alone. Why then had he felt so urgent a desire to set eyes on her in person? The answer is that he will lose her if he continues to trust to words instead of deeds. Now is the time for action, and action requires the evidence of the eyes as well as ears. But it is also that he's starving. He aches with a hunger that can no longer be ignored and will only be allayed by flesh on flesh, by hearing his own name spoken in a lover's voice.

Friday evening. Helen is getting ready for a party; she's showering, spraying scent between her breasts, brushing out her golden hair. The liquefaction of her clothes. She is in a slip of silk, standing before her mirror, heedless of her loveliness, her shoulders smooth and white, her arms as graceful as a swan's neck, a bracelet of bright gold around the bone. She leans closer to the mirror to paint her mouth, rose petals settle softly on the snow, she is lampglow, she is starlight, Helen, the beloved, who walks in beauty, like the night.

167

She telephones a number but says nothing; there is no one at the other end. There will be a record of the number on the other tape, which he will listen to when he has time, although he probably won't tell Rollo. Helen is not the target of Rollo's investigation, why should Rollo care to whom she talks or where she's going? A minute later she makes another call, she says: 'Allegra? Hi! I'm not yet dressed, which is why I'm ringing you instead of running up the stairs. Look, I can't quite remember – did we say that we'd meet there or that we'd go together? I know you said something about going via your sister's . . .'

Stephen cannot hear Allegra's answer on this tape. After she has listened to it, Helen says, 'That's fine, yes. And is Marlow coming too?' Then: 'Yes, don't worry, I'll be fine, I'll see you there. Bye now,' and she puts the receiver down, picks up her handbag, shrugs on her winter coat and knots her scarf and leaves the flat.

Stephen envisages her going: the staircase she walks down, her hand on the same banister that he touched, the door that opens onto the street; the slender figure pausing for a second on the threshold in the dark. But he cannot follow her to the party. He can picture it – held in a tall, white house in Notting Hill or Chelsea, a house with steps leading to a front door painted glossy black, on which is hung a wreath of holly; a lit tree is visible through a window. Helen hands her coat to an aproned maid and goes softly through an open door into a book-lined room, where a real fire burns in the hearth and there are real paintings that are not prints or posters on the walls. Beautiful women in flowing dresses, their bare backs gleaming, diamonds and pearls, and Helen, the fairest of them all. Champagne, palest gold, topaz, citrine, fizzing in crystal glasses, murmured talk of love and books and art. Or perhaps in a more modest house – Clapham, Fulham – both rooms on the ground floor filled with people talking, laughing, drinking mulled wine – scent of cloves and oranges – and later, dancing. It could be either, how can he be sure? He has to let her go that evening and wait till she comes back.

She's not very late. Probably she told her friends that she had to get up early for the carol service in the morning; she has a busy day ahead. She left Allegra at the party. And Marlow. Who is Marlow? Marlowe? Strange to have heard that same name yesterday; coincidence or not? She was singing 'O Little Town of Bethlehem' quietly to herself as she walked home through the dark and dreamless streets of London. She came back with her husband, faithless Jamie Greenwood. They hardly spoke to each other at all; evidently tired they went straight to bed. Did she ask him where he had been earlier in the evening? Does she know when he is lying? Where had he been in fact? That's another thing that doesn't matter – the truth, whatever that is. Stephen is in control now; he is creating Greenwood.

Saturday morning. Surer ground. Stephen's day before yes-terday, and he was with her then. As Helen gets ready to leave he reminds her that she will need her warm hat and umbrella. Snow falls and melts and turns to sleet. Helen in her pale coat, her tall black leather boots.

Saturday midday to midnight: nothing but the sirens in the distance heralding emergency, the traffic passing, an unanswered ring on the doorbell, the dog that sometimes barks. In a neigh-bouring flat that night there is a party. Stephen fast-forwards through it all.

Saturday midnight–Sunday midday: the tape that Muriel

had fished out from the bag that was delivered to the Institute very late last night. Someone had driven an unmarked van to the rear entrance of the building and the garage doors had opened for him – or for her. Did they simply sling the bag out or was there a formal handover that required signatures and conversation? Who took delivery of the bag and where did they store it before Muriel arrived? There is much that Stephen does not know. In this place there is a hidden cast of nameless people who keep things running day and night – operating the machines, locking and unlocking doors, watching the cameras that watch the vans arriving. They're like an army of ghosts or the faceless ones who drift through Stephen's dreams, and when he allows himself to think of them he feels that other dream-like sense of dread: that there are corridors beyond the ones he knows and rooms where no one but the nameless go and mirrors that are also doors that lead to where the real work is done in secret and in silence.

Stephen broke the orange tag. 03.21, and Helen and her husband fighting. That's a new sound to him and he couldn't tell what they were quarrelling about. 'We can't let her down like that,' Helen was protesting. 'I just don't understand why you said that to Harry. She's my mother. You were so unpleasant.'

'If we're going to talk about unpleasantness, I'd invite you to consider your own behaviour tonight. You have been in a sulk all evening. And you were rude to Harry.'

'I was not rude! It's quite clear he doesn't have a clue.'

Back and forth they went – accusation, counter-accusation, indignation and the original grievance, whatever it was, re-opening unhealed ones. 'You've never been fair to my mother,' Helen says tearfully, 'but yours can do no wrong. But remember that time she said that I was "*ordinaria*"? That's what she said, in Italian, as if I wouldn't understand her, and you didn't contradict her. You didn't stick up for me!'

'But she didn't say that! You're forever bringing that up but that's not what she said . . .'

'Yes, she did! She's never really liked me,' and on she wails, with 'That's not true and that's not fair . . .' until she can no longer speak for weeping.

At the centre of this there's something else upsetting Helen that Stephen doesn't understand: something about Allegra and always seeing Marlow too. They only met a month ago and already he's moved in and that can't be right; it's far too soon. He isn't right for her, there's something wrong with him – she's so shy and he's so bloody vain. Exploitative. She loves Allegra, she's a true friend, and a colleague, but that doesn't mean she wants to see Marlow all the time. Especially not at Christmas. The more upset she is, the more incoherent she becomes. Jamie tries to make some sense of what she's saying but not enough for Stephen to deconstruct the argument. It ends when Jamie tells her to shut the fuck up and Helen slams the bedroom door.

Stephen punched the air in vindication. He had known it all along. Girls like Helen – the pure and vestal, the innocent and the good – believe in reciprocity, that they must love if they are beloved. He supposed that Helen had met Green-wood when she was still a student, inexperienced and very young; he was probably the first man, the only man, she'd ever kissed. Of course she'd think she was in love. The moment he set eyes on her, Greenwood, determined and ruthless as he was, would have been out to get her, indeed to trap her, and she, once trapped, being of a constant nature, would have made the best of what she had. She might have been charmed by his raven hair and his romantic looks. But PHOENIX was the devil in disguise. And in the early hours of Sunday morning, Helen, like a damsel tested to the limit in the castle of an ogre, would finally have seen him in his true and cruel colours. She would know there was no future for her with Greenwood and his kin and that no amount of patience or forbearance or of love would turn this dissembler into a prince. Rescue was essential now.

After the bedroom door was slammed, a running tap and a chink of glass – water or more wine? Helen must have gone to bed alone. Good. Greenwood would have to spend the night on the sofa in the sitting room, which would not be nearly long enough for a man so tall. He'd have nothing but his overcoat for coverlet, no pillow for his head; he would be uncomfortable and cold.

Greenwood snored and stirred in the night but there was nothing else until 10.27 when Helen came out of the bedroom and, thirteen minutes later, left the flat without a word. Stephen knew where she was going. He had already seen that she went to church on Sundays when she was in London, and that she went alone. Greenwood woke at 11.44, before Helen was back, and began to make his breakfast. The tape stopped at a minute before noon, just as the telephone rang.

Thirty-six hours of recorded time, even scanned at speed, took Stephen to late afternoon. He kept his headphones on all day, and a deep look of absorption, defying Louise to give him extra work. Around him the other listeners were as focused but the atmosphere was calm – perhaps Department Four had found what they were looking for, or there were enough listeners in the Institute today to handle the extra load. He saw Louise in conclave with Ana, the Group II Supervisor, and a pair of analysts; maybe there'd be news before the evening. There was no sign of Rollo Buckingham. Stephen guessed that he could get away without a written report on PHOENIX till the next day, as Rollo would assume that everyone was still preoccupied by the explosion. While he waited for the second of Sunday's tapes, he would check the telephone intercepts and have a quick look in on VULCAN.

VULCAN was in a bad way. Stephen had listened to him on Thursday trying to make an appointment at the doctor's and being told that there were none available until next Friday at the earliest. He heard the old man fighting for breath enough to speak, and the receptionist's impersonal tone: 'Sorree,' she said, with the emphasis on the second syllable. 'We're extra-busy now because it's close to Christmas.'

But he might be dead by then, you stupid cow, Stephen said to her. Can't you hear how ill the poor man is? Because it's close to Christmas? What sort of excuse is that? Because it's Christmas you should be working overtime to heal the sick and get them back onto their feet so that they too can have their rightful share of the blessings of the season. But VULCAN, conditioned by his class and generation, by the abasement and humility of age, to take no for an answer if it was spoken by a medical authority, however spurious, meekly booked with Dr Mather at 9.50 on Christmas Eve and did not complain. There was no further traffic on his line that day or the next.

Because it's close to Christmas. Where would VULCAN spend the day, with whom? The ODINs, Stephen knew, would stay at home, as they had to do, having nowhere else to go. Last summer they had sent their daughter away for a week – the first time she had been anywhere without them, the first respite they had had in years – availing of a charity that sent disabled people on holiday to a boarding school in Suffolk. But when Diane came home she had a great bruise on her thigh, and there was not one word of apology or explanation. Anyway, as Mrs ODIN told her cousin on the telephone, they had missed her terribly. 'Everyone thought we'd be pleased to have some time off and to catch up on our sleep, but as a matter of fact we couldn't hardly sleep at all for worrying how she was. Because, if a person has no words to say whether they're all right or whether they're unhappy, how can you tell unless you look into their eyes?' It would be the three of them on Christmas Day, as usual, a weepy telephone call to Canada and a wheelchair decked with tinsel.

He ran through the rest of his caseload. Some of his targets will make a point of disregarding Christmas, a capitalist conspiracy if there ever was one, but they'll struggle to do anything that would interest the strategists when the rest of the country is half-asleep and slumped in front of the telly. Whether Stephen checked their telephone calls during the holiday or days later would make no difference at all. But what of PHOENIX? PHOENIX, who shared his living space as well as his telephone line with Stephen, who alone of Stephen's targets posed a serious threat to national security, whose every breath was meant to be recorded and yet whose Christmas plans were still unknown?

Then Louise was coming towards him, making signs to show that she needed to talk. Stephen removed his headphones. 'Good news!' she said. 'We're cleared for take-off on Wednesday afternoon!' Charlotte was following in her wake. 'Talk about the eleventh hour,' she said. Louise carried on down the long room but Charlotte stopped at Stephen's desk.

'Good weekend, or what there was of it?' she asked.

'I'm sorry about the baby,' Stephen said. 'I hope she's all right now?'

'She will be. Thanks for asking. For a while it was touch and go. Isn't modern medicine a marvel? She'd be dead without it. We are lucky, aren't we, to have been born when we were? I always think that, when people say they'd like to have lived in ancient times so that they could have had a chat with Shakespeare or discovered a new continent. I point out that they probably would have died at birth or, if not then, in childbed for certain.'

She sat down heavily on the edge of the desk. 'How's your tooth? I'm sorry I forgot to ask you on Friday. There was so much going on.'

'It's better now. It wasn't an abscess, the dentist said.'

'Teeth! Honestly you can see why people used to get them all pulled out on their twenty-first birthdays!' She bared her own. 'You've been keeping your nose to the grindstone. What's so interesting today?' Picking up his headphones, she waved them at him in an interrogative way.

'Nothing really. I'm just trying to catch up.'

'Mine have mostly gone quiet. Apart from my dear little fascist and even he can't get much action this week. His calls all go unanswered. Everywhere things are running down or about to close. Except for us. At your service round the clock and every day of the year. Have you ever done the Christmas shift? It's okay actually, a lot of Dunkirk spirit, and the Director comes round with mince pies; other kinds of spirit too, though not doled out by him.'

'Were you conscripted into it?'

'No, you get asked to do it if there's a real emergency like last week's and you have the right language or the background. When I did it, it was for Baader-Meinhof. Nothing happened in the end. *Plus ça change.* Except! That reminds me; did you know that there's going to be an official inquiry into what went wrong?'

'Went wrong?'

'Yes, about CUCHULAINN. Evidently something significant was missed. A warning. Sub-director Four is seething and Ana's talking about handing in her notice.'

'But was there a connection?'

'Who knows? As with everything else in here, it's anybody's guess. Martin's going round saying that the Department Four boys didn't actually have a source; it was just a rumour that a local rozzer happened to overhear. Which, if true, means that we were all fossicking around in completely the wrong places. Par for the course, I say. Anyway. Did you hear Lou-Lou saying that we had to take that extra hour off tomorrow or we'd lose it? So, I thought I might come in an hour later in the morning but then I thought no, maybe we could go to lunch together, you and me?'

Stephen looked up at her where she was sitting, her open, round and rosy face, her expectant smile, the faintest shading of dark fuzz above her lips. 'Well,' he said, 'that would have been nice but I'm afraid I already have another engagement.'

'Another time then,' Charlotte said vaguely, sliding from the desk onto her feet and walking off.

The working day was coming to an end. Muriel, hindered by backlogs and conflicting priorities and late with the second delivery of tapes, had just reached Stephen when all the lights in the room went out and the machines came to a sudden halt. Behind the blinds it was pitch-dark. The listeners stayed where they were, waiting for an announcement; Charlotte struck her lighter and the small flame flickered gold. After some time a voice came crackling through the rarely used address system: 'This is Security,' it said. 'There is an electricity failure, due to unknown cause. Staff are ordered exceptionally to draw open the black-out screens and to lock away equipment by the light of the street outside. They should thereafter proceed to leave the building in an orderly manner. There is no present danger. Do not attempt to enter the lifts.'

'Poor buggers who are already in them,' Solly said. 'They could be there all night.'

'And the people in the basement!' Charlotte added. 'No street light gets in there!'

'No,' Solly agreed. 'They'll all be striking matches and the building will catch fire.'

'Come on, team,' Louise said. 'Let's do as we are told.'

She and Harriet began to open the blinds and a sallow light seeped in. Stephen, reaching out his hand, felt for the envelope that Muriel had just dropped into his tray. He picked it up and tucked it into the inside pocket of his jacket before he joined his colleagues in the complicated business of making things secure in the almost undiluted dark.

'D'you want to go for a drink?' asked Solly. 'Seeing as it's early? Outside, because the upstairs bar won't be open, I don't suppose.'

Stephen hesitated. What would Helen be doing now? But then he thought how much he'd like a drink and how rare were Solly's invitations and he replied: 'Why not?'

Damian and Charlotte joined them as they fumbled their way down the dark corridor to a stairwell dimly lit by torches held in the hands of Security staff posted on the landings.

'This is exciting,' Charlotte said. Solly said it reminded him of the three-day week. 'Do you remember? We got used to doing things in the dark.'

'Wouldn't it be fun if we always worked by candlelight?'

'Yes dear,' said Damian. 'But we'd have no work. Unless we went back to the days of listening at keyholes or with our ears pressed to glasses on the wall.'

'Silence please,' a guard said, which made them laugh.

The world outside seemed bright by contrast and they blinked at each other in their little huddle on the pavement. 'Fox and Grapes?' asked Solly. 'It's by far the closest.'

'Is that the one with the stuffed bunnies in a case?' said Charlotte. 'Yes, let's go there, it's nice and quiet and it probably won't be crowded. I can only stay for a few minutes; I've got to get back to my sister's. God, I'm knackered. I really need a drink!'

'But isn't it out of bounds now?' Stephen said.

'Who cares? No one pays any notice to those stupid lists.' Solly laughed. 'I've seen half of Department Six in there on more than one occasion. That young Buckingham poncing around, and the other one, his chum, yeah, McPherson.'

'Ah, the dishy Marlow,' Charlotte said, rolling her eyes and flapping at her chest. 'Be still, my beating heart.'

*

178

The man behind the bar is the one who was there on Friday night but he gives no sign of recognising Stephen. Not so Alberic, who is standing at the corner of the bar, fussing with his pipe. He looks up when he hears people coming into the pub and at first does not pick out Stephen from the group. When he does he seems a bit surprised but immediately comes towards him, smiling and waving his pipe in a gesture of welcome. 'Capital!' he cries. 'I was exactly on the point of leaving in the intention of I telephone you. You have saved me the call! Tomorrow? Yes? You remember? Don't be letting me down? Let's meet at 7.15; the concert's at 7.30. Wigmore Hall. You know it? It's Oxford Street, or near. Brahms and Liszt. Hahaha. Very funny, don't you think, to be saying that in the pub! I'll be in the foyer!'

During this conversation the others had moved to the bar and Solly was getting in an order.

'Won't you join us?' Stephen says to Alberic, dreading his reply. But Alberic declines the invitation. 'Too kind,' he says, 'but I am in a dash. Tomorrow then. See you later, alligator.' And with that he bustles out, his coat over his arm, leaving a half-drunk pint on the bar behind him.

'Who's your friend?' says Damian, for the sake of politeness, it would seem, rather than curiosity, as he doesn't ask any other questions when Stephen answers vaguely that he is a casual acquaintance. But Solly is amused. 'Sly-boots,' he says. 'I've seen that bloke in here before. So you're a regular yourself? Out of bounds, my foot! You just didn't want us queering your pitch!'

'No one would want you two, queering or otherwise,' interrupts Charlotte, distracting Solly's attention. 'So, why is it out of bounds then, this nice pub?'

'Because once upon a time somebody must have seen somebody from a hostile agency in here. But everybody knows that no one but a half-wit would even think of trying to make a pick-up in a pub that's on our doorstep! So, you see, it's completely safe. That's why the operatives use it.'

'Unless it's a double-bluff,' Damian says quietly, but Solly isn't listening; he's asking Charlotte concerned and kindly questions about the baby. 'Open-heart surgery,' she says. 'Poor little thing. She has to be fed through a horrible tube.'

They take their drinks and sit at the table by the door. After Charlotte leaves, Stephen buys a second round but the other two do not stay long: Solly has to get home to his wife, and Damian, as always, has mysterious arrangements of his own. Stephen, left alone, decides he might as well have another pint of lager; what else is there for him to do tonight?

Tuesday

What is this quintessence of dust? Stephen, on Tuesday morning, woke from a dream in which he faced a firing squad, to those words hissing in his ear. It had been a haunted night, after his solitary evening. Returning to his flat he had felt as if he had been away for longer than two days; time was taking new, distorted shapes and the person who had left on Saturday seemed strange to Monday's man. I am growing old by leaps and bounds, he thought, and weary. Nothing tethers me to the ground; I am the spaceman lost in space, trapped in a tiny capsule, and doomed to circle round and round in the starlit blackness until his heart stops beating and his lungs no longer fill with breath.

He had stayed in the Fox and Grapes for a long time, drinking lager and then whisky. The rain was falling hard on his way home. Having transferred the tapes in their envelope from his jacket to his coat pocket, he did not take his hand off it until he reached his own front door.

Later he had fallen asleep to Helen's voice on his portable machine. Helen on the pillow next to him, whispering to him from Sunday afternoon. But it had not been her voice solely, for although Stephen tried to shut it out there had been Jamie's too, and they were making love.

In his dream the leader of the firing squad tied a bandanna round his head to close his eyes.

What is it that exists between a husband and a wife? Marriage is confounding. Stephen is intimate with Helen's and yet he does not understand it. How can a man and a woman slide between dispositions as swiftly as shadows moving on wind-blown water, how do they forgive? He knows that Helen is unhappy. Helen cries alone at night. Her husband is unkind to her; he tells her to fuck off. Her in-laws are contemptuous and cold. But out of the blue on Sunday, inexplicably, her mourning turned to dancing. Why? Why? Living with Helen and PHOENIX over the past two days has been like watching clouds fast-skimming over stormy skies and Stephen does not like it. Listening to the pair of them is giving him a heartache, making his head spin; it hurts to be always on the outside looking in. Why is Helen so easily deceived? Stephen can sympathise with early infatuation. But to allow herself repeatedly to be seduced after God knows how much time with him? Surely by now the scales should have fallen from her eyes to lie like flakes of old confetti trodden into dirt. Is the answer in that word 'seduced' – is that what keeps her captive?

Seduction, seducer. Even the sounds of the noun, of the verb, are sordid in their sibilance, like those other slithery words: espionage and blasphemy. And here's a key. She does not know that her husband is a traitor. If she did, her flesh would crawl and she would shrink from him instead of making love.

Making love. He would rather pluck out his own eyes than think of that. But the images are so much more disgusting now he knows who PHOENIX is, and so much harder to banish from the blank screen of his mind. Dark head hovering over golden one; flesh against soft flesh.

What is this quintessence of dust? Half a man, an incomplete thing, a man who is afraid of going to his grave unloved. No. No. These were words heard in a dream, they have nothing to do with waking life, or with the man who knows exactly where he's going.

This hunger is exhausting, though. Is it too much to ask: to love and to be loved?

On arriving at the Institute at nine o'clock that morning Stephen met Rollo Buckingham by the lifts.

'Glad I've bumped into you,' Rollo said. 'Was just about to give you a buzz. About time for a conference, don't you think? Should we aim for the Cube at two – meet me there unless you hear from me before?'

In the long room Louise was looking worried. 'Ah, there you are, Stevie,' she said. 'Muriel wants you. She's lost a tape and she thinks it's one of yours.'

A gush of fear sluiced through Stephen, followed by a wave of heat. But surely Muriel could not be searching for the tapes he took last night? He had left them both at home this morning, which might have been unwise. Then he recalled that other tape from days ago, which cracked when he hurled it at a metal cabinet. It is still in a drawer, with his socks and handkerchiefs, at home. He had somewhat vaguely thought that as it had been paired with an orange-label tape, Muriel might have accounted for the two together. 'I'll go and see her,' he assured Louise.

Muriel was in her scented cubbyhole, with her arcane ledgers spread open on the desk. She raised her head when Stephen knocked on the half-open door. 'Ah, honeybun!' she said. 'Now, PHOENIX. The tapes from 9 December, Thursday. The afternoon delivery – 12.00 to 24.00. I logged the orange-label coming back but not its usual companion. I must have thought that you were still working on it, although I know that usually the non-specials in this investigation don't take long to process. But that was on Monday last week: have you still got it in your cupboard? I'm checking because we're due a Security inspection any minute now.'

Stephen looked surprised. 'Offhand I really can't remember what was happening on the tenth, but I'll have a look at the duplicate report sheet, if you like. Oh, except that I've probably put that one out already for your pending files. I'm absolutely up to date.'

Muriel got tiredly to her feet. 'I'll find it,' she said. She unlocked the cabinet in which, as Stephen knew, she kept the safe-box, and pulled that box towards her by its handles. 'Allow me,' said Stephen. 'That looks very heavy.'

'I can manage,' Muriel said. 'But it is a bloody nuisance having to hoick it out.'

'Aren't this month's duplicates in the current pending file?'

'Not this one,' Muriel said.

He watched her fingers closely as she spun the lock on the box but her fingers were nimble and he could not read the code. She saw him staring and looked at him askance. He tried to seem indifferent to what she was doing but could not resist craning to see what the box contained. Muriel held the lid at such an angle that it hid the papers inside. There was evidently more than one file in it for she had to flick through several to find PHOENIX. It looked exactly like any other Individual Case File, except that its dun-coloured cover bore in red the words: TOP SECRET X LIST EYES ALONE.

She opened the file, turned a couple of pages and extracted

the duplicate report sheet. 'Here it is.'

9 December:
    Subject of interest arrived home at 19.33. Stated he had been
working late and further delayed by faulty bicycle chain. Made
one telephone call: to father. Arrangements made previously
for Friday 10–Sunday 12 confirmed.

'Oh yes, now I remember. Obviously there was nothing on
that tape that needed to be saved. I would have cleared it for
wiping and re-use. I'm quite certain that I would have put it
in my out-tray with the rest. I'm always extra-careful about
PHOENIX.'

'So am I. About it and all the other X lists. That's why I am
especially worried about the tape.'

'Could I have a look through that?' Stephen asked, holding
his hand out for the file.

'No,' she said. 'Do you need me to find another report?'

'No, it's all right. I'll check my casebook. But, it has just
occurred to me, you know what might have happened? As
there was nothing at all important on the tape and it was
a no-label, I wonder if I might just conceivably have had a
moment's inattention and put it in with ODIN? I seem to recall
that I had a lot to do with him that week.'

'But then I would have seen there was one extra,' Muriel
objected.

'You're an absolute wonder,' Stephen said. 'To keep track of
all those tapes and all those sheets of paper every single day, in
and out, it must sometimes feel like counting grains of sand.
I'm pretty sure that I bundled several of ODIN's no-labels in one

envelope last week and that the missing tape was with them.'

Muriel did not seem entirely convinced. She'd have to report it to Security, she said, but the fact that it was only a no-label would hopefully be enough to save her bacon.

Stephen said he hoped so too. 'When's your birthday?' he asked as he was leaving the room.

'May the seventeenth,' she said. 'Why do you ask?'

'Because today I'm going shopping!'

Muriel laughed.

Back at his desk, off the hook and pleased by having got away with the borrowed tapes, Stephen fabricated the weekend for PHOENIX on a new report sheet. He alluded to the real argument on Sunday morning but omitted all the detail. He claimed that Mrs PHOENIX was absent from the flat for several hours and that while she was away the subject of interest left it briefly. He reported an incoming call from Wednesday evening's male visitor, still identified by his first name only: Michael. *Call made from a call-box. Thanking subject for dinner.* He accurately described the subject's intended movements from now until 27 December, with an extra twist of his own.

There had indeed been a telephone call from Michael Bennet-Gilmour on the unlabelled tape that Stephen had quickly run through yesterday. He had called at 11.59 on Sunday morning to say thank you and how pleased he was that they were back in touch. 'What happened then was a long time ago,' he said. 'It should be forgotten now.' Greenwood made a sound of assent, with perhaps a note of hesitation in it, but said nothing to shed light on his friend's puzzling remark. Stephen let it pass. It did not add to the picture he was making.

Other telephone calls, and conversations between Jamie and Helen on Sunday afternoon, were festering like thorns in Stephen's memory. Listening to them in bed last night had made them all too vivid. Whatever her temper when she left silently on Sunday morning, Helen came back at 12.22 apparently restored. 'Hello!' she called from the front door. Jamie must have been in the bedroom, for his response was indistinct and then she too faded out of earshot for a time. When they were within hearing again, he was saying: 'I know that you were tired. We both were. We shouldn't have stayed out so ridiculously late.'

'Let's go back to bed,' she said.

Afterwards they cooked and ate cheese omelettes. They went for a walk by the river. It was dusk: silver-blue light, seagull cry, scent of cold grey water. They walked home through the park holding hands. White flowers on black branches, winter-sweet; the voices of children playing their last games before being called inside. A father swings a baby high into the air to make her laugh and Helen laughs with them. When he kissed her he felt how chill she was from the evening mist. On their return he made hot chocolate with cream.

While Helen was in the bathroom getting dressed to go out to supper with her godmother – a long-standing engagement – Greenwood rang his parents. His mother answered the telephone. 'We've sorted it out,' he told her. 'I'll definitely make the meet.'

Stephen had listened to what Jamie said on both sorts of tape and therefore as one-sided conversation and as dialogue. 'But not for Christmas?' Lady Greenwood asked.

'No. I'm sorry, Mamma. Helen feels that we must go to

Joan's. Yes, it's true we spent last Christmas there as well, but that's the thing when you are an only child.'

'But you did tell her that Joan would be most welcome here?'

'Yes, of course I did. But she didn't think that would really work. She's tired, she's a bit under the weather – I didn't want to make an issue of it. In any case, I don't suppose Joan would have changed her mind at such short notice. But I mean the main thing is we will be there. We'll get up early in the morning and drive down.'

'How long will you stay? And for New Year?'

'Only until Wednesday. Because then we are going away.'

'Just like that? All of a sudden? Where are you going to go?'

'I don't know yet. Paris, maybe. Or Vienna. Somewhere scenic and romantic. Venice. Biarritz. Somewhere with a really good hotel. It's a surprise for Helen, a Christmas present.'

'And a surprise for you, apparently. Do you intend to turn up at the airport and take the first available flight?'

'No! It's not quite that last-minute. I'll go and see the nice little man at Thomas Cook. The one you always use. He'll recommend a good hotel and he'll make the bookings.'

'Dear Mr Railton! He's been there so long; he must be about to retire. Where would Helen like to go?'

'I haven't asked her. I told you, it's supposed to be a surprise. Of course she knows that we're going to have a few days away, just the two of us, but she'll be expecting Norfolk or the Lakes.'

'Well then, don't forget to pack her passport. You know, Jamie, very good hotels can be very expensive.'

'Yes, but you only live once and anyway Claudio has given me some money.'

'Really? What for?'

'A late wedding present is what he said.'

'He told me he wanted you to have a painting.'

'Well, maybe he'll give us one another time.'

'*Allora, tesoro mio*, you are quite sure about the Boxing Day? You will be here? You will come home for that?'

'*Ma certo, Mamma; te l'ho promesso*. Look, I have to go now, Helen's finished in the bathroom – she might hear me talking. I'll telephone you from Joan's.'

'Who were you talking to? And why did you have to hang up in case I overhead?'

'It's Christmas, darling! It's the season of secrets! I was talking to Mamma.'

'Oh yes, right, I will phone mine.'

Helen's mother, Jamie's mother – so unalike they might as well belong to different species. They must have things in common: they were mothers, in sorrow had they brought forth children, but there resemblance ended. Jamie's mother with her operatic voice, her marked emphases, her swooping intonation, her implied inverted commas and something exotic in her speech, like the reverberation of a plucked string beneath the sharp notes of her precise enunciation, and Helen's with the soft tones she had passed down to her daughter, breath indrawn in the slightest of sighs, a way of listening, as if she were a piano tuner waiting for the silences between each separate note. In her voice the echoes of another land, much further west than the place where she now lives. Stephen was suddenly flooded with nostalgia for somewhere he had never been: a place where curlews cry and saints pray on lonely outcrops, listening to wild seas and the saddest of laments.

189

'Mum,' Helen had said, 'it's me. And everything is fine now, everything is fine. I'll see you tomorrow. Jamie will drive up on Christmas Eve. Yes, I'll take the train.'

Was that a break or a small sob he heard in Helen's voice? No, she sounded happy. That man pulls the wool over her eyes time and time again; if ever he thinks that she may see him clearly, he clouds her vision anew, a hobgoblin painting the juice of magic herbs upon her sleeping eyelids to make her madly dote. Oh God, will the only way to end this be by slitting Greenwood's throat?

When he had written his report, he put it in an envelope to give to Rollo later and then he asked Louise if he might claim his extra hour at lunch today. He told her that he had to be back by two o'clock, but, if licensed to leave a little early, would be able to do his Christmas shopping. She gave her permission and would have liked to hear where he was going and what was on his list but he pretended not to hear the enquiry implicit in what she said. Before he went out, having made sure that the people nearest him had their headphones on and could not overhear, he made a call to VULCAN's doctor. The same obstructive receptionist who had spoken to VULCAN last week answered the telephone. Stephen told her he was a neighbour and concerned that the old man was seriously ill. Could the doctor please go round today?

'We are very busy', the woman said, 'because it's Christmas.'

'I know that. But he's on his own and very poorly.'

'If it's an emergency, you need to call an ambulance.'

'It's not that bad as yet but he does need to see a doctor. He needs medicine, I think.'

Reluctantly the receptionist agreed to put VULCAN on the

list. 'What's your name, please?' she asked.

'Michael Bennet-Gilmour,' Stephen said on the spur of the moment, for no reason at all.

Outside, the day was strangely still and lightless. Stephen took the long way, through Shepherd Market and down Hertford Street toward the park, allowing himself more time for planning. He had no clear idea of what to look for when he got to the shop but if Helen did her shopping there, it must stock things she liked. In previous years he had not needed to give any thought to Christmas presents; he had always bought his mother a scarf from Marks and Spencer and, for whichever colleague he had happened to draw in the listeners' lottery, a bottle of wine. This time he was going to be more imaginative. He pulled his overcoat tightly round him and clasped his arms against the cold. From the bare branches of a tree a flock of starlings flew and swirled like cinders in the milk-white sky.

Harvey Nichols loomed over the street with its curving corner like the prow of a ship. It was another world inside: thickly scented, busy, brightly lit and very hot; a bizarre cathedral. For a moment Stephen felt like a refugee inside it but he knew he did not look like one, in his gentleman's coat and brightly polished shoes. He straightened his back. The entrance he had taken into the shop had led to counters piled with lipsticks and scent bottles; lights glinted off the glass, the varnishes, the colours, the painted ladies and their smiles. He inspected the rank of bottles closest to him; they were prettily shaped and bore intriguing names – Shalimar, Mitsouko, Vol de Nuit – and he considered buying one of them. He knew Helen's scent – the scent of freshness, of rose petals after rain, of falling snow, and a deeper element within it, a trace of musk – like lost Titania's

– but he did not know its name. He picked up a bottle and held it to his nose: the liquid inside smelled sweet and heavy, like violet creams; it would be quite wrong for Helen.

He wandered through the ground floor of the shop, past racks of scarves and leather gloves displayed on severed hands, bags and shoes and things to be worn in women's hair, until he came to jewellery. She walks in beauty, like the night; she doth teach the torches to burn bright; fairer than the finest gold she needs no adorning. And yet, to see the look in her eyes, surprised by diamonds.

Diamonds at first appeared to be not at all expensive. Hoops of them on gilt and silver were hanging on a plastic tree beside a till. Seeing Stephen eyeing them, a shop assistant asked if she could help.

'Are they real?' he asked.

'Yes, real diamanté. Four or five worn together look very elegant.'

Not quite sure, Stephen drifted towards a counter where the shiny things were in locked cases, and the price tags reversed so that he could not read them. Earrings, bracelets, chains of varying thicknesses and lengths; he had never looked at jewellery before. Most of it struck him as too glittery but there was one piece that stood out: a flower and crescent moon of gold and tiny pearls, with a diamond at its centre. 'May I look at that one?' he asked of a male assistant, who unlocked the case and reverentially plucked it out. 'We also do the chains,' he said. Stephen peered at the little label. It cost a lot of money.

'For your wife, sir?'

Stephen imagined the pearls on Helen's skin, nestling on her breastbone, and he answered: yes.

With the pendant and a fine gold chain wrapped and in his pocket, Stephen turned to finding a present for his mother. Did she actually own any jewellery other than the wedding ring and the watch she always wore? He couldn't really remember. There was a little drawer in her dressing table in which she kept some beads and a pin or two but nothing of any value. What would she say if he were to give her real gold? That he shouldn't have wasted his money on her, of course. Had it been sad to be a woman whom no man imagined wearing pearls against her skin? He returned to the girl with the diamonds and chose for Coralie a brooch in the shape of a flying swallow.

Now Christophine. Nothing on the ground floor of this shop was likely to meet Louise's rules on budget but Stephen was enjoying himself and didn't feel like going anywhere else. It was a real pleasure, this extravagance of love. He went back to the part of the shop where scarves were sold and spent time admiring the softness and the colours of them, running them through his fingers, finding for Christophine a square of silk in swirling peacock blues.

He had a little time to spare. On an impulse he took an escalator to the second floor. It delivered him into the midst of improbably miniature clothes, in white and blue and pink. There was a lacy cardigan with fasteners of ribbon on display. It looked too small for any human creature but the label on the hanger said that it would fit a child aged between 0 and 3 months. He supposed that Charlotte's niece, being quite new and having been so ill, must be very tiny.

He walked the quick way back to the Institute, his shopping bag in hand, stoking the warmth in his heart to keep it going.

He would need it as insulation against Rollo. The prospect of the Cube was loathsome. Had Rollo said 'conference' or 'meeting'? Conference possibly, but that would be of a piece with his usual self-importance. Stephen was also looking ahead with a certain amount of dread to the evening with Alberic. Why had he not made his excuses yesterday, in that awkward encounter in the Fox and Grapes? What had seemed last Friday like a generous burst of spontaneity now promised nothing but embarrassment. He hardly knew the man. What would they find to talk about for an entire evening? And anyway, where was he supposed to meet him? He was positive that Alberic had specified the Festival Hall but last night he had definitely said the Wigmore instead. Perhaps the man was mad. Shouldn't he forget the whole absurd idea?

Rollo had brought a sandwich and a cup of coffee with him to the Cube, which reminded Stephen that he had eaten nothing since a slice of toast at breakfast. He was alone but said that his Director was planning to join them later. 'We have concerns,' he added.

Stephen gave him the envelope with the report from the weekend and watched him read. Rollo was good at staying expressionless, and he took his time. When he had finished, he breathed in deeply and breathed out. Then he studied Stephen closely. Stephen looked away, but spoke to break the tension. 'Why does PHOENIX sometimes speak to his mother in Italian?'

'Because she speaks it, I suppose. She's from Argentina.'

'Don't they speak Spanish there?'

'Yes, of course they do,' Rollo said impatiently. 'PHOENIX speaks that too. But evidently some people from Argentina speak Italian. I don't know why, I just know that they do. He has family connections there.'

'Well that would explain his raven hair.'

'What?'

Stephen realised his mistake at once. 'Oh it's nothing,' he said. 'It's a quote. From Beckett, Samuel. I was only joking.'

'Please don't. We need to stay focused here. Let's go through all this carefully again. The wife was absent from the flat for several hours, and during that time the subject only left it once?'

'Yes.'

'And you don't know where he went?'

'No.'

'Where did she go?'

'To church, I think, but I don't know what she might have done afterwards; she wasn't talking to the subject when she got back.'

'Why not?'

'They had a fight. It says there. They are always fighting. It is not a happy marriage.'

'That is not my impression.'

'Excuse me, but you don't know what they are like when they are on their own. I see it all the time with married couples: one thing in public, quite another behind their own front doors.'

'But they will be together at Christmas?'

'For the barest minimum of time. He's leaving as soon as he can, as it says there, at crack of dawn on Boxing Day.'

'When the snow lay round about, deep and crisp and even. It's a quote.'

Rollo read the report to himself a second time and began to eat his sandwich. Ham and cheese. Stephen watched him as he ate, his working jaw, his straight white teeth. 'The Boxing Day meet,' he said at last.

'Absolutely,' Stephen said.

'That will be the twenty-seventh as a matter of fact – Monday. I may be there too, at Harcourt Mill.'

'I don't shoot myself,' said Stephen.

'Vienna?'

'That sounded likely.'

'May I listen to that call that you reported?'

'Absolutely. Oh no, wait a moment, damn, I think I've already sent that one out for wiping and re-use. Well, I'm sure I have. I'm sorry.'

If he was irritated by the answer, Rollo Buckingham didn't show it. 'Vienna,' he said again.

Stephen had known that mention of Vienna would ignite a reaction. Everybody knew that enemy operatives, banned from travelling freely outside London, preferred to meet their agents in the cities of nearby countries in which neither they nor the agent would be known to the local trackers. Paris, Brussels, Lyon, yes of course, but Vienna – convenient for Czechs, Yugoslavs, Hungarians and East Germans – was particularly favoured. 'Will you be able to follow PHOENIX there?' he said to Rollo.

'I don't know yet. There is something here that does not square with what I know from my other sources.'

Just as Stephen was opening his mouth to ask what sources Rollo meant, Binks pulled open the door. 'Frightfully sorry to disturb, but Rollo, there's a message from Sub-director Six for you. He's frightfully sorry but his other meeting is overrunning. He'll call you when he gets back and will fix a time for a conference later on. But it could be a bit late. He is frightfully sorry.'

'Thanks, Binks. We'll be finished in a minute,' Rollo said. 'Stephen, when will you be able to finish Monday's take?'

'Now. I mean this afternoon.'

'Good. Well then, we can fit in a meeting with the sub-director at close of play today.'

'Actually, I can't stay late today, it's not possible. I have another engagement. I am meeting a friend, we are going to a concert and I'd have no way of letting him know if I was going to be late.'

Now Rollo does look irritated. His lips tighten into a straight line but 'Tomorrow then,' is all he says.

Tomorrow? But yesterday Jamie Greenwood drove his wife to Liverpool Street in time for the 9.47 train to Woodbridge. Afterwards, Stephen supposed, he went to work. The flat stayed empty through the day, bereft of Helen. A barren place, a cold expanse of nothingness, as is anywhere and any time without her. Not knowing when she will come home, how shall he survive this time, these hollow days of desolation? She leans her head against the grimy window of the train and, in the fields she travels through, the cattle and sheep, the stalks of corn, form a guard of honour and salute her. The winter trees bow their bare branches in homage to her beauty. The train takes her further and further away and, because she is not here, there is no purpose in today. Stephen listened to the tapes of Monday but he didn't need to; he could have predicted that there would be nothing to report. PHOENIX came home late that night, alone. No one telephoned him and he did not say a word.

*

Coralie was at her kitchen table wrapping Mr Fisher's gloves. She had decided on a green pair this year, to make a change from blue or brown. To wrap up a parcel nicely was not as easy as it had been when her knuckles were less swollen but she did like the finished effect. She had already wrapped the jumper she had bought for her son. That jumper had been in her chest of drawers for weeks, hiding beneath her own clothes – not that Stephen would ever have thought to look. Every morning, as she was rootling around for a vest or a petticoat, she gave it a little stroke. It was gorgeous. So soft, so luxurious. She had made a special journey by taxi and train to Oxford just to buy it. Since he had started that job in London, her son had become very fussy about clothes. It was funny, that. He had never shown any sign of caring how he looked when he was at school. Mind you, of course he wore a uniform all day. Coralie approved of uniforms; great levellers they were, apart from looking smart. Just look at any soldier, any FANY. Spencer had never seemed as handsome in civilian clothes as he had when he was in the Army. Anyway, that jumper was one she'd seen being modelled in a magazine, it was in a feature called 'Get the *Brideshead* Look', which had also helpfully listed stockists. Stephen had a look of that Sebastian, only not so blond or girlish. Nor as susceptible to dangerous temptations, she must hope. No, of course not, he was a sensible boy. But it was a bit of worry that he didn't seem to have made many new friends in London. It never sounded very sociable, that office. Where else do you meet people except in the place you work? Well, he'd never been the sort of child who goes round in a great big happy gang; more of a loner, really, maybe a little shy, or maybe choosy. At school, though, there had been his good friend

Giles. She must remember to ask Stephen if he was planning to meet up with Giles during the festive season. Perhaps he'd care to come to tea? With a bit of notice, she could always rustle up some more mince pies. She'd like to see him again herself, now he'd got so famous. But just talk about girlish looks! Him in his tight white satin and his eyes made up like a geisha's. Speaking for herself, she'd go for Jeremy Irons any day. Although he'd probably make even more of a fuss about his cufflinks than her Stephen. Do you suppose it might put the girls off, dressing like an old gent in wartime when today's boys all went round in jeans? For her part, she really couldn't be bothered about what to wear, as long as she was warm and decent. Life was far too short.

The shortest day of the year, the longest night, but uphill from now on. These were good days, the days between the winter solstice and the eve of Christmas; all the lights on in the house and every single item ticked off on her list bar those she really could not do more than two days in advance. Her cards were sent, her presents wrapped, her cupboards full and the turkey sleeping the sleep of the just in the boot of Stephen's car. In her mind she ran through the last-minute list again: peel chestnuts, peel potatoes, peel parsnips, do sprouts, giblet stock and Stephen's stocking. Not many surprises in there, she was sorry to say! A tangerine and chocolate coins, because they were what he always had when he was a little boy. In those days she'd have put in a Dinky car and a Ladybird book – *Piggly Plays Truant!* – a bright rubber ball or a bag of marbles. Beautiful those marbles were, positively jewel-like, but costing next to nothing, except for the extra-large. And Britains animals! Stephen had adored those animals and played with them for years. You could get farm animals and zoo ones; he was always very stern about keeping them apart, lest the lion ate the lamb. Calves and polar bears and piglets – pink and black – and rhinos. Those were the days, oh dear! Now it was a bar of soap and a pair of socks. Mind you, this year's socks were really rather superior, patterned in a sort of Fair Isle, like the jumper.

Odd how Christmas involves a lot of peel. Chestnuts are the worst; you always get that inner skin beneath your thumbnails and it hurts. Just one of those things, like losing the end of the Sellotape, those minor irritations, small thorns in the flesh, which you need in life as a Christmas cake needs salt to give the sweetness savour.

Coralie got up and went to the living room to put Mr Fisher's present next to Stephen's under the decorated tree. The tree was looking a bit the worse for wear, it had to be admitted, rather threadbare, but what could you expect, when it had done such service down the years? Yet even so, it was brave enough, and gay enough, under its load of lights and tinsel. There! What else did she have to do tonight? Nothing. Put her feet up, heat some soup, watch *The Bridge on the River Kwai*. Snow was falling hard again; she drew her curtains closed.

The snow caught Stephen by surprise. Who would have thought it could snow again, so soon after last week's storms? It must have been falling for a while, silently, stealthily; it was already deep on roofs and pavements. Standing at a window of the long room, about to close the blind, he watched the thick flakes drifting down like dying birds, or shreds of cloud, and thought of the white sky he had seen earlier in the day. A skin of sky holding back the snow. *Vol de nuit*. To escape on the wings of the night, to soar above the long room and the Institute, to start again from the beginning, in a new place, a new story – if only it were possible. Behind him Louise was calling the group together. 'Two things, chaps,' she said. 'One, don't forget the party! As if you could! I vote we do our pressies just before. And two, have I got everybody's leave sheet? Harriet, you're taking Thursday off, aren't you? Christophine? Good! Stephen, did you give me yours?'

'I don't know what I'm doing yet,' he said.

'Well, I'm afraid that last-minute requests for leave will probably not be granted. With Department Four still running around like headless chickens and something very odd afoot in Department Six, we'll almost certainly have to have some holiday cover. That reminds me Stevie, could you manage an hour or so of overtime this evening? Martin's off sick for the rest of the week and Ana's tearing her hair out next door.'

'I'm frightfully sorry but I have to leave on time today. I'm meeting somebody at six.'

'Never mind, I'll see if Solly can do it. I thought you might be busy,' Louise said, without irony or rancour. 'I'd do it myself but for the rehearsal, which of course I cannot miss.'

Stephen nodded sympathetically. He was used to Louise's habit of assuming that he and everyone else knew all about her outside life, the people in it and its small events. Charlotte clearly did. 'Will there be tickets on the door?' she asked. 'Oh, I forgot to tell you, I got those tickets for Cockney Rebel! Yes, I know, petal, not your cup of tea! Actually, Steve you might like . . . ?

'As a matter of fact I'm going to a concert tonight,' he interrupted. 'Brahms piano sonatas.'

'All right, all right, Mr Clever-clogs! I bet you're going in white tie and tails with your Oxford friends?'

'I adore Brahms,' Louise began to say but Stephen did not wait.

'I must pack up', he said, 'or I'll be late.'

'Don't forget your umbrella,' Charlotte said.

He didn't have an umbrella. Snowflakes fell upon his hair and combed their chilly little feelers through it, shivering his scalp. He stood irresolute on the street outside the Institute and felt the coldness of the pavement through the thin soles of his shoes. Where should he go now? He couldn't have stayed on at work, for fear of being found out by Rollo Buckingham. He wasn't dressed for this weather. This December was turning out to be so strangely cold; what if the sun had spurned the world for ever, condemning it to endless winter? If he were to stay here any longer, would he be frozen to the spot? Suddenly he felt as if he really could not move at all. But he must. People were coming out of the Institute; he would be observed. Should he just go home? Another cheerless night, alone? Or might he find a refuge in the quiet of the staircase outside Helen's flat, where an element of her will linger still? I need to know that she is near me, he said to the darkness; tell me where to go.

And of course it was entirely obvious: the Wigmore Hall. He didn't expect Alberic to be there; the man was probably some sort of fantasist. But there was no reason why he could not buy himself a ticket and attend the concert. What better bridge to Helen than an evening of the music that she loved? And in the strange dominion where their souls connect, she might hear that music too.

He had time to kill. The invitingly lit doorway of the Fox and Grapes across the road promised instant shelter from the snow if he dared defy Security again. Why not? It was warm in there. He would tuck himself away in the corner furthest from the bar and hide behind the paper.

He was on his second whisky and halfway through the crossword when he heard the voice of Rollo Buckingham ordering two pints of IPA. The pub was busier than it had been on Monday and a small crowd was standing near the bar, forming a screen for those who were, like Stephen, sitting down. He opened his newspaper to its full extent and peered cautiously round it. Buckingham, in his beautiful coat, was paying for the drinks. There was no reason why he should look in Stephen's direction now but until he left the pub he was a barrier between Stephen and the exit. If Stephen were to get to the Wigmore Hall by seven, he would need to set off soon. He watched as Rollo, taller than anyone else in the room, shouldered his way to the opposite end and then he saw with a sinking sense of inevitability that the other pint was for Greenwood. The two men stood close together, near the door, talking intently. At this distance Stephen was unable to hear what they were saying. He felt like a rabbit in a snare, trapped unless it chews its own paw off. He also felt affronted. Security's instructions were explicit: this pub was out of bounds. How arrogant it was of the two men to behave as if the rules did not apply to them.

It was almost half past six. He gulped the last of his drink and considered his next step. He could stay here, with his empty glass, and hope that Buckingham would not need the gents'. If he did, he would have to push straight past him. But if Stephen did not make a move quite soon, he would miss the concert. Perhaps that was the better choice? Alternatively, he could turn his collar up and sidle out, hoping that Rollo would not notice. If he were seen, would Rollo acknowledge or ignore him? Then it occurred to him that Rollo might be working. He could be in this forbidden place for operational reasons, in which case he would definitely not acknowledge Stephen, although he might report him to Security tomorrow. But why would he be with PHOENIX? Was he using PHOENIX as a decoy? Or tricking PHOENIX into thinking he was still a trusted colleague? Or detaining PHOENIX for a while in order to give Technical the clear run of his flat or their shared office at the Institute? Perhaps there were investigators at this very moment searching through his drawers for illicit material or hidden codes, as Stephen himself had done. If he stayed here, unseen, and watched the men, he might learn more about this enigmatic case.

Each time someone entered or left the pub, the door banged loudly and cold air whistled in. It was that blast of air which announced the arrival of Sub-director Six a few minutes later. He did not come right in but stayed by the door, holding it open, summoning Rollo and Greenwood with a crooked fore-finger. Immediately they put their glasses down on the nearest table and followed their leader out.

How tiresome this evening was turning out to be. Stephen considered tracking the three men but on balance decided against it. Twenty to seven. Did he have still have time to get to Oxford Street? Yes, if the concert did not begin until half past and he took the Tube, he probably did.

He went to Bond Street, fairly confident that he knew the way from there. On the way he tried to remember if he had ever been to a concert of classical music before. When he was at school perhaps? Music did not exist for Stephen as a child, except as hymns, theme-tunes and advertising jingles. Had he ever heard his mother sing? Did she sing when she was by herself? Helen had opened his heart to the possibilities of music. Was it Chopin, Alberic had said, or was it Brahms or Liszt? Helen plays a piece of Brahms – an intermezzo – and when he first her heard playing it, he had been entranced. He did not know its name then but as chance would have it the piece was on one of his new records; someday he will ask her to play it just for him. There will be a long room, bare but for a white sofa and a grand piano, French windows open to the night, and the curtains billowing, and she will rise and move to the piano, her lovely fingers on the keys, a drift of jasmine on the air.

It came as a surprise and an interruption to his thoughts to find Alberic waiting impatiently beneath the glass portico of the Wigmore Hall.

'Ah, there you are at long bloody last, my friend! I had given you up for lost and was on the point of going in when I said to myself: just give him two more minutes! And it's a good thing that I did!'

'I'm sorry. Did you say 7.15? Delays on the Jubilee Line; the snow . . .'

'Of course, of course! It is ghastly weather! Cats and dogs! No, as it is snow not rain we should better say polar bears and penguins. Come, let us take our seats, the performance is about to start. I already bought a programme.'

Stephen followed the hurrying Alberic into the small, warm and very red concert hall. They found their seats in the middle of a row towards the back. Lights shone on a glittering cupola above the stage and Stephen's impression was of an ecclesiastical space until he saw that the figure he had taken for the risen Christ was some other form of deity in a monstrance of gold rays, attended by maidens bare but for their hair or wings. Even so, there was an air of worship.

Alberic held the programme up for Stephen to read: *Franz Schubert – Winterreise D. 911.*

'But you said Brahms,' he whispered.

'So I got it wrong,' Alberic whispered back. 'But this is better, no? More suitable for the season. Ssh!'

Stephen, silenced, settled in his seat as a man and a woman in evening dress walked onto the stage. He had no foreknowledge of what he was to hear; he didn't know the significance of the title.

The woman took her place at the piano. She paused there for a moment, staying very still. The man stood, also without moving, his head bowed; their stillness like a fine mesh falling invisibly upon the audience and drawing it together, tensed and reverent and hushed. Into that stillness dropped the first slow, quiet notes of the piano and the man straightened his shoulders, breathed in deeply, and sang.

He sang without a break for an hour or more, an hour in which Stephen lost all consciousness of time. He was transfixed. Never in his life before had he been so affected by something he could not translate nor put in words. He did not know the meaning of the words the man was singing but he understood them. He understood the singer's sadness, his loneliness, his sense of alienation. He knew this was a journey of a kind and that its end was madness. At times the piano part seemed almost to console, twining with the voice like a companion on his way, but at others it kept its distance. It was unbelievable how desolate this music was. As it neared its end Stephen's eyes were full of tears and he could not stop them falling. Slow, haunted chords. One last despairing question, one final, quiet, inconclusive note. The loud applause that followed it was as rude an awakening as a drench of icy water, shocking Stephen back into the present. He wanted it to stop. How could he make so sudden a transition from the reverie he had been in to the conviviality of the cheering people round him? He became abruptly aware again of Alberic, but he could not trust himself to speak.

On stage the pianist and the tenor – that same man who had sung so truthfully of death – were also smiling, bowing and behaving as if the world were a welcoming and happy place. The singer stretched his hands out to the audience and it answered him with even louder clapping.

Alberic turned to Stephen. 'The best thing about the piece is that it's short. My favourite kind of gig. Have you heard it before? It's good, no? Winter journey. It makes me think of the retreat from Moscow. Napoleon's troops wore sackcloth on their feet instead of boots, trodding on deep snow. Here, you can keep the programme. It has the lyrics in it. Do you know the German? Have you eaten yet?'

Stephen, still in a daze, considered this last question. Had he eaten yet? Yet? Since when? Perhaps not since that piece of toast at breakfast. He did remember that he had not had time for lunch. Had he forgotten to be hungry? 'Er, no,' he said.

'Me neither. Nothing, not one bite, after my boiled egg this morning. Go to work on an egg, as I always say! And soldiers! Haha, no? I was flat out all day and now I could murder a horse. Would you join me for dinner? I detest eating on my own.'

'Well, yes, all right,' Stephen said.

The snow had ceased falling and the night was clear and bright; a full moon Stephen saw, to lighten the longest night. As if he had heard Stephen's thoughts, Alberic said, 'Look, how white the moon, how beautiful on snow.' He knew a good place in Covent Garden near the Strand, he went there often; it was only a short walk away from here. Evidently he also knew the way through Soho's back streets, although it seemed to Stephen that he chose a complicated route. Do not dodge pointlessly in and out of doorways, he reminded himself for no particular reason.

The restaurant was large, decorated lavishly with paintings thickly hung, with mounted antlers and stuffed game birds, and would clearly be expensive. Stephen wondered awkwardly if Alberic might expect him to pick up the bill but he, mind-reading for the second time, said as they were seated in a quiet corner, 'You should know that I am my own manager when it comes to my expense account, which gives me an advantage over you, I guess. It is one of the rewards of a life in business. God knows that they are few. Every time I come here I order the same thing, the terrine and the steak béarnaise, but you might like the oysters, or the duck – have a look at the menu. Let's have some champagne.'

Champagne comes ice-cold in flutes and words tumble out of Alberic apparently haphazardly, not expecting answers: Müller, Schiller, poems he had to learn by heart when he was at school, *Kennst du das Land, wo die Zitronen blühn,* do you know the German? The people of the north are always hungry for the south and who can blame them when they live for months on end in total darkness; can you think how dark it was in the times before electricity or gas? On nights without the moon? In northern lands, those long, long nights, no light at all, is it any wonder that the stories are of ghosts and hellish things? Have you ever been in a place where there is no light, where you truly cannot see your hand in front of face, as the saying goes? Yes, I myself have seen that dark: you may as well be in your grave. Except there are the Northern Lights, of course. Have you ever seen them? Incredible, quite incredible, the colours and the shapes, the night sky full of living light, I saw it from a ship, if you saw it you would believe in magic. Red lights and gold and green, and flying in the sky like, what's that creature called, a dragon. Red and green. The colours of Christmas, no? In Christmas I do not believe but still I think it right to have some colour in the winter. Do you go to many parties? But yes, of course you do, young man.

More champagne before the food arrives; sweet wine with foie gras says Alberic, ordering a bottle of Gewürtztraminer, a name that Stephen has read in books but never before heard said. 'At home, when I was young, we would drink a good Tokaj,' Alberic continues. 'You know, in the old times, in this country, but of course you know this already, at Christmastime kings were made to serve their servants and servants were made kings. Or lords maybe. Yes, that is the word, lords, lords of misrule. A great custom, I always say, we should bring it back into every office, every Christmas party, what do you think?'

Stephen says he doubts the Director would approve, and wishes that unsaid, but Alberic lets it go without remark. He does not wait for a waiter to pour wine but fills Stephen's glass and his; the cold white wine and, later, the warm red. Meat, tender in the mouth. The taste of blood. 'The point is that the ordinary rules of normal life, I mean the rules of everyday, they can be broken, how do you say, suspended, and that's good, that's healthy. You know I think of those soldiers in the trenches in the war who sang '*Stille Nacht*' to the enemy on Christmas Eve and played football. But afterwards, the next day, they started to kill each other once again.'

A pause. More wine. You really have to try the crème brûlée. It is brought to Stephen in a fine white dish, candlelight strikes off silver, glass, the glassy sugar slivers into shards, sweetness on the tongue, intense. On the other side of the room a beautiful woman is eating the same thing – or what looks like the same thing to Stephen; a white dish – she slides a spoon slowly into her mouth, relishing the slick of it; he watches her take the cream onto her tongue and suck the smooth base of the spoon; he does the same. More wine. Coffee and Armagnac, were there ever words as liquid and as lovely as those two? A poem.

Alberic lifts his glass to clink it against Stephen's: 'Here's to you, Stephen, my friend,' he says. 'Shteefen,' a softening of the consonants, an elongated vowel. Stephen looks at him. His features are somehow undefined; if Stephen were later to be asked for a description, he would find it hard to give. A man of indeterminate age, of indeterminate origin, his hair much the same no-colour as his skin. Despite his constant animation there is something slightly forlorn about the man. 'To you,' Stephen responds. 'And to a happy Christmas.'

'So, what do you do on Christmas Day? Do you spend it with family or friends? With your girlfriend? You have a girlfriend, no?'

In Stephen's pocket the crescent moon of gold and pearl glows as if it were alight in its little casket. Does he have a girlfriend? He looks at Alberic and Alberic smiles back. 'There is someone I love,' he says, 'but it is complicated.'

'A boy, therefore . . . ?'

'Oh no.'

'Ah, I see. She's married. That is the way so often. You know, sometimes I think that marriage is essential, not to married people but to lovers. The truth is that love cannot survive longer than a few years in a marriage. Oh yes, in the beginning the husband and wife, yes they are in love and they tell each other – actually they believe – that love will last for ever. But then the ordinary things, they come along – work and getting out of bed on Monday mornings, paying the gas bill, children, buying school shoes, not tonight I have a headache, those unpleasing noises – what's the word – slopping, squishing? – when he drinks his tea. And then, if they are lucky, the man and woman become friends. But if unlucky, enemies. Either way, the time has come for another to step in. To rescue. This is what I try to say: marriage is essential because adultery is the truest form of love and the one is impossible without the other. Ask the poets. You were never married, were you?'

'No. But you are?'

'Yes. And I will say my wife is my best friend. But as for love . . . or lovers . . . '

'Shall I show you what I bought today for her Christmas present?'

Stephen slips the box from his breast pocket and passes it over the table to Alberic.

'But it is already wrapped!'

'Yes, but you can open it. I will wrap it up again, in some other paper.'

'No, no, it will be impossible to make it so nice again. Describe it to me, please.'

The words themselves are jewels in Stephen's mouth. A crescent moon, and gold and pearl. Oh, she doth teach the torches to burn bright; he says her name, he tells her name out loud. Helen, Helen, Helen. And Alberic is smiling still but not looking straight at Stephen, looking down instead at the pipe which he is carefully filling. His concentration is all on it: on tamping down the tobacco shreds, on striking first one match and then another, the small flame burning, breathing deeply in. Eyes averted; it's the invitation of the father-confessor or the driver; it's an invitation that Stephen, in the warmth of this man's company, with his fingers laced around a goblet full of liquid fire that tastes of incense, grapes and Christmas, in these rich surroundings, unhesitatingly accepts.

He tells Alberic the story. Not the entire story – he is not a fool – he omits to say that he knows Helen only through the medium of a secret investigation. Nor does he mention eavesdropping but to make some sense of the affair, he does hint that Helen's husband is a suspect in a case of espionage. He describes in full an unhappy marriage, Helen's solitude, the arrogance and the snobbishness of the husband and his own precipitous falling into love. He tells of watching Helen in her pale coat walking alone across a park.

While he speaks he listens to himself. It is a long time since he heard his own voice at such uninterrupted length. The story he is telling strikes him as finely structured and compelling but it appears that Alberic is only giving it half an ear. He nods from time to time encouragingly, but also keeps glancing round the restaurant as if looking for a waiter; he re-lights his pipe and fiddles with a knife. It is only when the story ends that he looks up and meets Stephen's eyes full on.

'You must be adventurous,' he says. 'So where is the lady now?'

'Now?'

'Yes, at this moment, now.'

As this is a question that Stephen has asked himself so many times, he marvels to hear it asked by someone else. If he needed a sign to set the seal on a new friendship, this is it. He stops to think. Where is Helen now? It is past eleven on 21 December, midwinter's eve. She is at her mother's house. When Helen is in London, Stephen can picture what she's doing but, knowing nothing of where her mother lives, tonight he has only a shadowy idea. Perhaps she is just now getting into bed in the room where she slept when she was a little girl, where her dolls and childhood toys are on the shelves and the curtains are sprigged with pale pink roses. She has on a long-sleeved nightdress of white cotton and her feet are bare.

'She is staying at her mother's house in a place called Orford, which is in the county of Suffolk, on the east coast of England,' he tells Alberic.

A small shift is apparent; Alberic's attention stiffens almost imperceptibly and becomes acute. 'Orford,' he repeats. 'Of course I know of it. As I suppose you do?'

This Stephen fails to understand. Why should Alberic think he must know Orford? Why does Alberic? He had never heard of the place before Helen mentioned it. Now its sole significance to him is its connection with her. His puzzlement is evident to Alberic.

'Working in Defence? Do you never have to visit Orford Ness?'

Stephen rallies quickly. Orford Ness means nothing to him either but, conscious of the need always to maintain his cover, he shakes his head in a knowledgeable manner and informs Alberic that such places do not feature in his particular line of work.

'Yes, well, I hear it is a place that is famous for the birds, for waterfowl,' says Alberic. He is himself a great enthusiast for birds, he adds, calling for the bill. He spends as much time as he can with his binoculars in places like the Heath; he once saw a bittern. When the bill comes he does not examine it but slides a quantity of cash beneath it, refusing Stephen's offer to split it with an airy wave.

They wait by the restaurant door while a waiter goes to get their coats. 'I must remember my umbrella,' Alberic remarks. Then, as if suddenly struck by a good idea, he seizes Stephen by the shoulders, 'We should go!' he says. 'To Orford Ness!'

'What, now?'

'No, not now, tonight; it is possibly too late. But tomorrow. Or the next day, maybe. I have been thinking about Christmas. It is not nice to spend the holiday alone. Not really. Not when everybody else is with their families and friends. I contemplated skiing but I don't have now my passport; it is being renewed. Anyway, there is nothing I adore as much as discovering a new part of this green and pleasant land. But it not much fun alone. And to be completely frank, not really practical for me. So come with me! Please, please! It will be good for me of course, but even better for you! For you may find your lady – just imagine: she is walking on the beach alone and you are there, and she speaks to you and then your life will change.'

'Why not?' says Stephen, laughing. He is charmed by the man's impetuosity but this latest invitation is pure fantasy and moonshine spun out of the solstice, which will not outlast the night. 'Super!' cries Alberic. 'I will telephone you tomorrow or when I can.'

Outside, on the pavement he embraces Stephen, putting both arms around him, holding him close, before pointing him in the direction of Leicester Square. 'I go this way,' he says, indicating the opposite direction. '*Hasta la vista*, goodnight, *ciao*, see you very soon, *mon brave!*'

Stephen, swaying on the Tube, unsteady on his feet on the short walk home, is flying high on promises and hope. The spell of tonight's music binds him still but the melancholy of it has ebbed to leave behind the legacy of beauty. And by sheer chance, by the sort of luck that seldom strikes in real life, he has found a friend. No, more than a friend: the uncle he never had, a guide and a purveyor of advice and sympathy and kindness. His name shall be called wonderful. Tomorrow is a new day, champagne is delicious, friendship is a very fine thing indeed.

But in the dead of night he woke, his heartbeat racing, in the vise of dread. He had not closed his curtains and now, at the bedroom window, he seemed to see small white faces staring in out of the darkness. Small white hands pressed up against the glass. Children wandering abroad and lost? Who is he and what has he done – this self-deceiving fool, this thing of rags and dust?

Wednesday

Stephen had forgotten to set his alarm clock and did not wake until after nine on Wednesday morning. His sheets were tangled sweatily around him; he must have had a fever in the night. For a while he did not know what day it was or what he should be doing. Then, seeing the time and coming to his senses, he tumbled out of bed.

'Delays on the Central Line,' he told Louise by way of justification when he got to the Institute but she had more important things in mind than Stephen's lateness. Something must have happened in the night: Ana and Martin from Group II were in anxious conclave round Louise's desk with an analyst from Department Four, and the atmosphere was tense.

'What's happening?' he whispered to Charlotte as he passed her.

'Not sure. It's something to do with CUCHULAINN. Somebody was killed last night but I don't know who or where. We'll get the gen later from Lou-Lou, I expect.'

Work that day was scheduled to end at five o'clock because of the Christmas party. Reminded of this by Charlotte, Stephen remembered he should have brought the party food with him. Now he would have to go shopping at lunchtime, a nuisance as he would rather have had a quiet sandwich in a pub; his head was aching badly. Muriel came past on her morning round. 'No sign of that tape, I don't suppose?' she asked.

'Oh, I'm afraid not,' Stephen said, cursing himself inwardly for having left all the tapes behind this morning in his rush. He had intended to slip them back into the system; he must be sure to bring them in tomorrow. The new tapes that Muriel delivered were from Tuesday morning. With Helen away, he could see no point in listening to them; whatever PHOENIX did or did not do in reality was immaterial to him. But he had nothing else to fill the day and was afraid that Rollo might at any time come hunting. He'd be safer in the shelter of his headphones.

The morning dragged sleepily on. For ODIN and his wife, life was relatively smooth: Diane had had a tranquil couple of days; the consultant had said her heart was bearing up, her wheelchair was mended and now they were enjoying their Christmas preparations. Mrs ODIN said that Diane loved the tree. There was nothing but unanswered calls on VULCAN's line. When no one was watching, Stephen dialled VULCAN's number himself but still got no reply. Probably the old man was feeling better, after the doctor's visit, and had gone out for a breath of air or to do his shopping. Stephen would try him again later.

It was not yet lunchtime but, if he slipped out now, he could be back before Louise had even noticed he was gone. He unhooked his coat from the rack by the door as unobtrusively as he could but was halted by Solly shouting out across the room to him, using VULCAN's real name. 'Hey Steve! What do you know about old Jacky?'

'What about him?'

'Come over here and have a listen.'

A comrade on the telephone on Monday to one of Solly's regulars, saying he was a wee bit worried about old Jacky. He'd been calling him at various times of day for the past two days now, but the old man never answered: could he be off on his holidays? But no, both men agreed, Jacky wasn't the type for winter cruises, nor for late nights neither. They knew he lived alone. There was a son but he was somewhere else – was it Australia? Was there anyone else who lived closer to Jacky than they did, and could pop round more easily, in case? Happen there was nothing to worry about but all the same, it was unlike old Jack not to pick up his telephone. Opposite problem on the whole – once you had him on the line it was a hell of a job to get him off it – no one like Jacky for a natter. In the end they couldn't come up with anyone in Motherwell; the caller would give Mick a bell, Jacky was like a father to him although he had a lot on his hands just now, what with the strike and all.

Stephen imagined VULCAN coughing tar and coal dust from his lungs, stranded between breaths, panicking to reach the next one, failing, drowning, falling, dead. Comrade, courageous fighter. No. The obvious explanation was that the doctor whose visit Stephen had requested yesterday had packed VULCAN off to hospital straightaway. That would certainly be the best place for him: a nice clean bed and nurses to fetch him cups of tea and wish him a merry Christmas. The old man safe in striped pyjamas, not all alone and hearing the ringing of the telephone but too weak to reach it.

'I don't think there's anything wrong,' he said to Solly.

'Should you mention it to his strategist?'

'I will, when I see her next.'

He put his coat on in the corridor and hurried from the building. Another day of bitter cold. Time felt unreal to him and oddly still, as if the hours had turned to ice and he was imprisoned in them. He told himself it was only because he had slept so badly.

Where do you buy cheese near Piccadilly? Stephen didn't know. He usually bought food in the corner shops of East Acton. Charlotte and Louise regularly shopped in Oxford Street but he wasn't sure where and didn't have time to look. Rollo Buckingham would be bound to know the best shops. What would Helen do? She'd go to a delicatessen in Soho, or a stall in a street market, where the cheesemonger would greet her by her name or call her darling. They would have a serious discussion and he would give her slivers of his cheese to taste before she chose one. How did people learn these things: the right cheeses, the right wine? He faltered on the icy pavement of White Horse Street, seeking inspiration, and then remembered Fortnum and Mason. He had never been inside it but it was a food shop, wasn't it, and it was nearby.

Again he found a sanctuary from the cold and from the world outside. Why had he not known earlier that there were such places – opulent, heated like greenhouses full of tropical plants, heavy with scent and colour? A man could simply stand there and get warm. But he was surprised how much the cheese and biscuits cost. 'JOBLESS TOTAL NUDGES 3 MILLION', read an *Evening Standard* billboard by the Ritz.

It turned out that he need not have done his shopping that day. When he got back to the long room he was met by Charlotte looking important and Louise with a harassed expression on her face. 'Where have you been, Stevie?' she scolded. 'You're turning into the Scarlet Pimpernel. I can never find you. We have a situation. CUCHULAINN is Alpha now. We've had to postpone the party; we've no choice. But isn't it lucky that we hadn't already made the sandwiches? I've been up to Catering and begged a roll of tinfoil off them; the quiches and the ham will just about squeeze into the fridge and Solly says he'll store the sausage rolls at home. It's not the end of the world.'

'Coo,' said Charlotte, 'look at Stevie's bag! Dead posh!'

'Well, I do hope this isn't going to get in the way of anything else that you had planned this afternoon. Things are difficult enough at this time of year as it is.'

'I'm sorry?' Stephen said.

'Oh yes, no I mean – I'm sorry, I should have made it clear. The thing is that it would really help if you could share the Alpha monitoring with Charlotte. Martin's off, as I said, and Harriet simply has to catch the train this evening or she just won't be able to get to Colonsay and now that you've done quite a lot of CUCHULAINN and most of your own cases are suspended . . .'

'Come on, Steve,' Charlotte broke in before he had a chance to speak. 'Pack up your kit! We're going in five minutes.'

Stephen locked his things away, including the bag of cheese, and followed Charlotte down to the basement garage, which was empty except for a few cars and a small white van.

'Where are we going?' he asked her.

'They never tell you. They just take you there.'

A man emerged from a side-door, cocked his head enquiringly at them and, at Charlotte's answering nod, opened the back door of the van. He motioned them inside. 'You have to sit on the floor.' He climbed into the driver's seat, pulled a cap onto his head and started up the engine. The garage doors slid open and they drove straight out.

'I feel like I'm being kidnapped,' Stephen said.

'How do you know you're not? Maybe Louise has tricked us and we're being taken hostage. Six months in a cell for us. Only, your folks would pay the ransom. If, that is, they actually want you back.'

'Keep your heads down, please,' the driver said over his shoulder and then nothing more for the forty or so minutes of the drive.

'We're heading north,' said Charlotte confidently, although she and Stephen could see nothing from their uncomfortable position on the floor. When they stopped, the driver turned to them again. 'Stay here, please. Keep your heads right down and don't make any noise.' He got out of the van and locked the door.

'Oh God,' Charlotte hissed. 'I hope they're not going to make us do the monitoring in here! It's so bloody cold and I need a wee.'

Her nearness was reassuring. That hostage-fantasy was meant merely to amuse but even so Stephen felt a sharp-edged pang of fear in his guts. He was finding it difficult to breathe. What if something were to befall the driver and prevent him coming back to let them out? How long must he and Charlotte stay here, trapped in this white prison, while snow cascaded on them and hid them from the world?

'Do you suppose that in the event of nuclear attack, you and I are essential personnel?' Charlotte said in a low voice after minutes of silence.

'What?'

'You know. The list of essential personnel who would be whisked away into the bunkers at the first sound of the warning bell.'

'What warning bell?'

'It must be a siren actually. A klaxon? Five minutes' warning, isn't that what we'd have?'

'Five minutes doesn't sound long enough to get anyone into a bunker.'

'Well, it could be that key people get an earlier alert. But anyway it's true. There is a list, and there are special underground shelters all across the country, built for people like us in case of war.'

'They had bunkers in the last war – Churchill had one.'

'Those were not the same. Those were designed as shelter from the normal sort of bombs; these are proof against nuclear attack. Beneath the streets of London there are comms rooms, canteens, larders full of tins and water, dormitories, sick bays, even operating theatres, all equipped and airtight to keep us safe from nuclear fallout. So they say. We could be down there for months. Think of that. You and me and Lou-Lou living together for months on end, while above our heads there was total devastation.'

'We wouldn't be key personnel.'

'Yes we would. Even when the Reds were raining nuclear bombs on us, the strategists would want to know what the miners and the dear old boys were doing.'

'They would all be dead.'

'That's true. Have you any idea what really happens in a nuclear attack? Third-degree burning of the skin, melting of the eyeballs, rupture of the eardrums . . .'

'Why do you know all this?'

'Everybody does. Besides, my brother-in-law is a submariner and they know a lot about attack drill. They . . .'

She was interrupted by the return of the driver in the cap. He unlocked the back door, half-opened it, put his head in and said quietly: 'Please count down two minutes before exiting the vehicle. Walk in an easterly direction, holding hands. At the bottom of the hill, turn left into Arcadia Street. Small block of flats about halfway down on the left-hand side, Arcadia House, flat number 3. These are the keys to the entrance and the flat. Let yourselves in. Exit the van as quickly as you can.'

'A two-minute warning,' Charlotte murmured. 'Steve, I hope you're counting.'

They did as they were told. Charlotte's hand was cool and firm in Stephen's. 'Why are we holding hands?' he asked.

'So that we look like an ordinary couple, you idiot,' she said.

The flat consisted of two grubby and sparsely furnished rooms. In one, Damian and Aoife were sitting on a single bed pushed up against the wall, both wearing headphones. On a low table in front of them were two tape-recorders built into overnight bags and connected to a small square suitcase that contained a mass of wires. These, Stephen saw, ran from the suitcase into the skirting board.

'For this relief much thanks,' said Aoife, taking her head-phones off. 'We're bored to tears. It's completely quiet up there. I bet Department Four have got it wrong.'

Damian slipped his headphones off and handed them to Charlotte, who immediately put them on. 'Shall I make you some coffee before we go?' he asked. 'There's milk, *mirabile dictu*.'

Charlotte freed an ear to hear him. 'Is there anything to eat?'

Time and again Stephen has imagined this: the urgency, the excitement, breathing when the target breathes, two hearts beating in one rhythm. But it is Helen's breath that he wants now, her heartbeat, not a stranger's. From above him comes the sound of a vacuum cleaner, 'Someone's upstairs,' he whispered.

'Of course,' said Aoife. 'He is doing his housework. He can't hear you unless you're very loud.'

'But nothing's happened so far?' Charlotte asked.

'Nothing. He has the radio on. We must have heard the Human League ten times, but that's better than Cliff Richard. So, you're on till eight, I guess? Good luck. The comms radio is there if you need to call an operative and the legs are out there somewhere, watching. But hey, Steve, don't try to take a look! Keep the curtains closed!'

'We know, we know,' said Charlotte. 'We don't need a lesson.'

'Keep your hair on,' Aoife said. 'We're off.' She tied a scarf around her head, waited for Damian to button up his raincoat and blew a kiss from the door before she closed it.

Stephen sat down on the bed beside Charlotte. 'What now?' he mouthed.

'He's still hoovering. We both need to listen, though, in case one of us misses something crucial.'

Stephen put on Aoife's discarded headphones. They were still warm. He drank some of the coffee. Charlotte had made herself as comfortable as she could, using a stained pillow as a backrest and sitting cross-legged on the bed, shoes off. Her feet were surprisingly small and shapely. He listened for a while to the vacuum cleaner and, when that stopped, the scrape of furniture being moved across the floor, the music on the radio and the voice of the announcer. There was no other voice. He felt himself drifting into sleep and shook himself awake. What would Helen be doing now? Hanging a silver star onto a tree, walking along a beach alone, where the salt-wind strokes her face and blows the gold hair off her forehead? Thoughts of Helen are as lifeblood constantly pulsing through his veins. She is his still point; the fixed foot of the compass to which he must return, however far he strays. What is this – this dismal room in a dingy flat in an unknown part of London, the unknown man in the flat above, now pacing up and down like a creature in a cage, the woman sitting close to him, her blue skirt rucked up around her thighs – but a deviation from the purpose of his story?

Charlotte nudged him awake and leaned over to push an earpiece off. The V-neck of her jumper showed the line between her breasts; she smelled of smoke and roses. 'I'm going to make more coffee – Damian's was filthy. Do you want a cup? Will you be okay on your own for a few minutes? I need to use the loo.'

In the flat above the man had finished his cleaning. He had also switched the radio off. It was very quiet. Charlotte came back with coffee, a packet of Rich Tea biscuits and an ashtray. 'Look what I found,' she said. Stephen ate two of the biscuits, letting the dry crumbs soften to fill and coat his mouth; Charlotte searched in her handbag for cigarettes and lit one. They sat side-by-side, attending to the absence of sound, cut off from the sounds outside and the sounds they themselves were making by their headphones.

Boredom is the condition of the listener. They might have to stay like this for hours, Stephen thought. Charlotte was apparently rapt. He was drowsing off again when Charlotte dug her elbow in him. He heard the sound of a doorbell and reflexively stood up to look out of the window and down at the street below. Charlotte pulled him back. The man upstairs must have pressed a button to open the main door; there was half a minute's pause before the front door of the flat was opened. This visitor, whoever it was, had come straight past the door of Number 3 on the way up, a thought that thrilled but also brought with it a sense of danger. Stephen had been told nothing at all. Who were these people and what might they be doing? Were they gunmen or bombers?

The exchange that took place between the two men upstairs was brief.

'You are to come with me,' the first man said. 'The boys are waiting for you.'

'I have things to do; I'm not planning on stirring out tonight.'

'Yeah you are. The boys are wanting a couple of answers. Better they don't ask you the questions here. They would like to see you now.'

'Ah look, I'm grand here on my own. I haven't been too well. Tell the boys I'll meet them tomorrow.'

'Come on, Danno. Don't make it any harder on yourself.'

There was a scuffling, thudding sound and one of the men cried out. The sound of a body hitting something hard and solid – a tall cupboard or a wall? – and stifled distress. Charlotte picked up the two-way radio. 'Keep listening,' she mouthed at Stephen. He could not hear what she was saying but he saw how competent she was, and calm. He heard the door of the upstairs flat slam shut. Then silence followed.

Charlotte removed her headphones and gestured for Stephen to do the same. 'They've gone,' she said.

'I don't understand. What happened?'

'Not good news, I'd say, for Danno.'

'Who did you talk to on that radio?'

'The operative on duty.'

'What did he say?

'He said, "Fuck." Then he said, "That's not what we expected." Then he thanked me.'

'What *did* happen, though?'

'Well, it was pretty obvious, wasn't it? Danno's in big trouble; the boys probably think that he's a nark.'

'You mean an informer?'

Charlotte reached over to the suitcase with the wires and flicked one of the switches on and off. 'Just checking,' she said. 'Sometimes the microphones work two ways; we could be being recorded too. But we're not.'

'You seem to know a lot about this stuff.'

'Yes, well, before I was a listener, I worked in Tech.'

'Did you? I never knew.'

'You never asked.'

'So, what do you mean, a nark?'

'Steve, you went to Oxford; you're supposed to have a brain. And you've been through training. You know how the world works. All these groups are riddled with narks – all busily telling on each other, all in a great muddle, like a mass of tangled knots. Danno might have been working for us. But then he got caught. Or at least suspected. As I say, his career prospects are not good.'

'But the operative will have called the police, surely; they will intervene.'

'Maybe. If Department Four can safely cover its back. But if another informer is involved or . . . Oh come on, you know the score. Poor Danno.'

'What do we do now?'

'We wait here until someone arrives to stand us down. Would you like a cigarette for once?'

'No thanks.'

'Did you never smoke?'

'I'm considering taking up a pipe.'

'My dad smokes one,' said Charlotte.

While they waited they kept their headphones on in case anyone should come back to the upstairs flat but no one did, and they had nothing to do until eventually a message came by radio that they should leave the flat and make their way back to the place where they had been dropped off.

They switched off lights, checked the curtains and locked the door behind them. 'Put your arm around me,' Charlotte said. Linked like that they walked back up Arcadia Avenue and the hill. Ahead of them they could see the small white van but just before they reached it Charlotte stopped. Turning her face to Stephen's she kissed him on the lips, a hard, full kiss. 'Just in case,' she whispered. But in the van on the way back she said nothing.

The driver dropped them off in the garage of the Institute. Stephen had been waiting for Charlotte to suggest a drink or something to eat when they got back but she did not and nor did she say anything when they entered the lift. She pressed the button for the ground floor and when the lift stopped, she smiled goodbye and said she would see Stephen tomorrow.

He went on up to the third floor. He could still feel Charlotte's mouth on his, unfamiliar and unnerving; he rubbed a finger on his lower lip. The long room was dark and empty, everyone's belongings locked away. Along the corridor there would be listeners from Group II working through the night but their door was closed. Stephen sat down heavily at his desk. What should he do now? A profound weariness washed over him; he hardly had the strength to move; if only he could lay his head down on the cool surface of his desk and rest here for a while. But soon a guard would come prowling through the room: safer not to be found here with no reason. His sense of being a prisoner grew. The lines of light that edged in through the slatted blinds were like the bars of a sealed cage. He was very thirsty. Eventually he hauled himself up and unlocked his cupboard. It smelled of cheese. And there was something else that was not quite right: his in-tray had been moved. He was almost sure he had left it in its usual place; he always kept his cupboard tidy. But now it was shelved to the right of his card indices, not to the left. Well, he must have had an aberration when he put his things away in a hurry this afternoon. He closed the door again and double-checked the lock.

He knew he should go home now and find himself some food. But the pockets of his coat were filled with stones; there were shackles on his feet. Come on, he said to himself, aloud. Come on. A drink would help. He could look in at the Fox and Grapes, just for the one; the fire would be burning. If Alberic were there by any chance, they could have a drink together, or somebody else might feel like striking up a conversation. He wouldn't mind some company right now; his head was full of death and the night was altogether far too quiet.

'Sign here, please,' the guard at the entrance said as Stephen left. 'Do you have any idea how late it is?'

Thursday

Ana was in the long room lamenting to Louise on Thursday morning. 'I'm in no mood for a party. It was a debacle. Martin is beside himself. After all the work we did, to think that the bombing could have been pre-empted . . .'

'I know, I know,' Louise said soothingly. 'It's very sad. But worse things happen on a big ship. Sometimes that's how it goes. It's not your fault, Ana, nor Martin's.'

'Nevertheless, there will be an investigation.'

'Pretty grim, huh?' Damian said, collecting Stephen's coffee mug and eavesdropping on Ana. 'So, what did you do last night when it was over?'

'Nothing. I was bushed. Are we actually going to have the party?'

'Yes, it's now or never. Louise says it would be a crying shame to waste the food. Don't forget to tell your strategists and operatives, if you want them to be here.'

Stephen let that go. He had no intention of inviting Rollo Buckingham or anyone else to the listeners' party or of being there himself for any longer than he absolutely must. He'd leave as soon as everybody was too drunk to notice. Meanwhile there were yesterday's tapes to get through.

He checked on VULCAN first. An almost blank tape; again unanswered calls. GOODFELLOW, on the other hand, had been unseasonably busy setting up a solidarity front with the striking miners and trying to get it funded by the Soviet Embassy. To transcribe his several telephone conversations took up a satisfactory amount of time.

Stephen was minded to ignore the two envelopes that held the PHOENIX tapes. It seemed ridiculous to write a report on PHOENIX's Tuesday evening when he and Rollo already knew that PHOENIX had been at the Fox and Grapes. Could he not tell Rollo there was nothing to report? NTR – so easily said and done. But on second thoughts he realised that would be far too risky. He had to make quite sure that his reports and whatever Rollo knew from his own observation tallied absolutely. Above all, he must not betray by the smallest slip or indiscretion that he knew who PHOENIX was; it was vital to maintain the pretence of ignorance. If Rollo were to find out that he had been conducting his own private investigation, Stephen would be in real trouble. He was on the thinnest skim of ice and he had known it from the moment he set eyes on PHOENIX. The worm of anxiety that had hatched last Saturday morning was growing fast and chewing on his innards. Safer then to listen to the tapes.

21 December 1981:
    Subject of interest arrives at 22.51. Difficulty fitting his key into the front door lock and collisions with items of furniture suggest he may be drunk.
    23.27: Subject makes call to unidentified male. Lengthy conversation in Spanish, not understood.

Stephen did not listen to Jamie's side of this call, knowing that he'd hear them both on the unlabelled tape. In any case, it was interrupted by the changeover just after midnight. He had predicted that there would be nothing on the new tape – Wednesday 00.00–12.00 – except the subject's departure for work at around his usual time. But in fact at 08.47 the subject received a telephone call.

These calls were a major inconvenience. Enmeshed now in another narrative, the last thing Stephen wanted was to take outside evidence into account. But he had to admit that both calls were potentially significant. The first, when he listened to it in full, was evidently to a close friend or a relative: the conversation was long and the tone was intimate although Stephen thought he could detect a note of strain. By his voice the other speaker was an older man. The second call was from a woman, identifying herself by name as Allegra, ringing from upstairs.

'I didn't wake you, did I? I thought I might just catch you before you left for work. It was a really good evening, wasn't it? That band is amazing. God, though this morning I don't half need the Alka-Seltzer! So anyway, we were wondering if you might be at a loose end again tomorrow, seeing as you will still be on your own?'

Greenwood made polite but noncommittal noises that did not stop Allegra ploughing on. 'We're going to have supper at the Bistro Vino in South Kensington and we'd adore it if you joined us.' He declined at first, saying he had a meeting after work tomorrow and an early start on Friday but she was persistent and cajoling and Greenwood in the end gave in.

Stephen considered the possible implications. The first call was unusual. In normal circumstances he would have asked a linguist to translate the words he did not understand but the classification and the delicacy of this investigation meant that without authorisation he could not pass the tape to Ana or to Tomás, who together dealt with Spanish. But even if he could, he'd rather not commission an independent record of the call. Perhaps he should simply keep it to himself until after Christmas. Yes, that would probably be best.

The second call was mystifying too. Stephen recognised the name Allegra: Helen had telephoned her last week and asked about going to a party; later she had spoken of her in connection with a man named Marlow. Marlowe? He hadn't given Allegra any thought but, as Helen had implied that she lived upstairs, she must be a neighbour. So why, if she was in regular contact with Helen and Jamie, had Allegra been so insistent on seeing Jamie again tonight? Could it be that she wanted to see him on his own, apart from Helen?

Any minute now he would receive a summons from Rollo. Or Rollo would come striding into the room without forewarning. What was Stephen going to tell him? He had to work this out. He also had to find a way of returning to the system the broken cassette tape and the other two that he had borrowed. In outline he had a plan for this. With so many things on his mind, it was not until later that he thought about the seal on the second of the PHOENIX envelopes. It must have been intact when he took the envelope from his in-tray or he would have noticed, but there something about it that was vaguely troubling him.

From the end of the room Louise called out: 'Hey, team! Could I have your attention? Do, please, gather round. As we're going to have the party in here, could we get everything cleared away by five? Now, Muriel would like to brief us on what's going to happen over Christmas.'

Muriel, standing on a chair, announced that there would be no late delivery this afternoon. Telephone intercept would continue automatically, with the product available after the twenty-eighth. Coverage would also be maintained on all Bravo targets, unless otherwise instructed by an analyst or strategist. Tapes would be registered on Tuesday. There were no Alpha operations scheduled. If anyone knew of an investigation that might call for extra cover between now and then, would they please tell her at once.

'Super,' said Louise. 'It sounds like we are all going to get the holiday we need, a decent break. And you all deserve it! Well done, everybody, for a great year's work! You're real stars! However, to be on the safe side, I'd better have your contact numbers over the next few days. Here's the list, please fill in yours and pass it on. Anyone who needs a lunchbreak, do take one but, wherever you're going, or if you have a meeting, please be back by three. We're going to do our pressies then, to get into the party spirit. Don't eat too much lunch; I might have a little something to go with the lovely parcels! After that I'd be glad of volunteers to get the room ready and set out the food.'

At this rate, Stephen thought, there might just be a chance of evading Rollo. It was nearly one o'clock. Except he didn't know what Rollo had arranged about recordings. Were eavesdropping devices easy to switch off? Or would they continue to hear nothing in an empty building, unregistered and unrecorded?

Just then the red light on his telephone flashed. It was Rhona Gray, the strategist whose cases included VULCAN and Solly's Communists. 'Might I pop down?' she asked.

'I was just on my way out.'

'It won't take long.'

Rhona was likeable and efficient; on an ordinary day, Stephen would have been quite pleased to see her. Now all he could think of was escaping from the room. The longer he was there, the more likely he'd be caught before he had had time to get his stories straight. He watched her impatiently as she stopped to greet Louise and then to talk to Solly. When at last she got to Stephen, she said: 'Thanks for the invite to your party!'

'Um, I don't . . .'

'It's all right, Solly already asked me – I'll be there! But I didn't come to chat about the party. I came to tell you that VULCAN is dead.'

'What?'

'Strathclyde told me just now. He's been dead some time, apparently. A milkman called a neighbour and the neighbour called the police. Did you not know that anything was amiss?'

'I knew he was not well. He had an appointment with the doctor.'

'But he didn't ring anyone else?'

'There were a few unanswered calls.'

'I'll get the numbers traced. Look, I don't want to make a big thing of it, but I would have liked to know about the unanswered calls.'

'But what could you have done?'

'I could have got the fuzz to check on him, via another party. They have loads of informers there.'

'I'm sorry. Poor VULCAN. I'll miss him, he was sort of like a friend.' I loved that man, he wanted to say but couldn't.

'Yes, well, they're all growing old, that lot. But his end was rather sad. Anyway, could you do me a last write-up after Christmas? Then we'll formally close the case and that'll be the end of that.'

'Am I interrupting?'

Stephen, his thoughts full of VULCAN's last imagined moments and the possible consequences of Rhona tracing the unanswered calls, had not noticed Rollo until he was looming above his desk. 'Not at all,' Rhona said. 'I was just leaving, thanks.'

Rollo said: 'I've come to see if you'd like a pint?'

'What?'

'Have you had lunch?'

'Not yet. I'm running short of time. I have a lot to do this afternoon.'

'I won't keep you long. I thought it would be nicer to have a drink together than going to the Cube. Let's go up to the bar, come on.'

I'd rather the guillotine, thought Stephen, allowing himself perforce to be led by Rollo who, disdaining the lift, took the stairs two at a time. Trailing behind him, Stephen could not but notice the unscuffed leather of his perfect shoes.

The bar was heaving. This was the only place where members of the Institute could loosen their guard a little, and learn each other's names. Those who did not drink or who disliked that hot dark room must stay in the tight circles of their sections, knowing no one but their immediate colleagues. Today, with the staff in an end-of-term mood, the bar was especially popular. On any normal day it was fine to get a little drunk; today you could get plastered.

'What will you have?'

Stephen tasted the inside of his mouth. His tongue felt as if it had been harshly sanded before being coated with a sour, thick paste. He wanted sweetness on it – syrup, honey – not the prickling yeast of beer, but now was not the time to depart from the persona he had invented. No one – and Rollo least of all – must be allowed to see the vulnerable flesh beneath the shell.

'I'll have a pint of Courage, please.'

'Why don't you wedge yourself into that corner by the window? No point both of us fighting through the mob.'

For the second time that week, Stephen watched Rollo's gilded head rising above a field of duller ones – the greys, the hues of mouse, the pinkish scalps – and the crush seeming to part before him, yielding the way. He was a sun king, beautiful, and sheer hatred coursed through Stephen.

Rollo came back with the beer and a glass of orange juice. 'Cheers,' he said. He drank his juice in two gulps, put the glass down on the window sill and lit a cigarette. 'Often the best way of having a confidential chat is to do it in a crowd. So, you going anywhere for Christmas?'

'Oxfordshire. And you?'

'Snap, as a matter of fact. Parents, not far from Chipping Norton.'

'That's nice.'

'Yes, it is actually. Taking the whole time off? No more overtime or extra duty?'

'Not unless I'm asked to do some. Which reminds me: what arrangements have you made for . . . ?'

Rollo stopped him before he could say the word. 'That's what

I want to talk about. I'm pulling the plug on it today. We've got as far as we're going to get and that is far enough. There's just one more thing to look at and so we're going in tonight.'

'In where?'

'Into the flat, of course.'

'But he's not going to Orford till tomorrow.'

'That's right. But he won't be at home tonight.'

'How do you know?'

'I just do. And so do you, I think. You must have heard the call.'

'I don't know what you're saying. I'm not up to date. I was just getting to yesterday's tapes when you came in; I've been away on operational duty.'

'I heard. Louise said, when I asked where you were yesterday. But anyway. If you could wrap up whatever's left, in the interests of tidiness, I'd appreciate it. We'll take the stuff away when we go in tonight.'

'And that's it? Just like that? You're not going to tell me what it was all about and who Jamie was spying for?'

'Ssh. No names! Please keep your voice down, Stephen. And no, I can't tell you any more than you already know. I said in the beginning that I couldn't give you any information about this investigation. But there is one thing I want to ask. You didn't report it, but did you ever hear the subject mention an unexpected gift of money or money coming from an unusual source?'

Claudio has given me . . . A late wedding present is what he said. No, it's true he had not reported that but why should he do so now? Why should he tell Rollo anything when Rollo had lost all interest in the case?

238

'No, I don't remember any unusual references to money.'

'Okay, fine, that's what I thought. Well, thanks very much for all you've done. My Director said to pass on his thanks too. And, of course, I do not need to say that this investigation stays top secret even when it's closed. Do you want another one of those?'

'No thanks.'

'Right. I'll be off then. I might see you later at the party; when does it kick off? Okay then, thanks. If I don't see you, have a happy Christmas.' And Rollo turned on his heel.

Stephen is drifting unsecured through infinities of dark, a diver cut off from his air-supply; not in this world, falling, falling; he has forgotten how to breathe. He opens his mouth to call for help but no sound comes out and even if it had, no one would hear him. Helen, Helen, oh let my cry come unto thee, after this my exile. The room is rocking round him; he is suffocating in the noise and smoke. What he needs is strong drink to thaw his leaden nerves and warm the chilled marrow of his bones.

Some time later Stephen made his way back to the long room. While in the bar he had arrived at the idea of pleading a recurrence of his toothache, collecting his coat and going home. But he had forgotten the ritual of the Christmas presents. When he walked into the room, he found the listeners waiting for him, sitting in a circle around Louise's desk. On the desk were a plate of mince pies, a bottle of Asti Spumante and six clear plastic cups. 'Where have you been?' Louise asked mildly.

To ensure the anonymity of givers, the presents had been piled together in Louise's out-tray. Stephen had left his two parcels, both wrapped by shop assistants, in his cabinet on Tuesday; now, retrieving them, he saw that Christophine was not part of the waiting group. 'Have you labelled yours?' Louise asked.

'Was I supposed to?'

'Silly sausage! You know the Santas have to be top secret!'

'Well, this is for Christophine.'

'Oh, what a pity she's not here; she'd already booked an extra day; she was sad to miss the party. Give it to me. I'll make sure she gets it on Tuesday when we're back. What smart paper! And so beautifully wrapped. Harriet's not here either; I wonder if she caught that ferry? Who's the other parcel for?'

'That's not actually a Christmas present.'

'Oh? All right. Now, who's for a glass of bubbly? Charlotte, would you be a duck and pass round the mince pies? Made to my granny's recipe!'

One by one the listeners of Group III unwrap their Christmas presents: the bottles of wine, the soaps, the bath salts and the chocolates. Muriel has been adopted by the group for the duration. Stephen's present is a contraption of suspended metal balls that click rhythmically together when they are set in motion: 'It's meant to help when you are anxious,' Greta says.

The wine is fizzy in the mouth, the filling of the pies is piercingly sugary. Stephen takes another when the plate comes round again; Damian refills his cup. 'Here's to us!' Louise says, toasting her team and laughing.

The smaller parcel is still on Stephen's lap. 'So, who *is* it for?' asks Charlotte. 'For you, in fact,' he says. Charlotte, already the recipient of the bath salts, blushes deeply and the others look on, amused. She accepts the parcel and asks Stephen if she should open it now or later. He says later, but is overruled. Slowly, carefully, Charlotte peels away each scrap of Sellotape, leaving the paper intact; there is a second layer of white tissue within. She unfolds it and lifts out the tiny cardigan, white and as delicate as cobweb; she holds it up.

'Isn't that a bit small for you?' says Solly

'It's for the baby that was sick, Charlotte's baby,' Stephen says.

Charlotte, not having spoken, looking stunned, now stands up says: 'Oh, Steve!' and starts to cry. Once she starts, she cannot stop. She stumbles past Louise, Solly and Damian to Stephen and, bending clumsily, she throws her arms around him, her face pressed to his shoulder, sobbing still. He keeps his own arms stiffly at his sides, at a loss to comfort her, and Louise says: 'Stevie, that was so dear of you!' and breaks the spell. Everyone is smiling now and handing the cardigan around, the better to admire the lacy wool, the silky ribbons. 'Who'd like another pie?' asks Greta.

Outside, more snow is falling. 'We must close the blinds,' Louise says. 'And now I'm off to the kitchen to make sandwiches – does anybody want to help?'

'I will,' Muriel says, and Charlotte goes with them.

Now what? Having eaten mince pies with his colleagues, smiling and nodding all the while, is it too late to say he is in agony and really must go home? Stephen is feeling rather giddy. His head is like a snow globe, if he shook it, it would fill with a thousand flakes of muddled thoughts. This is terrible. He cannot leave and yet he cannot stay. It's like being stuck in quicksand with no idea how fast the tide is coming in.

He went back to his desk, put his headphones on and

pretended to listen to a tape. In fact, there were none he had not already scanned. Having lost two targets in one day, and with OBERON away, ODIN putting up his Christmas lights, even GOODFELLOW expected at his mum's – everyone going about their lives in ways that could not be of any interest to even the most obsessive strategist – there was nothing for him to do except sink deeper in the sand.

It was half past four. He wrote his last report on VULCAN, listing the times of all the calls the old man did not answer, apart from the ones that Stephen had made himself; noting that he had not been heard since Thursday, exactly a week ago; writing in his flowing hand: *Nothing further to report.* To whom could he report his own sorrow? Who would share with him the horrifying thought of VULCAN slowly dying all alone, or the guilt of knowing that there was something he could have done to save him? He slid the report sheet into an envelope and marked it for the final time: *Confidential for RWG/Department Two.* If she – Rhona – asked for checks to be done on the telephone line, she'd find the secret number of the Institute, and what would she do then? With luck, she would not bother to make enquiries but would accept instead the evidence of the last report. For her the case was in the past and easily forgotten.

Damian was the only other person still working at his desk, clacking away at his typewriter keys, his headphones firmly on. The rest of the listeners had already stowed away their papers and machines, and gone. Stephen began to tidy his. He stacked his empty in-tray underneath the out-tray, in which he placed Rhona's envelope and the finished tapes. Cleared for wiping and re-use. He put his blank report sheets, his pins and paper clips and treasury tags, into the top drawer of his desk. The borrowed tapes were still in his jacket pocket. As he was about to seal them in an envelope, it occurred to him that he might never have a record of Helen's voice again and he slipped them back. After a second's thought he put the tape of Greenwood's recent telephone calls into his pocket too.

Wearily, stiffly, like a much older man, Stephen got up to move his things from his desk to his safe cabinet. In the cabinet he saw the Fortnum's bag of biscuits and cheese. Well, it might as well be used. After he'd locked everything else away he would take it down to Louise and Charlotte in what was called the kitchen, although it only contained a fridge, a kettle and a sink.

The kitchen was at the end of the corridor, beyond the rooms of the other two groups and Muriel's small office. Passing Muriel's door, he noticed it was open and he had a new idea. He looked inside: she was not there, but files and folders were piled on her desk.

This was strictly against the rules. Security came down heavily upon anyone caught leaving documents and files unguarded. In the long room there had to be at least one listener in attendance if a cabinet was open. Muriel must have popped out for a moment, taking an uncharacteristic risk.

Stephen looked up and down the corridor. Voices and laughter were coming from the kitchen but there was no one in sight. He ducked into Muriel's room. He had meant to drop the broken tape into one of her trays but, as there were no trays on her desk, he poked it into the narrow space between the back of the nearest cabinet and the wall. If Security should spot it there before she did, Muriel would be in real trouble but Stephen couldn't help that.

Then he saw that the door of the cabinet in which she kept the safe-box was wide open. He was irresistibly impelled towards it. As if in a dream he withdrew the box and it was unlocked too. If this was a dream, he was desperate not to wake.

PHOENIX's file. P. In the second half of the alphabet. He didn't have time to flick through all the files in search of it; he could at any moment be discovered in the act. Instead he pulled out a handful from the middle of the pile and stuffed them into his carrier bag. As quickly as he had entered, he left the room and went on his way to find Charlotte and Louise.

At the far end of the room a table, pitchers full of something green, bottles of beer and wine. The room is filling with people: Ivan, Vladimir, Magda, Adam, Edouard, Imran, Rafiq, Aoife, Mohammed, Thaddeus, Natalia, Ana, Martin, Muriel, the listeners of Group III and their selected guests; more of them keep pouring through the door. Invitations to the listeners' Christmas party are sought after: it's an unmissable event. The Sub-director of Technical Services and Support is there; the Director himself is rumoured to be putting in a brief appearance; strategists, analysts and operatives have descended from the top floors for the evening. Thaddeus has connected his tape-recorder to a pair of large loudspeakers and in place of whispering voices music is crashing out.

Stephen does not recognise the music, which is already at a volume that discourages conversation and will get louder still. That's good. He doesn't want to talk, he wants to drink this emerald liquid which tastes of mint and lime; it's cool, it's cleansing, it's clear streams through mountain meadows, icy waterfalls. He takes a pitcher from the table; he will walk around the room filling people's glasses – in that way he will look like a belonger, like a host, and he can fill his own. 'Hello,' Rhona says, smiling at him and holding out her glass, 'What's in this? Is it absinthe?'

'It might be, I don't know.'

'Well, absinthe makes the heart grow fonder, so they say.'

'Chasing the green fairy,' Adam, standing next to Rhona, says, and Charlotte, coming up to join them, laughs with pleasure. 'That's what Edouard calls this concoction – *la fée verte*.'

'Is absinthe the same as wormwood?' Rhona is asking but Stephen turns away before Adam can answer; he doesn't need to know. Wormwood, bitter gall. Drink it down, this Lethean cocktail, it slides like green ice down the throat and numbs your tight-stretched nerves. First chill, then stupor, then the letting go, have another and pour what's left into the nearest glass, the bass notes of the music thud.

Solly is circulating with a plate of sausage rolls, Louise is tendering sandwiches: ham, cheese, tuna and salami; there's more cheese on the table, the Stilton Stephen bought. Cheese and pineapple on sticks. Don't fuss about food, it sticks in the throat, you could easily choke to death on a cocktail sausage; besides, it soaks up the drink and turns it into moss. Or swamp-grass. Marsh-grass, samphire, sapphires and garlic in the mud, no that's not it, marram, the grimpen mire where the monsters live. Grendel in the snake-infested depths, oh lend me your sword and shield, why is this pitcher empty?

The music is different now, as Ivan has changed the tape. It's the music of the steppes, of bareback riders on wild horses, of the tundra, of the frozen wastes, it's Leningrad sorrowing for Petersburg, it's homesickness for places never visited and it brings the sting of tears to Stephen's eyes. But it is making Ivan happy, and Thaddeus and Rafiq; they have linked arms, are kicking out their legs and dancing and others are joining in. No one seems sad at all. Martin has the highest kick, the onlookers clap and cheer.

'Stevie, do you feel like passing the quiches around?'

'I'm quite happy doing drinks; has Edouard gone to mix another jug?'

Indeed Edouard conjures up more nectar and Mohammed calls out that it is time to hear some real music. A babel of melody, stridor, stramash, how is it that it plucks your heartstrings, makes them quiver, my monkish life is quiet but for the ringing in my ears. Tintinnabulation, hark now I hear them ding dong bell, 'Don't forget the avocado dip,' Greta is instructing Solly.

Now there is another tape, reversion, and he does know this: it's Giles; it's Giles's number-one hit and it is strange to hear that high voice in this room, *mon semblable, mon frère*, when we were boys together we did not know the men we would become. If I had known what I know now, I would have lived my life another way.

Charlotte is swaying through the crowd, holding out her hands. 'It's your best friend!' she says, 'Come on, Steve, you've got to dance!' He resists, he ardently protests, he stands his ground, his legs stiff and his feet firmly rooted to the carpet but she will not be daunted. She grabs the jug that he is clutching to him, thrusts it at Damian who is spurring her on, seizes Stephen by the hand and drags him to the cleared space at the other end of the room where there are couples dancing. Giles's taunting voice, his heart-breaking voice, and the drum beat throbbing and Charlotte with his hand in hers, flourishing her free arm and waggling her hips. The music slows and she draws him to her, throws her arms around him, she is as tall as he is, he can feel her breasts against his chest, he links his arms around her waist, her mouth an inch from his, scent of smoke and wine. Stephen's head is spinning, the entire world is spinning, the drum beats are his heartbeats, she is hot against him, human in his arms and solid, and he is leaning a fraction closer, her mouth a moth-wing's width away, when horrifying-ly he sees over her shoulder Rollo Buckingham and PHOENIX, twin cocks of the walk, the dark and the fair, both swaggering toward them through the knot of dancers. Charlotte, intent on him, is oblivious to them until Greenwood claps both hands across her eyes and holds them there as blindfold. 'Guess who?' he says, and his voice is not his own. Charlotte, letting go of Stephen, tugs at the hands to break their clasp, twists round and greets the man: 'Oh Marlow McPherson, you wicked thing!' she says and she is laughing. 'What do you think you're doing – you gave me quite a fright!'

The white rim of the toilet bowl is cold against his forehead, the floor of the cubicle is lurching, he is sicking up green slime. He must get out of here, he must go home, if he just waits a little while, maybe the world will steady down. No one else is here as witness, he can stagger to a basin, sluice his face and drink some water from the tap. The water helps. The basin is next to a window, he can open it, he does, and icy air flows in on him like judgement.

Later he will not remember how he managed to collect his coat and his belongings from the long room and to leave with-out a word to anyone, not even a goodbye. He will remember

Charlotte looking bewildered and upset. Even if he could have found the words to tell her why he turned from her abruptly when she was trying to include him in her bantering with Marlow, why he staggered like a man poleaxed straight out of the room, he could not have spoken them. He felt himself to be literally dumbfounded. The ground beneath his feet would never again be solid.

He will remember encountering a security guard at the main door of the Institute and becoming confusedly aware of the top-secret folders he was carrying in a Fortnum's bag and the orange-label tape in his pocket. 'Been at the party on the third floor?' the guard had asked. 'No need to sign the late list, sir.'

What might have happened on his way home has vanished into a black crevasse of memory but he does recall that as he was fumbling with his keys at his front door, the telephone inside was ringing and ringing. He cannot be sure exactly what was said, though through successive waves of nausea and misery he registered that Alberic seemed rather irritated. He'd been trying to get through to Stephen all evening and he tried yesterday as well; has Stephen forgotten what they have agreed?

Then what else could Stephen do but agree again? And, having concurred with some arrangement, of which the only distinct element is that Alberic will come to fetch him in the morning, he also recollected that he should telephone his mother.

Is there a word for the day before Christmas Eve, or the evening of the day before? There should be, shouldn't there? – in honour of the mother. He was born at dead of night – well, according to the carols – it came upon a midnight clear, didn't it? – that glorious song of old – and everybody knows that first-time mothers tend to take a very long time in labour. For Coralie it was two entire days. Or thereabouts. She'd heard tell that it was quicker next time but as she'd only had one go at it, she couldn't say, herself. Nowadays they advise you to bide at home as long as you can bear it and only go to hospital when the pains are coming fast. You see them on the telly – women making cups of tea in their immaculate kitchens with nary a groan or grimace until the final moment, when off they trot – no, off they drive, as passengers in reliable cars – escorted by their husbands, to shiny, modern hospitals where they are greeted by beaming midwives and said husbands tenderly massage their aching backs. It had not been like that for her. Spencer, far from kneading the small of her back, was somewhere else at the time: in the pub, perhaps, or in someone's bed. Someone else's bed, that is, not hers. All right, that might be a bit unfair, but given what happened afterwards it's not impossible, although improbable, you'd have to say, and the worst of it, of what happened later, was that little Stephen saw it. God knows what it might do to a child, to see his daddy rutting away, a bare white bottom like a rising moon, bumping up and down above a stranger. Stephen had never mentioned it and she had never asked – well, she couldn't, could she – I mean, how could anybody talk about a thing like that? Spencer. He said he was at work. He'd turned up when it was done, clutching a bunch of tulips. Tulips never were her favourite flower – too stiff, too upright, reminding Coralie with their buttoned-up cups of guardsmen in their busbies, or regimented rows of graves. If only Spencer had brought armfuls of wild roses, honeysuckle, lavender, flowers that grow shyly in hedgerows and hold the scent of summer. Coralie had set sweet peas on Henrietta's grave. And that must have been hard for Spencer too; she must be fair.

Anyway, in all likelihood, His mother must have begun her labour the night before Christmas Eve. Poor thing. Such a hard time she must have had – jolting through the frosty desert on a stubborn donkey, no one with her but her geriatric husband; her mother and her womenfolk a long way off – and then to find no shelter but a stable. They describe it as a stable, which makes it sound reasonably dry and warm but chances are that it was actually a cave. A dark place – lightless except for one dim torch – stony, damp and very cold. And outside, the snow. That star, the bright star shining in the sky, obscured by snow and in any case invisible within the cave. The ox and ass – for all their soulful understanding, and doesn't legend have it that birds and animals can talk on Christmas Eve? – still having to be true to their beastly natures and standing deep in dung. The stink of it in steaming heaps, the black stone of the stable wall streaming with icy water and in the middle of it all, a maiden labouring on her own. There is no pain in the world to match the pain of childbirth, no matter whether you are giving birth to human twins or to the Son of God.

Who cut the cord of Baby Jesus? Who wiped away the blood? Mary, you must have been so lonely and afraid but be thankful that you never had to worry about Christmas. Not that Coralie is worrying now. It is too late for that. All that can be done is done, and she is glad she had the foresight to extract the giblets from the turkey before it took up its residence in Stephen's car. Groping in its cavity, now she came to think of it, was fittingly obstetric – but the result is that she has already made the stock. There it sits, sherry-brown and fragrant, in the fridge.

She has resisted the temptation to prepare the sprouts tonight; she'll do them tomorrow. It's too late now or maybe it's too soon. *Stille Nacht, heilige Nacht*, earth stood hard as iron, water like a stone. Stephen will be home tomorrow. Together they will listen to the carols from King's; at bedtime he will hang his stocking by the gas fire and, last of all, he'll lay the baby in the manger, according to tradition. Yes, Coralie is looking forward to tomorrow, Christmas Eve. But it is late now, and the snow's still falling – who can that be, ringing on the telephone? It stops her heart, that shrilling in the middle of the night; in the silence of the night it warns of death.

Christmas Eve

Another persistent ringing woke Stephen in the morning. The sound had pierced his dreams and snaked deep into them before he came to consciousness, and for some time he could not tell if it was real or not. Then he realised that there was someone at the door: Alberic, oh God. He had forgotten. Even now that he was awake, he could not properly remember. He didn't think he had invited Alberic to the flat but perhaps he had; he had certainly given him the address. He got out of bed and immediately needed to lie down. His head had never hurt so much and his eyes refused to focus. If he lay down and ignored the doorbell, would Alberic go away?

Evidently he would not. Now, from the bedroom, Stephen heard him rattling the letter box and knocking on the glass of the bay window at the front. There was nothing for it – the upstairs neighbour must have heard him and might come down to find out what he wanted – Stephen would have to let him in. He put on his dressing gown and shuffled to the door.

Alberic was wearing a camel-hair coat, carrying a suitcase and looking very sleek. 'Rise and shine!' he said. 'At long bloody last. Good morning, my friend. You surely took your time about coming to the door; you must have been sleeping the sleep of the dead.'

'What time is it?'

'It's twenty past nine. We should be off if we will make the most of daylight and the birds.'

'What?'

'At Orford Ness, of course.'

Memories were slowly filtering into Stephen's mind, like drops of rain through thickest undergrowth. Orford. Yes. A plan that even in a daze of wine and music he had dismissed as nothing more than a midwinter night's delusion. And now it seemed the man had really meant it. Fleetingly he thought of making some excuse why not to go; the implausibility of the idea was evident in spite of his befuddled head. But there was Alberic, expectant, standing on the doorstep, somehow credible, and in Orford there was Helen. A fact, whatever else. And otherwise what else was there but vast eternal deserts?

'Come in,' he said. 'I'll go and get dressed.'

Alberic in his shades of caramel and sand followed Stephen into the front room. Stephen, seeing it through his eyes, was uncomfortably reminded of its shabbiness, of the worn and greasy patches on the sofa, the dingy carpet, the pervasive odour of oven chips and takeaways and the fried fat of past meals that hung there always and was almost tangible, as if the molecules of grease had over time become a sort of net.

'Would you like some coffee?' he asked, trying to remember if there was any milk.

Alberic looked around him. 'No thanks. We could stop for breakfast on the way if you are hungry.'

On the way? He hoped that Alberic knew where they were going. Suffolk: country clothes? Still befogged he put on light-brown corduroy trousers, a checked shirt and a tweed jacket; polished brogues. Now at least he looked like the man that

253

Alberic expected, the man he wanted the world to see, even if his furnishings belied him. He had not anticipated a visitor to the flat so soon.

Had Alberic suggested that they would stay the night? Stephen, slowly reassembling the scattered shards of memory recollected: yes. It was Christmas Eve. He packed his toothbrush, his shaving things and some spare clothes in a bag. He still felt very weak and very sick and the events of last night's party were as incomprehensible and enigmatic in his memory as a dream.

When he went back into the room he found Alberic intently studying the contents of his bookcase. The Fortnum's carrier bag that Stephen had brought home was not where he thought he had left it, on the floor beside his coat, but placed neatly on a chair. Catching sight of it he remembered those folders – well, too bad; there was nothing he could do about them until after Christmas. He hadn't even looked at them last night and he didn't yet know if the PHOENIX papers were among them. He left them where they were. At the last minute he also remembered Helen's present. Thank heavens it was still safely with the brooch he had bought for his mother, in the pocket of his other suit. He put both small parcels in his bag.

'Super!' said Alberic. 'Thunderbirds have go? Where do you leave your car, then? Is it on the street?'

'My car?'

'Yes.'

'Oh, I think I thought we'd go in yours.'

'The brakes are making trouble in my car. It's better that you drive.'

'But I don't know the way.'

'No problem! We will follow signs and it will be straightforward, totally.'

Miserably, shakily, Stephen locked his front door and
unlocked the passenger door of the Datsun, which was parked
outside where he had left it on Sunday morning.

'Your car is the colour of my toothpaste. Maybe I would put
my suitcase in the boot?'

Stephen opened the boot for Alberic. Inside it was the
turkey bought with his mum on Saturday that he had completely overlooked. There it squatted, pallid and peculiarly
baleful, like the complicated residue of an act of necromancy.
Alberic said nothing but set his suitcase down beside it. Stephen could only hope it would survive the journey. It would
get rather warm, being driven about all day – might it start
to rot? Should he ask Alberic to wait while he tried to stuff it
into his fridge? No, it would never fit even if he took out both
the shelves and the other contents; the fridge was tiny, otherwise he'd have stowed the turkey there before. He looked at
it helplessly, enquiringly, as if it might be able to suggest its
own solution. But it could not and he was in no state to find
one either.

Abandoning any sense of autonomy, he got into the driver's
seat. He needed a rest, he was suffering from the aftermath
of shock and it was easier to let Alberic take charge. But for a
terrifying moment he could not remember how to start the car.
Which was the brake and which the clutch? What should he
do when he had turned the key? The close proximity of Alberic
was disconcerting; he was not used to passengers, apart from
his mother, and the interior of the car felt very small.

They set off, jerkily. 'North and east,' said Alberic. 'North-east.

Turn left at the end of the road. We head for the North Circular, is my guess.'

North and east. The maze of outer London's roads and Stephen blindly trusting to an internal compass that had mostly been untested, to steer round Wormwood Scrubs, over railway lines, through Willesden, Harlesden, Stonebridge, Brentfield, past factories and houses, office blocks and shops; death has undone so many; Craven Park. He met the main road with relief: keep to it and carry on. You couldn't go straight on a circular road, that's a contradiction in terms. Who are the people living in these places where the snow is falling softly: Chadwell Heath and Romford? At Colchester there are signs to Ipswich.

Alberic's eyes were closed, he might be sleeping, it was hard to tell. The snow had given way to rain and Stephen went on driving east as if dreaming, guided by the signposts. He barely noticed the other traffic on the road. His windscreen wipers were inadequate but he could not stop to clear the glass: he must go on because otherwise he would not be able to start again, because the rolling of the wheels, the roar and rush of cars and lorries round him, the staccato rhythm of the wipers – Marlow-Marlow-Marlow – filled his head and drove out thought. At any cost, he must not let his mind retrieve more memories of the night before. His heart was beating irregularly, but sickeningly fast, and the fuel gauge was showing that he was running low but he'd take a chance on that, as he must on so much else. He had no idea how many miles there were to go: three-score miles and ten? Can he get there by light of day? Yes, but it's anybody's guess if he'll get back or what he'd find when he arrived.

Towards Woodbridge it was as if he and Alberic had crossed

into another world. Suburban sprawl and main roads ceded to fields and woodland, the rain stopped to catch its breath and pale sunshine streaked the clouds. Stephen wound his window down and scented saltwater on the breeze. A faint trace of a childhood pleasure stirred in him: anticipation of the sea. The incoming rush of air woke Alberic or made him open his eyes.

'We're nearly there,' said Stephen.

'Oh, tally-ho! What a great driver you are. From now on you will be known as Sterling Moss.'

The closer they got to Orford, the more animated Alberic became. 'There's a song,' he said. 'Do you know it? "*Oh, we do like to be beside the seaside*" – how does it go on?'

'I hope you're not going to be disappointed,' Stephen said, noting the flat land, the absence of sand or beach.

'Ah no, it is truly delightful to be here. We will walk to Orford Ness and quickly spot the birds. Look, the sun is shining on us, what a sign that is. It's a perfect day for your lady-love to be going for a stroll.'

'And there's a rainbow to the west.' A rainbow, that's a covenant – if only that were true, if only you could still believe in promises, in God.

Stephen stopped the car next to a church and they both got out. Alberic, it seemed, was determined to stride out at once in the direction of the sea but Stephen was not sure if he could stand unaided, far less walk. 'I think I need something to eat,' he begged.

Alberic looked a bit annoyed. 'There don't appear to be any restaurants here,' he said.

'There's a pub over there.'

'Okay, but will they make food today, on Christmas Eve? I

imagine not but if you really want, we'll see.'

It was a nice pub, warm, with woodsmoke sweetening the usual smells of beer and cigarettes. Walking into it was like walking into a party – no one was drinking on his own and everyone was talking to each other as if they were old friends. Stephen felt a strong desire to be befriended by them. They were welcoming to strangers; from behind the bar a woman smiled.

'You place the orders,' Alberic insisted. 'I'll take a bitter lemon.' Unaccountably he did not seem to be his usual self and he chose to sit at a table as far away from the people round the bar as possible, in the dimmest corner.

Consulted about food, the landlady looked doubtful. 'It's Christmas Eve,' she said. But, seeing Stephen's stricken face, she proposed a round of sandwiches and soon enough they came: satisfyingly thick ham in buttery white bread. With a Bloody Mary they worked like medicine and Stephen at last began to come alive. In spite of the wretchedness that was silting up his veins, it could almost be enjoyable, this seaside jaunt with Alberic. He would shut out of his mind his shattering mistake, for now; he would seal it up like radioactive waste encased in concrete and it would not undermine him. Just because he had been wrong about identifying PHOENIX did not mean that he was wrong about everything else. Although he might not know what PHOENIX looked like, he could still maintain he was a double agent. He'd be able to explain his reasoning to Helen, gently, carefully, when the right time came. And, although he might not have come to Orford of his own accord, lacking an address for Helen or a confident plan of action, he now felt sure that it was right to be here. In this misty, watery place he was near to Helen, and any minute now she could walk in through the door of this congenial pub and say hello to him.

But Alberic rejected his offer of another drink and made it clear that he did not approve of Stephen having one. Like a man with an appointment he constantly checked his watch. As soon as Stephen had finished, Alberic bustled him back into his coat and out of the pub door.

'That way,' he indicated.

They walked down to a quay. From a tall flagpole a Union Jack was flapping in the breeze and the wide river at their feet was khaki-brown. Across the water, over the gracile masts of sailing boats, they saw a desolate place of shingle and a collection of strange buildings – a tall black tower and barrack-blocks, two flat-roofed open structures that looked something like pago-das, listening masts, and a lighthouse in the distance – but it was immediately apparent that there was no direct way to it except by boat. Alberic cast wildly around and tugged uselessly at a lifebelt hanging on a wooden post as if he hoped to use it as a float. There was no one else about.

'Is there a ferry, do you suppose?'

'If so, there are no signs.'

'Maybe, if we go that way, we will find a bridge,' said Alberic, pointing to a path that led up onto the river wall and down-stream to their right.

Stephen followed him. The sickly sun had long since changed its mind and bowed out in favour of dark cloud but its brief spell of warmth had begun to thaw the topmost snow to slush. Alberic, pausing only to re-light his pipe, ploughed on. Grass patched with ice on both sides of the footpath, and to their left the salt marshes and the shingle of the Ness. At the river's edge a heron, standing as absolutely still as if it had been sculpted out of stone, and staring at the water. While Stephen watched, it all of a sudden darted its beak downward and withdrew it; something trapped in it writhed in a silver flash.

The river did not narrow. After less than a mile Alberic and Stephen reached a point at which the boundaries of land and water became still more confused: before them lay what might have been an island, and the path curved back inland; evidently there would be no bridge.

'We must return,' said Alberic. 'We must find a native to show us another way.'

Rain that had begun tentatively and softly, a scattering of drops that might have been sea spray, now grew more determined and a wind blew in from the North Sea.

'It's cold,' said Stephen. 'Why are we are trying to get there, what is there on the other side?'

'We'll see. I must say I am surprised you do not know. Now, hurry up. You will be warmer if you walk faster and you do not complain.'

They retraced their steps, huddled now against the driving rain. Alberic's camel-hair coat was pocked with mud, his city shoes presumably soaked through. In this weather there will be no one in the streets or on the quay, thought Stephen; even dedicated walkers will be sitting by their fires, at home or in that cosy pub. What hope is there of finding Helen now, in this place of marsh, mud and saltwater, where nothing but a belt of stone restrains the terrible sea?

Stephen was wrong about the complete absence of people. When he and Alberic got back to the quay they saw a man in yellow oilskins sorting out some tangle or other in the bottom of a rowing boat. 'Go ask him,' said Alberic, prodding Stephen with an elbow.

'Why don't you? I don't know what to ask. I don't know what we want to know or really why we're here.'

'You must be the one to ask in case I will not understand his rural accent. Ask him how to get across to the other side of the water.'

Through the sound of wind and clattering lanyards, Stephen called down to the man in the boat, who looked up in some surprise, his head below the level of the ground.

'I say, could you very kindly help us? We're trying to find a way that will take us over there, to that side of the river.'

The man was mightily amused. 'Well,' he said, 'you could walk there but you couldn't do that from here – you'd have to start from somewhere else.'

'From where?'

'From Aldeburgh, in point of fact.'

Alberic, listening intently, poked Stephen again. 'We will go there in the car,' he hissed.

'Oh, right. Well, thanks, that's very helpful. So we simply make our way to Aldeburgh and from there it will be obvious, the path?'

'It may. It's quicker, of course, by boat.'

'Of course. So, I don't suppose . . . ?'

'You don't suppose quite right. But mind, when you find the way, and it's a fairly long one, you won't be let onto the Ness.'

'Why not?'

The man laughed out loud. 'It's the Ministry, isn't it? Everybody knows that it's a prohibited place under the Act. Mind,

261

they're not testing bombs there any more, it's all radios and suchlike now, but it's top secret still, and besides, the previous tenants left behind enough unexploded ordinance to blow you and your friend to kingdom come.'

Alberic intervened. 'As a matter of fact,' he said, 'my friend here is an official of the Ministry of Defence and he actually has clearance.'

'Then clear your own way, squire. No boat round here will land you except you have a permit from the powers that be in writing. An official permit. Now you'd best make tracks for Aldeburgh, if that's where you're going, for this rain will come down harder soon and later there'll be snow.'

'Thanks,' said Stephen, turning after Alberic who had begun to walk away in the direction of the car. He caught him by the arm. 'Look, I'm sorry but you heard what he said. This is becoming a wild goose chase; now that we've seen enough to know we'll never get there, we should simply cut our losses and drive home.'

'What does it mean, a wild goose chase?'

'A hopeless quest. That's what it means – a mission doomed to fail.'

Alberic gave Stephen a disdainful look. Rain was dripping off his nose. 'I am disappointed. I took you for a man. To come all this way, for nothing? Let us chase that wild goose then. If you never try, you always lose.'

Goaded, Stephen squelched after Alberic to where they'd left the car. He wanted to protest. He wasn't here for gulls and avocets. He couldn't care less about the Ness. He was here for Helen. But now the weather was so grim that waterfowl were seeking shelter and no one but a mad boatman would dream of being out of doors. He opened his mouth to speak but something about the set of Alberic's shoulders made him close it. This new steeliness of Alberic's was a powerful deterrent and Stephen did not even dare suggest they stop for a hot drink.

As they neared the car, Stephen remembered the necessity of petrol; perhaps there would be somewhere on the road to Aldeburgh; a place that he already knew to be about ten miles from here. If not, they'd be stuck. He considered alerting Alberic to the situation but, once again noting that stern profile, kept his counsel, while hoping he had taken the swift onset of darkness into account. What they also needed was a map.

In the car, Alberic relit his pipe and closed his eyes again. Stephen kept his peeled for garages but there were none along the road. He calculated that he had enough fuel to get to Aldeburgh and back, but not to London, or to Didcot.

They came into Aldeburgh by the main road and followed it to the centre of the town. Even in the rain Stephen could see that it must be a lovely place but he was not in a position to appreciate it now. 'Get as near as possible,' Alberic instructed. 'From here we will walk south.'

'But it's a very long way away,' objected Stephen.

'No it's not. We came a roundabout way by road but now we go straight down.'

In dreams, in nightmares, this is what you do: you stumble over shingle in your slippery-soled shoes, you sink deep into it and the hard stone sucks your ankles; although you trudge for miles, you get nowhere. In the end you are exactly where you started; there can neither be an end nor a beginning when time has stopped, when sky and sea and land are of one substance and that barely substance but a nothingness of grey. Only the black struts of the groynes define an edge, and a flock of birds. The struts are the twisted limbs of the dead and when the birds, disturbed and nervous, take wing and swirl into the air, they disappear against the stormy water. When the cold rain turns to hail the cruel sting on your face is mirror of the stones in which you're drowning. You're a prisoner or a slave, you're completely worthless, and the wind – it is so loud it is deafening your ears, you will never hear again. In the distance, but always in the distance, never coming closer, is that wilderness of concrete and barbed wire where hidden bombs tick in their shallow graves. You have crossed these battlegrounds before: the monstrous towers of Didcot that overhung your childhood also cast their shadows on Harwell's nuclear reactors: the Atomic. Radiation seeps into the ground and into water, from there into your teeth and bones. Daddy worked at Harwell, he was a war hero but no one ever told you where he'd gone; it must have been the Bomb that got him and vaporised him like an angel in a halo of white light. In infant school we all did bomb drill: quickly, everybody, duck beneath your desks, stick your fingers in your ears and do keep calm. If you stick your fingers deep into your ears you hear the sea, the whisper of the sea not the thunder that the sea is now. Mrs Medlicott in her shell-pink jersey, cradle my head between your breasts, be haven, harbour, place of rest, this nightmare drags on and on.

Abruptly his fellow-traveller halted. He had been tramping steadily ahead of Stephen, saying nothing. Now he said: 'It's getting dark.'

'It is.'

'Soon we shall not see our hands before our eyes.'

'That's true.'

'Better we go back now and try again tomorrow?'

'Much better.'

There'd be time to dissuade Alberic from his cock-eyed plan this evening, when they were in the dry and in the warm. But warmth and shelter were a long way off and there were miles of shingle still to go in the gathering dark and biting cold. When later he recalls that winter journey, Stephen will hardly know how they managed to stagger back to Aldeburgh through the scourging rain but somehow they did, and finally they reached the sanctuary of the car. By then both men were drenched and shivering hard. There was snow in Stephen's bones in place of marrow. 'What now?' he asked.

'We find our hotel and we change our clothes.'

On the long trail back, Stephen had sought to fortify him-self with images of snugly curtained rooms, thick carpets, roaring fires and rare roast beef, a traditional hotel in keeping with Alberic's sumptuous tastes, a place where Helen might possibly call in for a glass of wine with friends on Christmas Eve. But it soon turned out that Alberic had a different sort of establishment in mind. Having consulted a note he had made in a small black book, he directed Stephen back onto the main road in the direction of Woodbridge and to a breeze-block prefab building that adjoined a dismal-looking roadside inn. There were no other cars in the car park and no one in the vestibule or in the unlit bar, although the door was open. Stephen, trailing water, expected Alberic to walk straight out again, seeing his mistake, but no, he marched up to the counter and banged his fist down hard upon a bell screwed into the wood, next to a plastic Santa. After he had rung it several times, a boy quite clearly roused from sleep, emerged through a beaded door screen.

'Reservation in the name of Stevens,' Alberic said tersely.
'One room was it?' smirked the boy, handing Alberic a key.

The room provided no surprises but at least there were two beds. As soon as the door had closed behind them, Alberic began unselfconsciously to strip off all his clothes and when he was quite naked, he hung his sodden coat and suit on hooks fixed to the wall. Bending to open his suitcase, he took out of it a white towelling robe and a pair of slippers. 'I'm going to have a long hot bath. Did you see a bathroom?'

'Along the corridor, I suppose.'

'Okay.'

Left to himself, Stephen took off his coat and jacket. He had a clean shirt in his bag but no other trousers; if he pressed himself against the rusting radiator that was just warm to the touch, this pair might dry a little. Luckily this morning he had remembered socks. Parting the grimy slats of a venetian blind he looked through the window at the late afternoon outside. What next? he asked himself aloud.

Quite a long time later, Alberic came back. 'Your turn. But I should warn you that the water is not running hot. However, it is somewhat less chilly than the rain.'

'It's snowing now,' said Stephen.

In his tepid bath he tried to scoop his scattered and fragmented thoughts together. The haze of unreality that had pervaded the whole day – and the past fortnight maybe – had been scoured away by the rain and hail, and it was as if he had been flayed. His hopes had formed a soft layer against the asperities of this world – thistledown and velvet – and now that they had gone, he was cruelly exposed. He looked down at his flaccid body, lapped by an inch or two of brackish water, and hated

266

what he saw. He needed a new strategy, a new suit of armour. But first he needed petrol and the answers to some questions: why hadn't Alberic booked that dismal room in his own name and what was he really looking for in Orford? Stephen had chosen to believe him when he said he loved bird-watching – or at least to close his ears to any undercurrent – because he didn't have the heart for disbelief. And the man had said that he was lonely. That was something Stephen understood. Things sometimes must be what they seem or all men would be lost in the cunning passages and the wilderness of mirrors. Stephen had had enough of living life as if he were enclosed by icy walls, and to free himself had placed his faith in what he saw before him. How else do people love? But God only knows how he should live now, in the knowledge that he had been so mortifyingly wrong.

He got out of the bath, dried himself approximately on an exiguous square of towel and put his wet trousers on. It was almost as cold inside this flimsy building as it was outdoors. In the room, Alberic was lying on one of the beds, his head propped on a pillow, an incongruously white sprawl against the orange of the dirty counterpane. His robe was untied and had fallen slightly open, revealing pale skin sparsely stippled with grey hair. He looked Stephen up and down. 'Have you no dry clothes?'

'I have a shirt. And socks.'

'You are going to catch your death. Better you borrow a pull-over; there's a red one in my suitcase.'

'Thanks.'

Stephen undid the catches of the case with caution, afraid of what it might contain, but there was nothing in it except neatly folded clothes. The red jumper was very bright and adorned with a motif of golf clubs. Stephen put it on. 'We're running low on petrol,' he said.

'So now you tell me? Why you don't think of it before? Where do you think you will find some, tonight or tomorrow?'

'Possibly I should go and look for a garage now.'

'If you ask my opinion, yes. You should definitely go, and you should hurry. Things will not stay open late tonight.'

'There's bound to be somewhere on the main road.'

'Well, you hope.'

'Do you want to come with me?'

'No. Thank you, I stay here.'

'What about dinner?'

'I will probably make do in the bar next door. I am sure that they sell crisps.'

'I'm hungry.'

'For a change! If you do find a petrol station, you can also buy some food.'

'I had rather imagined that we would spend the evening in Orford.'

'There was nowhere in Orford we could stay.'

'Oh, but, Helen . . .'

'Ah. Yes, so here is an idea: you go and see if you can find her too. After you have found the petrol, okay?'

'Shall I take the room key?'

'I shall not lock the door.'

Stephen put his tweed jacket on over the red jumper, collected the crescent moon from his overnight bag, picked up his sopping overcoat and said goodbye. Alberic, apparently intent on lighting his pipe, said something in reply that he did not hear.

Snowflakes like particles of dust milled in the sulphur light outside the door of the motel. Now there were lights on in the bar. Someone in there would tell him where he could buy some petrol; he went in. The sleepy boy was lounging on a bench with a girl whose blue hair stood around her head in spikes like a sea urchin's. Ooh, they couldn't be sure, at this time of day, and it being Christmas Eve and all, but he could try a place about ten minutes down the road.

Indeed there was a small garage a couple of miles away but the owner was just locking up. 'Sorry, mate,' he said. Desperation swept over Stephen like a tidal wave. He'd never get out of here. He caught hold of the man's hand. 'I have to get home for Christmas,' he pleaded. 'My mother is dying. This Christmas is her last.'

The man began the slow process of unlocking the pump and the doors. When the tank was full, Stephen followed him into the garage and spotted some tourist maps of the area on a little stand. He bought one and tipped the garage owner. 'Safe journey then,' the man said. 'Sorry about your mum.'

'Thank you. And a merry Christmas.'

One task successfully accomplished. Now for the rest. Stephen got into the car, studied the map and took a new way back to Orford.

It's Christmas Eve. Coralie Donaldson is staring abstractedly at the glowing filaments of the gas fire in her sitting room, holding her son's Christmas stocking on her knee. The stocking was once his father's: an old Army-issue sock, sludge green. Every year since Ste was one – twenty-seven years therefore – this sock has been set reverently beside the fireplace or, when there were no fires, by the closest equivalent, and yes, of course, a gas fire needs no chimney but that's never been the point – and tonight she does not know what she should do. She's in a very melancholy mood. This should be the happiest of nights but instead a deep grief has drifted over her like the dust that falls when you take some long-abandoned object off the top of a wardrobe, or the threads that mat in your mouth when you walk into a spider's web that you had not seen was there, and that almost choke you. That's how she feels: as if something too difficult to swallow was sticking in her throat. Should she put the stocking there, as Stephen would, if he were here, and fill it later, as she always did? Should she lay the Baby Jesus in his manger? In the old days Stephen had loved these rituals. And now they're nothing but a shared amusement, a small diversion for the two of them, but then that's not nothing, is it?

A cold foreboding of a time when she would have to spend her Christmases alone crept over her. She knew how lucky she had been. Stephen was a good boy and a loyal son: he'd never once said that he would rather take a holiday away at Christmas, or go skiing, or spend the time with friends. Young people do, don't they? They jet off to exotic places like Jamaica in search of winter sun, which is perfectly understandable when you consider how interminable and drab the English winters are. Sun is good for aching bones. But Stephen's never expressed any such desire, although he must know people with nice big country houses where Christmas would be fun. The sort of houses where they have trees as tall as real trees in forests, scenty pines, and huge log fires in their halls. Other people's children of necessity spend Christmases with in-laws, leaving their own mothers to make shift as best they may. One day Stephen will have in-laws – well, she ought to want him to have in-laws – but it's not that thought which is making her feel sad. It's hard to put a finger on why she feels afraid but it's obvious why she's worried. He had sounded very strange in that telephone call last night. Ill maybe, or maybe drunk, although that's not a possibility she'd welcome. It has crossed her mind that he might have made the call under duress. How else to explain its oddness? She had seriously considered informing the police. Called away on Christmas Eve for operational reasons? Well, yes, if it were wartime, that would be reasonable, what else could you expect? No respecter of high days and holidays, the enemy; emergencies happen in their own time, not to plan. But it is peacetime now. Or more or less. Stephen's job, as far as she knows, and though she asks no questions she is not ignorant, has not before these past few days required him to work out of hours and at weekends, so what is happening now?

And besides the worry about Stephen, she has many practical concerns. As always, by this time, she has everything all spick and span and ready for tomorrow: the spuds are in their water bath, the carrots and parsnips scraped, the sprouts prepared, the stuffing in the fridge. Stock, bread sauce, brandy butter, mince pies, yes. The one thing there is left to do is to pop the turkey in to roast. But when? Stephen had been so vague. I'll get there, Mum, he'd said, or rather, slurred. But when? He didn't say. He couldn't say and now she's in a quandary. A turkey needs at least six hours, even when it's on the small side, what with time to rest and so on. Normally they would eat at one. She'd set her alarm for five o'clock; leaving plenty of time for a cup of tea and unforeseen occurrences, she'd have the oven heated up and the bird in it at seven.

It was actually a miracle that she happened to have Mr Fisher's number. Being an old-fashioned gentleman, he didn't like the telephone, preferring to communicate by letter. But a while ago, last May it was, she'd happened to run into him at the entrance to the library and he had mentioned that he was about to have an op to cure a contracture of his hand. Oh, she'd said, you must let me know how it all goes but you might not be up to writing, seeing as it's your right hand that they're doing, and he had said that she could always telephone. So she'd noted his number with a pencil on her library ticket and, strangely, she had never got round to rubbing it off. When Stephen rang last night, she'd known exactly where to find the number in the morning: oh my goodness, otherwise she would have been in a pickle. Imagine Mr Fisher turning up as usual, punctual as ever, looking forward to his Christmas dinner and there being nothing to eat but vegetables and pudding. As it was, it had been awkward trying to explain the change of plan but he had understood; after all, he was in the Navy in the war. He'd assured her that she should not worry on his account; he'd fend for himself; he would decorate his fishfinger with a sprig of holly! But she couldn't bear to think of him all on his own on Christmas Day and missing his nice dinner, and in a flash of inspiration, while she was on the telephone, she'd suddenly thought: why not? Why not have their meal in the evening? Say seven o'clock? And Mr F, bless him, had been rather tickled by the scheme, remarking that it was somewhat unconventional but at his age that was no bad thing. When all is said and done, a change is as good as a rest. So that turned out all right, he'd appear at half past five and they would have a glass or two of sherry. But. But that was assuming Stephen came home by noon. And what if he did not? Coralie has no means of getting hold of him; she has no idea where he is. All that she can do is fret and pray and hope that he is not in trouble.

She already knows that she will not sleep a wink but it is almost midnight and she really ought to go to bed. She gets to her feet, pressing hard down with both hands on her knees for leverage, switches off first the fire and then the light. The last vestiges of heat flicker like glow-worms in the dark until they gradually fade out. Coralie pulls aside a corner of the curtain and sees the snow; she watches it falling for a while and then, leaving Stephen's stocking unfilled by the extinguished fire, she slowly makes her way upstairs.

It's Christmas Eve. In the windows of the cottages and houses where the curtains are not closed, there are small scenes: children playing, children watching television, families in kitchens, tables laid for meals, a young girl combing her long hair; and in all of these are lampglow and the look of warmth. People are in shirtsleeves, not double thicknesses of wool. Doors bear wreaths of holly, candles are lit on mantelpieces, in front gardens coloured lights bloom on the boughs of trees. Stephen, roving through the town, peers hungrily at these illuminations of domestic life, coming as near to the windows as he can, invisible to those within, he hopes; like a famished creature cast out of its pack, he prowls the quiet streets. Few walkers are out on this cold evening and those who are have their intents and purposes and hurry past him, swaddled in dry clothes and shielded from the snow by their umbrellas. No one stops to talk to him or ask him what he's doing and even if some kindly passer-by were to see that he is lost, Stephen could not ask her for directions. How could he explain that he is searching for the house of a woman he only knows as Joan, who may live in this little town where the river is messenger to the open sea, but equally might live in one of the secluded houses on its outskirts, and that he needs to tell this woman's daughter that he loves her?

Framed in one of the bright windows a woman in her kitchen, gazing out but seeing nothing in the darkness, spoons something crimson into her mouth and tastes it lingeringly before re-filling the spoon and lifting it back to her mouth. In a second window a tall blonde woman seen from the back, and Stephen's heart misses a beat, but when she turns he sees that she is old.

Systematically he explores each narrow street and looks into every window still unscreened but as night falls and darkness deepens, more curtains and blinds are drawn. It is almost eight. At the quay the river-water slaps against the stone and the lanyards on the masts of the moored boats clatter and clink on wood and steel. Now no one is about. But light is coming from the pub along the road, and in the bar a lively fire is warming the small cluster of people gathered there. The landlady of earlier in the day has been replaced by an older man who warns Stephen that he will be closing early but cheerfully serves him a double Bell's.

What alchemy or transubstantiation turns liquid into flame when it is swallowed? Shutting his eyes and leaning against the upright wooden back of the bench close to the fire where he is sitting, Stephen pictures the golden drink as a dragon's tail whisking through the passages of his body, bringing heat where there was frost before. For the first time in hours his teeth stop rattling in their sockets like unsteady tombstones in a gale. He buys another double. It is good but not good enough to thaw out his numbed faculties of reason: his mind is still too frozen to conceive of his next step.

Around him the group of friendly drinkers is beginning to break up; people are leaving the bar, calling out their Christmas greetings from the door. 'Last orders, gents,' the old man says: time for Stephen to have another whisky and a chaser of Adnam's mild to soothe his throat. There is nothing to eat but peanuts and pork scratchings; they will do. It's Christmas Eve. He smiles to himself. It's Christmas, Steve. Unbidden, the image of his mother flickers before his eyes: what will she be doing at this moment? Better not to ask that question but to scrub the thought of her from his imagination. She will be all right tomorrow; he'll make sure of that. Better also not to dwell too long on images of Helen either. She is not alone tonight but with her faceless husband; will she share her girlhood bed with him, be forced in its narrowness against the wall by his inconsiderate bulk, by his repellent smells? Who is he? What will he have brought for her this Christmas? The gold moon and its attendant pearls shine in Stephen's pocket.

He is now the last customer and the publican is sweeping the floor and raking the fire in a pointed manner. It's time to leave. He'd rather not go out into the cold again or join Alberic in that comfortless hotel but he can't stay here: it's getting late, it's Christmas Eve; he has nowhere else to go.

On leaving the pub he almost trips over a blackboard propped up against the outside wall. There's a piece of chalk tied to it, a small streak of whiteness in the dark. On an impulse Stephen kneels to wipe the surface with his sleeve, erasing anything already on it, and with the chalk he writes: I love you, Helen Greenwood.

It is a relief to find the room in darkness and Alberic asleep – or lying still at least – when he returns. As quietly as he can, he takes off his clothes and gets into the empty bed where the slithery sheets smell of mould and damp like the clothes that even the desperate leave unbought at jumble sales.

This is the first time in his life that he has shared a bedroom with a man. In the bed beside him, inches from him, Alberic makes no sound at all. Perhaps he is dead. If he could, Stephen would stay awake on guard throughout the night but he is so tired, so bone-achingly weary, that he can't help sinking into sleep.

While he is still in the shallows of sleep, a realisation comes to him that jolts him back into alertness, but it comes too late. How stupid he has been. It is one minute before midnight, on the eve of Christmas: he knows where Helen is. She's in the church with the solid tower where he left his car this morning. He did not need to enter it to know that there will be stained glass and candlelight and choristers and scents of dust and stone. There will be a crib, and a baby with its father and some sheep. And there will be singing: Come and behold him, born the king of angels, and now the carols are over and the service is ended. If he were to get up and dressed and into the car, would he get there in time? No, Helen is at the church door now, wishing the vicar a happy Christmas, stepping out alone into the snow.

Which way did she go? The snowflakes are soft as kisses and moonlight makes a path for her along the dark and dreamless streets beneath the watchful stars. Stephen is halfway out of bed and scrabbling for his trousers before he knows that he has lost her. At a house with shuttered windows she stops to find her key. It's hushed inside the house; the dog stirs a little in its bed but it knows Helen and it does not bark. She had asked her husband and her mother not to wait up for her; they are both asleep.

In the drawing room her stocking hangs beside a fire which now has died to barely smouldering embers and for a while she kneels by it and weeps. What does she weep for, Helen? She weeps for endings, truths discovered far too late, for betrayals and for loss, and loss of love.

Why had he not remembered midnight mass until it was too late? He could have been there with her. He could have knelt beside her in a pew and shared her hymnal; their fingers would have brushed against each other's on the page and she would have spoken to him. With the sting of his own tears on his face and in his ears, Stephen slowly drifted into sleep, and in the silent night outside, the falling snow.

Christmas Day

He woke to a shaft of sunlight and an empty room. Alberic was not there, nor was his coat, but his suitcase was still lying on the floor. He must have gone out for breakfast or a walk. Stephen pulled the thin blankets and the sticky sheets closer about him and considered the day ahead. Whatever else, it must include his mother. He had to get to Didcot soon. Yesterday he'd barred his mother from his mind but she was back in it this morning and he knew how worried she must be. His heart tightened when he thought of her hobbling across the kitchen in her purple dressing gown, wondering what had happened and if he were ever coming home. She'd be anxious for her turkey. Could he leave Alberic to make his own way back to London? If so, the drive would probably be quicker – cross-country, instead of south, then north and west. But there would be no trains today. Perhaps Alberic would choose to stay here longer, to do what-ever he was doing by himself? Definitely, that would be best. And definitely it would not be wise to ask him any questions now. With his newly abraded vision he can see that Alberic may not be quite the harmless friend he wanted to believe in. But he does not want to be told the truth; that would be too dangerous now.

And Helen? Stephen watched dust dancing on the beam of light and saw that, wherever she was this morning, he would never find her. It was hopeless to pace the streets of Orford yet again, for only by a miracle would she appear and, if that miracle occurred, it would take another for her to be unaccompanied. On Christmas Day no one who is loved is on their own. She will be with Jamie, or her mother, with other people maybe – Stephen cannot know. His strategy, such as it is – and he would admit it is contingent – has only ever been to contrive a time and place where they could talk alone and unobserved.

But unexpectedly on the sunlight comes an answer, like the answer to a prayer, or a miracle indeed. He may not know where Helen is now but he knows where she will be: at the place of the hunt in two days' time. The meet on Boxing Day, which is not on Boxing Day – how insulting that Rollo had assumed that fact would need to be explained, and how aggravating that it did – but on the next day, Monday, the day after tomorrow.

Stephen can see it so exactly it as if he had already been to that mill house on the edge of a village in the Cotswolds on a late December morning. The road that leads to the village runs above a river valley; on either side of it, stone walls, lone trees standing sentinel, and fields shaped to the gentle contours of the hills. Sheep, white against the white of snow, and crows on wintry branches, like black notes on a stave, hungrily awaiting the coming of new lambs. The frost on the branches is so deep that they are sheathed in ice.

There is a turning off the road: an ancient lane, hemmed by leafless hedgerows, leading through fields and meadows to the river; hawthorn and bramble, and contorted roots which clutch at the frozen earth.

A narrow humpback bridge. The river, flowing through its low arch, swirls and eddies, a swan is circling with it, its neck an echo of the arch when it plunges its bill deep into the water.

279

Over the bridge, following the path and the river where it curves and forms a crook half-islanding gardens and a house, and he's there, at Harcourt Mill.

No one has ground grain here in a hundred years. Nothing is left of the mill but ruins and nothing interrupts the river except the threat of ice. The house has grown fat over the years on the remains of the mill, eating up its walls and land, swelling from workman's home to this long stretch of pale stone set around a courtyard. Frosted flagstones and in the centre, a marble fountain – a naiad bending from her waist and pouring water from an urn but the cascade arrested, turned to sculpted ice.

In this white world, a blaze of sound and colour. Voices calling, horses stamping, their hooves ringing on the stones, jangle of metal upon leather, riders in bright scarlet, white-cravatted, dogs snarling, yapping, their din merging with the neighing horses and the braying men into one great clashing discord. Hot breath steaming on the air. Stephen, leaning against a slender yew and hidden by its branches, watches as the riders, hounds and horses throng, a woman moving between them with a silver tray of cups, and shouts, instructions, laughter split the morning air until, at a horn's piercing command, they turn and wheel and clatter one after the other out of the courtyard, over the bridge and off towards the hills.

Then silence. Stephen waits patiently until the sounds of the hunt have died away and the world is once again suspended in cold and the lightest mist. There are stone steps rising to the porticoed main door of the house but he knows a better way, through a wooden door at the end of the west wing, which admits him into the garden by the river. The path is bordered by a mass of palest green and by stems of willow that hoar frost has embroidered with traceries of crystal – each leaf, each twig distinct and clearly outlined in the winter light. No one else is in the garden; no one but Helen in the house.

Helen is on the side of the hunted not the hunters: she will have watched the pack depart and breathed in the new stillness with relief. Since earliest morning she's been longing for this moment when the house is empty and nothing disturbs the quiet but the murmur of the river and the chiming clocks. She opens the door of a room that her husband's family seldom uses – a room in the west wing, where the windows open straight onto the garden and white silk curtains billow in the breeze. There is nothing in this room but a sofa and a grand piano and, on the floor by the piano, a vase of winter jasmine. Helen lifts the lid of the piano and props it open, takes her place at the piano stool. Bowing her head as if in prayer, she strokes one hand against the other, runs her fingers down the keys: ivory white, a string of notes, a minor chord. But then a small shift in the light attracts her, the slightest of passing shadows, and she looks up to see Stephen at the window, framed against the willows, the cold sunlight on his hair. She knows him at once. Because souls sing beyond the reach of bodies, they recognise each other, and Helen stands up to open the window and let Stephen in.

A need to pee that could no longer be ignored broke into Stephen's chain of thought and he got out of bed, clutching a blanket to him. It was bitterly cold in the corridor and toilet. When he returned to the room, he found Alberic sitting on his bed, examining the map that Stephen had bought yesterday. He must have seen it sticking out of his coat pocket. Or perhaps he had been through the pockets first.

'Good morning, old boy. I trust that you slept well? It's a beautiful morning, the sun is shining and the rain has gone.'

'Have you been for a walk?'

'I went to get myself a breakfast. I woke early. But there is nobody about, not in here or in the bar. I can only suppose they have all forgotten we are here. They've buggered off because it's Christmas. Fortunately there is that kettle over there, and tea, but if there's one thing that I detest, it's powder milk. Still, it will have to do. I make you a cup?'

'Yes please.' Stephen felt a marked reluctance to get dressed in front of Alberic but at the same time it seemed foolish to struggle with his trousers underneath the blanket. He was glad when Alberic turned round to fiddle with the kettle. 'So, what plans have you made today?' he asked.

'You clever boy to find a map. We would have done better to have it yesterday. In the night, I was thinking we would walk again today. But now I see that it is not so easy and I cannot be positive that we can cross the boundary.'

Stephen, emboldened by his own firm plans, was suddenly decisive. 'I am quite positive that we cannot. There will be barbed wire, electric fences, dogs, security: we would be arrested.'

'But not on Christmas Day? Surely the guards take holiday as well? Come on, my friend, let's have a go!'

'No. You go if you want to. I'll drop you off in Aldeburgh now.'

'Stephen! Stephen, please!'

Shteefen. He will not be swayed. 'I'm sorry but I have other things to do.'

'Well, but it will not be fun if I stay here without you. Also I think there is no public transport.'

'I think you're right.'

'Hey, don't be angry with me. We make a compromise. We drive back to Orford, from where there is a pleasant view, okay? Because all I want is a photograph or two for my family album. Like a souvenir, you know? Something to remember with, like those papers that you "borrowed" from your work. I try to get pictures of everywhere I visit in this country so that when in the end I leave it, I will remember and look back. I would have bought a postcard but I saw none. And yesterday it was so cloudy. Today is better: clear and bright; actually, a very good day for being outdoors. Your girlfriend: does she have a dog? For if she has a dog, she will have to take it for a walk.'

Stephen heard the implied threat and it chilled him to the bone. But he stood his ground. 'I will drive you to Orford because that is not too far out of my way. But I can only stop there for a minute. If I leave you there, will you get yourself back home?'

'No, actually I think I will be washed up on a beach.'

'Stranded. Yes, you might.'

'Not precisely safe then, not for you, and nor for me?'

'All right. I'll take you back to London. We must get going now.'

'Stephen, you are a brick. I knew that you would get it.'

They left the motel room without seeing anyone at all. There was one other car in the car park and for a moment Stephen thought he saw a flash of movement at a window of the inn but when he looked again there was no one there. If the world had ended in the night, and he and Alberic were the sole survivors, he would not have been entirely surprised. The day was clear but the air so cold it hurt. The car was suffering too and to begin with would not start: the engine stuttering and dying again and again and each time making Stephen feel more trapped and hopeless. Alberic, having said nothing, got out, opened the bonnet and did something to the spark plugs which brought the car shuddering back to life. 'I am a jack of all trades,' he said, fastidiously wiping oil off his fingers.

Alberic was right that there would be people out and about in Orford. Not many – some on their own with dogs, a family, two couples heading for the river – but all of them smiling and greeting each other as they passed, as if Christmas made strangers into friends. Stephen and Alberic parked at the quay. 'Will this do?' Stephen asked.

'Please, let us walk just a few yards along that way, where there is a better view.'

A view of what? Of a stony place, a wasteland, the junkyard of cold warriors and, beyond it, the implacable sea. A place prohibited within the meaning of the Official Secrets Act, the sort of place that fascinates the foot soldiers of secret war. A place those soldiers could not reach without the help of some unwitting fool to give them cover. Stephen saw it now through Alberic's sharp gaze. Now he knew why Alberic would not give his own name or use his own car, why he chose to stay out of the way, a rat hidden in a sewer. He closed his eyes so that he would not see the man taking a miniature camera from his pocket and pointing it across the water.

They had walked some distance towards the massy church, uphill, and were out of sight of the quay. 'Hurry up,' Stephen said, starting to go back the way they'd come. His guts were liquefying in fear but he would not have Alberic observe it. He would stay outwardly composed and get away from here as fast as possible. Once he had left Alberic in London, he would not see him again.

When the quay came into view, Stephen saw two cars parked right next to his. There had been no other cars when he and Alberic arrived. Three men were standing by them. Dog walkers from out of town, he hoped, or perhaps they could be sailors. But when he came close enough, he saw that one of them was a uniformed policeman.

Stephen nodded casually to the men as he and Alberic drew near them. One, in a plain dark double-breasted jacket, stretched out his arm to bar the way. 'Good morning, sir,' he said, his voice courteous and calm. 'Is this your car? In which case, could you kindly come with us? Without your friend. We would like to ask you a few questions, so if you would please get into that black car over there.'

Alberic, beside him, was trying to shake off the uniformed policeman's firm grip on his shoulder, and furiously protesting outrage and innocence in a rush of muddled words that included immunity and holiday snaps and seagulls but Stephen already knew there was no point resisting. The evidence was there. He could see the operative on duty in the Institute this morning taking the telephone call from the police and making his way down to the underground repository where thousands of names are held on alphabetically ordered cards: Donaldson, S. S., red-carded to show that he is a member of the Institute. There will be protocols in place to deal with this emergency. The film in Alberic's camera will be developed straightaway.

The searchers will be sent to Stephen's flat where they will find the folders and the tapes lying where he left them, in plain view. What can be said in his defence? Treachery once was punishable by death.

Stephen saw all this with total clarity but right there on the quay Helen was disappearing before his eyes like a white bird against a wild wave's crest, like summer snow, and he knew that he would not see her again. She would live her whole life without him and never even know of his existence except as a minor story in the news.

Alberic, still protesting, was being bundled into one of the cars; a driver was waiting in the other, with a rear door open. Without a word Stephen got in, while the plain-clothes officer watched him carefully and the cold wind blew across the shingle spit on the far side of the water.

Friday

In the long room it is quiet, on a morning in late winter, on the last day of the year. At their isolated desks the seven listeners keep their shocked thoughts to themselves, incapable so soon of putting words to them. Charlotte's eyes are very red. Louise has a note in front of her of the many times that Stephen Spencer Donaldson signed the late list without authority and the folders that Muriel is missing. Damian will never know if he did the right thing or if he should have kept his suspicions to himself; Steve will get a minimum of twenty years, they say, and more if he's unlucky.

Elsewhere in the Institute, Security is checking through its partial records of the times when L/III/SSD was seen in places where he had no excuse to be. On the seventh floor, Rollo Buckingham is reviewing the reports he knows were falsified because the information they contain directly contradicts the first-hand evidence obtained by Marlow McPherson, his colleague and close friend.

Several thousand miles away, in a windowless room in an inconspicuous building in the suburbs of Buenos Aires, an analyst is writing a report on the British Government's undeclared attitudes to the islands that it calls the Falklands and she calls Las Malvinas. All that she knows of the source of the intelligence that will justify invasion plans early in the spring is that it is secret. And, in the long room, Christophine still wonders about the parcel she was given when she returned to work on Tuesday, and the square of silk in iridescent blues that the parcel contained. Soft to the touch and beautiful and obviously expensive – what was in his mind? she asks herself. There was so much love behind that gift, and imagination; what in heaven's name was wrong with that young man?

Acknowledgements

I am very grateful to Anna Webber, Hannah Griffiths, Victoria Millar and Arabella Currie for their advice, encouragement and warm support.

Quotations are taken from the following sources. In addition there are references in the text to the Bible and to the works of Baudelaire, Byron, Dante, Donne, Herrick, Keats, Marvell, Marlowe, Christina Rossetti, Shakespeare and Shelley.

p. 34 *My mother wore a yellow dress, gentle, gently, gentleness*: from Louis MacNeice's 'Autobiography', in *Collected Poems* (Faber, 2007). Courtesy of David Higham Associates.

p. 161 *Lay your sleeping head, my love, human on my faithless arm*: from W. H. Auden's 'Lullaby', in *Collected Poems*, edited by Edward Mendelson (Faber, 2007) © The Estate of W. H. Auden. Reprinted by permission of Curtis Brown, Ltd.

p. 245 *First chill, then stupor, then the letting go*: from Emily Dickinson's 'After great pain a formal feeling comes'. Reprinted by permission of the publishers and the Trustees of Amherst College from *The Poems of Emily Dickinson: Reading Edition*, ed. Ralph W. Franklin, Cambridge, Mass.: The Belknap Press of Harvard University Press, Copyright © 1998, 1999 by the President and Fellows of Harvard College. Copyright © 1951, 1955 by the President and Fellows of Harvard College. Copyright © renewed 1979, 1983 by the President and Fellows of Harvard College. Copyright © 1914, 1918, 1919, 1924, 1929, 1930, 1932, 1935, 1937, 1942 by Martha Dickinson Bianchi. Copyright © 1952, 1957, 1958, 1963, 1965 by Mary L. Hampson.

p. 245 *sapphires and garlic in the mud*: from T. S. Eliot's 'Burnt Norton', in *Four Quartets* (Faber, 2001) © The Estate of T. S. Eliot; reprinted by permission of Faber & Faber Ltd

NOTE: The calendar for 1981 has been shifted slightly to allow Christmas Day to fall on a Saturday.